JADE'S EROTIC ADVENTURES

BOOKS 16 - 20

VICTORIA RUSH

VOLUME 4

JADE'S EROTIC ADVENTURES: BOOKS
16 - 20

COPYRIGHT

For the uninhibited...

BOOK 16

THE COSTUME PARTY

1

I woke up to the sound of my best friend Hannah calling me from the other end of my house. She'd let herself in early on a Saturday morning and for some reason was yelling at me as she ran up the stairs.

"Jade!" she hollered. "Where are you? I've got some exciting news!"

I rolled over and squinted at my clock on the nightstand. It was a little past eight. Saturdays were the only day of the week I allowed myself to sleep in, and I was more than a little ticked at her rude intrusion.

"Aren't you up yet?" she called. "Get up—you're not going to believe what I just heard."

I rolled over and wrapped my pillow around my ears as she dashed into my bedroom. She paused for a minute smiling at my feeble attempt to block her out of my morning daze, then she pounced on the bed below my curled-up knees.

"Wake up, sleepyhead!" she squealed, pushing my shoulders to rouse me from my slumber.

"This better be good," I said, raising my pillow a few inches and peering at her through thin eyes. "You know how much I worship my weekend sleep-ins."

"You'll be glad I woke you when you hear what I have to tell you," she said. "Besides, you're gonna want to get up and begin planning your day right away. We're going to need a few extra hours to go shopping."

I pulled my duvet cover over my shoulders and huffed.

"What could possibly be so important to drag me out of my soft and cozy bed this early in the morning?"

I peered outside, looking at the gray clouds hanging low in the late October skies. I was in no hurry to venture out into the chilly autumn air.

"Only the biggest private shindig of the year. Steve Bannon is hosting his annual Halloween party at his mansion on the lake, and we're invited!"

"Isn't that the party with all the A-list celebrities? How did you score an invitation?"

Hannah peered at me with a wicked look in her eyes.

"Let's just say I know somebody who knows somebody. Someone with whom I may have pulled a few strings to earn some special favors."

"I bet that's not the *only* thing you were pulling to earn those favors," I said, raising an eyebrow.

"Possibly," she smirked. "But I apparently impressed him enough with my naked gymnastics to land an invitation to this special event. Except this year, it's got an extra twist. This time it's going to be a *nude* costume party."

I lifted my head and propped the side of my face on a crooked elbow, suddenly intrigued.

"Isn't that an oxymoron? How can you be in costume and naked at the same time?"

Hannah smiled and handed me a gold-embossed card inscribed with fancy calligraphy writing. I felt the raised surface of the script on the tips of fingers, rubbing it gently trying to divine its meaning through my still bleary eyes. Somebody had gone to a great deal of effort to create an invitation card on par with the most extravagant wedding.

I pulled myself up and leaned against my headboard, slowly reading the message.

You are cordially invited to attend my annual Halloween costume ball at my estate overlooking Lake Michigan.

This year I've added a special twist to make it even more interesting. You're encouraged to wear as little or as much trappings as you feel comfortable—including nothing at all beyond a simple mask. With everyone baring a little more than usual, who knows what kind of shenanigans might break out, and we're always mindful of protecting the anonymity of our special guests.

Of course, I encourage everyone to be playful and creative with their choice of costumes, as this is always the highlight of the event. As in previous years, there will be a special prize for the best costume of the evening and we hope you'll be suitably daring and inventive.

Feel free to bring a partner and let down your britches! As always, what happens at the Bannon residence stays at the Bannon residence. I look forward to seeing you this Saturday, starting at midnight. We'll all have a ghoulish good time!

I peered up at Hannah and grinned.

"No RSVP?"

"There's no need with a Steve Bannon invitation," she said. Everyone who's invited always goes. It's the go-to event of the year in the Chicago area. Models, actresses, rock stars, billionaires—everybody who's anybody in this town will be there. There's even a rumor that the Governor and his wife will attend this year's event."

I looked down at the card, rubbing my fingers over the embossed script.

"The invitation says you're allowed to bring a partner. Was that a condition of your little tryst with your friend—that you accompany him as his plus-one?"

Hannah peered at me devilishly as a tiny curl formed on the sides of her mouth.

"When I told him I had a friend who was even prettier than me and had a body to die for, he didn't hesitate to hand me an extra invitation. *You're* my plus-one, girl." She pulled another card out of her purse and handed it to me. "You know I'd never pass up an opportunity like this without bringing my bestie along to share in the fun."

I looked at Hannah with a quizzical look and shook my head in confusion.

"How are we ever going to find a decent Halloween costume on the Saturday before the end of the month? All the costume stores will be sold out of the best stuff."

Hannah kicked off her shoes and lifted the covers, then scooched in excitedly next to me against the headboard.

"I've been searching online for some ideas. We don't have to wear anything too elaborate, and there's no reason why we have to stick to a Halloween theme. Remember, this is a *nude* costume party. We already look pretty hot for a couple of girls nearing middle age. The less we wear, the better. Let's flaunt it while we've still got it!"

She pulled an iPad out of her purse and tapped the screen. A website opened showing a collection of sexy models wearing risqué costumes. She scrolled through the images, commenting on the various themes.

"Just look at some of these possibilities. We can play any role we like, wearing as much or as little as we please. Most of these costumes can be put together with a simple trip to Walmart and maybe a bit of needle and thread. Plus, we can easily remove one of two pieces from each outfit to reveal a bit more skin. The most important element is the headpiece. We just need something to conceal our identity and highlight our girly figures with a bit of flair."

Hannah paused at a picture of a sexy blonde wearing a Playboy bunny costume. She wore a tight corset and a rubber mask that covered the top half of her face with tall ears pointing up in the air.

"What about this one? You have to admit, it's pretty hot. You'd could even dispense with the bodice altogether and just keep the bunny tail on your naked ass. Imagine the looks you'd get prancing around his mansion in that costume!"

The images of sexy half-nude models wearing unusual masks

reminded me of my encounter at the Fantasy Feast naked dinner party. Suddenly, I became mindful of the wetness that had begun building between my legs.

"Not bad," I said, shifting my weight uncomfortably off the wet spot on my sheets. "Show me some more."

Hannah flipped through a few more images and stopped at a picture of a sexy maid wearing a lacy dress, holding a feather duster in her hand. Her firm tits pressed against the flimsy fabric, creating an irresistible focal point from the sensuous shadows on her bosom.

"How about this?" she said. "You'd look stunning in this outfit. You'd be covering up just enough to drive every man and woman at that party absolutely crazy. And imagine all the fun you could have teasing the naked guests with your little duster!"

"*Intriguing...*" I said as I squeezed my thighs together, trying to quiet my burning clit.

The more images Hannah showed me, the more turned on I got. Whether it was from me imagining myself in the costumes or imagining myself playing with the guests dressed up in the provocative outfits, was unclear. Either way, the more my mind began to ponder the possibilities, the more excited I became about going to this event.

"The only problem is, it will be difficult to cover my face without looking unnatural in that outfit," I frowned. "Show me more costumes with masks."

Hannah refined her search by typing in the words *sexy mask costumes* and the screen refreshed showing a new set of models in racy outfits. Many of the themes revolved around superheroes, with the male models sporting Batman and Superman motifs and the female models wearing Wonder Woman and Batgirl-type costumes.

"Not very original," I frowned. "I bet there'll be a ton of superhero costumes among all those egotistical celebrities. I'm looking for something a little different."

Hannah paused for a moment, then tapped on her photo library pulling up an image of me wearing a business suit painted on my naked body.

"Remember that time you went to the nude bodypainting workshop? You're a graphic artist. You can be virtually anything you want and show off all you wish with a little bit of well-disguised paint. Whether it's Catwoman, Black Widow, or Wonder Woman–all these characters wear is a mask and tight outfits to show off their beautiful physiques. You could even dress up like Mystique in the X-Men movie and wear absolutely nothing other than a full coat of body paint."

"Been there, done that," I said. "If I'm going to really enjoy myself, I want to wear something I've never worn before that will absolutely blow everyone away."

"You sure are a tough customer," Hannah said, shaking her head. "Let's try something a little different..."

She reopened her browser and typed in the words *naked masquerade costumes*. A gallery of Google images popped up with a collection of half-naked men and women.

"*Now* we're talking," I said, squirming on the bed as I scanned the toned bodies of the sexy models.

"Look at that one," Hannah said, pointing at the screen. "It's a picture of Rihanna at last year's Met Gala dressed as Nefertiti. With her sheer lace dress and silver headdress, it doesn't leave much to the imagination. A bit more makeup around the eyes, and you'd be able to mask your identity quite easily."

"That's pretty hot," I said, beginning to feel the sheets getting wetter and wetter between my legs. "She definitely looks fuckable. But it's been done before. I don't want to wear something half of these people will have already seen."

"Damn, girl, you're *impossible!* Remember, less is more. The idea is to show as much of our bodies as possible to attract the attention of all these beautiful people. You could get away with a simple mask, a painted emblem on your chest, and a shiny belt. Who really cares what you're wearing as long as you get the attention of the guests?"

"Humor me for a little longer," I said, squeezing Hannah's leg. "I'm starting to get a few ideas. I just need a bit more inspiration."

Hannah began flipping through the images more quickly until one picture suddenly caught my attention.

"Wait!" I said. "Go back a few frames. I saw something

interesting..."

She scrolled back until an image of six men dressed in contrasting costumes popped up.

"That's the one," I said, scanning the image slowly.

"*The Village People*?" Hannah said. "That might be okay for a gay guy, but how could you possibly look sexy wearing any one of those cheesy costumes?"

My eyes darted back and forth between the sexy cowboy wearing chaps and the indian warrior wearing a feathered headdress and a skimpy loincloth. Suddenly I nodded as a mischievous smile formed on my face.

"What?" Hannah said. "What could you possibly be thinking?"

She glanced down at my breasts peeking above the covers, noticing my hardening nipples.

"Because I know gay dudes—even ones with hard bodies like these guys—don't do it for you. Where is your mind going with this idea?"

"I've decided what I'm going to wear," I said, crossing my arms over my chest. "But I'm going to keep it a secret until we get to the party. It'll be all the more fun and surprising if I reveal it at the last second. But I promise you, it'll be one-of-a-kind and extremely provocative."

Hannah's eyes darted across my face, trying to imagine what I had in mind.

"Now you've got *me* all excited thinking what you're going to do. Judging by your obvious state of arousal, your head is already at the party. Can I crawl under the covers with you and have some fun fantasizing which one of those costumes you're going to wear?"

"By all means," I said, disappearing under the covers with her. "Just imagine me as one of those hot dudes with his clothes off."

"Mmm," Hannah purred, slithering between my slippery thighs. "I'd rather imagine you as a hot *chick* with her clothes off."

"In a couple of days," I said, spreading my legs further apart and pulling her face into my steaming crotch. "You might be able to have it both ways."

2

Just after midnight on the day of the party, I pulled my car up beside a call box in front of a large wrought-iron gate protecting the entrance to Steve Bannon's estate. After providing our names and the identification numbers on the front of our invitation cards, the gates opened and we followed the curved driveway up to the front of a giant French-styled chateau. As a parking attendant approached our car, I turned to Hannah seated next to me and smiled.

"It's show time," I said.

"Not a moment too soon," she huffed. "I've been dying to see what you're wearing under that coat ever since you picked me up."

I'd intentionally worn a long western duster to cover my body all the way from my shoulders to my ankles. Part of it was meant to surprise Hannah when I finally reached the event, but it had much more to do with my desire to shock everyone else once I got in the front door. I reached behind my seat and pulled a thin black mask out of a bag on the floor and wrapped it around the top of my face.

Hannah's forehead wrinkled as she looked at me, still confused.

"Let me guess: Kato, Zorro, Nightshade?"

"You're moving in the right direction with the first two," I smiled, reaching back into the bag and pulling out a pair of western boots.

"Cowboy boots?" Hannah squinted. "I don't know my cowboy characters quite as well—"

"Maybe this will help," I said, donning a white Stetson.

Hannah looked at me blankly for a moment, then her eyes lit up, recognizing the familiar image of the famous cowboy with the white hat and black mask.

"The Lone Ranger?"

"Yes, but with a little twist. You'll have to wait for the full reveal until we get inside."

"You're such a tease," she said as I handed the attendant my keys and we stepped out of the car.

We paused for a moment, taking in the full scale of the Bannon estate close-up. The four-story mansion extended almost a hundred feet in either direction, with tall arched windows and ornate brickwork. The bright spotlights illuminating the front of the house lit up the entire courtyard, reflecting off Hannah's shiny Batgirl outfit.

"Holy shit!" she exclaimed. "This place is gigantic. We're going to have to drop *breadcrumbs* to not get lost in there."

"More like *caviar* or *foie gras*," I chuckled. "Something tells me everything about this affair is going to be top shelf."

"What are we waiting for?" Hannah giggled, rushing ahead of me toward the front door.

My gaze drifted down while I soaked up her tight ass in her black latex outfit. She had a beautiful hourglass figure, and the tight Batgirl costume highlighted every curve of her sexy body. I smiled as I imagined the two of us mingling among the high rollers. But I had a feeling they'd be focused on someone *else's* ass tonight.

With the large double entrance doors pulled back, we peered into the bright marble-floored foyer as we approached the front steps. A large crowd of costumed guests had already begun to gather in the main ballroom, and we could hear soft jazz music wafting out into the courtyard.

"Good evening ladies," a man wearing a crisply tailored tailcoat and black tie said as we stepped into the entrance hall.

He looked at my long shawl and smiled.

"May I check your coat, Madam?"

"Yes, thank you," I said, turning my back to assist him in its removal.

When he pulled the cape off my back and viewed my naked backside, I heard him gasp. To complement my Lone Ranger disguise, I'd chosen to wear a tight-fitting black leather vest and long black chaps with nothing underneath. My tight ass poked out the back of the open leggings, and I could feel him running his eyes up and down my body as he hesitated hanging my coat in the closet.

But when I turned around, both Hannah and the doorman took a step back in shock. On the front of my open pants, I wore a large dildo fashioned in the shape of a man's cock and balls, framed by two silver pistols on either side of my hips. The long phallus slapped against the sides of my naked thighs as it swung from side to side.

"Holy *fuck*, Jade!" Hannah squealed. "That's *outrageous*! Where did you ever come up with that idea?"

"Remember the Village People picture you showed me a few days ago? I decided to borrow elements of both the cowboy and the indian characters to create my own design." I shook my hips to juggle my equipment and smiled. "I thought it would be kind of fun playing *both* sides of coin, so to speak."

"Uh—*yeah*," she said, flicking her eyes between my tight bosom spilling over the top of my vest and my faux genitals. "I'd have to say you pulled it off. With that getup, I expect you'll be the center of attention all night long."

"Um," the doorman said, shyly interrupting. "May I have your tickets, please?"

"Of course," I said, rustling my rubber balls as I fished in the pocket of my chaps for my ticket. When the butler turned to collect Hannah's ticket, I could see the front of his pants tenting in obvious arousal.

"Enjoy your evening," he said, motioning for us to enter the ballroom.

"Oh, I have a feeling we will," Hannah winked, as she nodded toward the lengthening pole pushing down his pant leg.

A waiter approached us with tall glasses of champagne on a silver tray and did a double-take when he noticed the swinging package between my legs.

"Whoa boy," Hannah said to the server, taking two glasses off his unsteady tray. "We wouldn't want you to spill your load before we've sampled the goods."

As we moved into the main entrance hall, the patrons milling in small groups began to turn around to view the newly arriving guests. Suddenly, the gentle buzz of group conversation receded until the only sound we could hear was the hum of the background music. Everyone was so stunned taking in my outfit, they were literally dumbstruck with their mouths agape.

Many of the guests had chosen to wear predictable Halloween costumes with little bits of flesh showing here and there, but nobody was letting it all hang out quite as brazenly as I had. Amid the predictable sprinkling of ghosts and goblins, there was a profusion of superhero figures and Disney characters bedecked in various stages of undress. I shook my head at the lack of imagination of the high-powered group and began to wonder if the event was going to live up to Hannah's hyperbole.

"Damn, girl," she said. "It looks like you're going to be this evening's scene-stealer. You've already stopped the show. I don't know what everybody's thinking right now, but that thing looks so realistic, they must be wondering if you're a legit tranny wearing that impressive package."

I smiled a crooked grin, suddenly feeling self-conscious with all of the eyes in the room surveying my exposed body. Fortunately, a handsome couple dressed as Anthony and Cleopatra began to approach us, providing some distraction.

"Welcome to our little costume party," the man said, extending his hand to Hannah and me. "I'm Steve Bannon and this is my wife

Genevieve. You'll have to excuse me, but I don't recognize either of you under your—*interesting* disguises."

I was taken aback by how handsome the eccentric billionaire looked close up. With his square jaw, dimpled cheeks and thick head of salt-and-pepper hair swept back in a dense poof, he looked like a slightly older version of the famous actor Patrick Dempsey. He wore a loose toga draped over his well-muscled chest, and I could see his pecs flexing as he shook my hand.

But I found his wife even more beguiling. Wearing a tight-fitting gold-lamé dress slitted at one side of her hips and a pretty beaded headdress, she looked like a dead-ringer for a young Elizabeth Taylor. As I ran my eyes shamelessly over her luscious figure, I felt a sudden dampness building under the weight of my latex balls pressing against my flaring clit.

"Jade," I introduced myself, not yet wanting to reveal my full identity.

"Hannah," my partner responded, politely shaking their hands.

"It appears that you two have already captured the attention of my guests," Bannon said, turning to appraise the congregation still gazing awkwardly in our direction. He extended his arm in the direction of the main hall and nodded. "Please, come in and mingle. There are so many fascinating people to meet. I'm sure we'll catch up with the two of you a little later this evening."

"I'll look forward to that," I said, smiling at Genevieve, lingering for a moment longer at her dazzling figure. She returned the gesture, widening her eyes as my member twitched while I held my palm over the handle of one of my six-shooters.

"Holy shit," Hannah said, as Bannon and his wife melted back into the crowd. "Did you see the way he was looking at you? He was practically *raping* you with his eyes. Something tells me this is going to be a very interesting night. It seems the men are even more enamored with your disguise than the women. Either there's a lot of bi-curious guys in here, or they're attracted to that whole futa thing."

"I dunno," I said. "I'm showing off a lot of *girl* parts too. Who's to say what they're more attracted to? But did you notice his wife? I'd far rather get into *her* pants."

"It's too bad that thing isn't animated," Hannah chuckled, glancing at my pendulous dick. "If you could actually get it up, you could probably have your way with just about everybody in this place."

"Who knows?" I said, winking at Hannah. "In my current state of arousal, I wouldn't be surprised if this thing had a life of its own."

Little did she know how much truth in this statement I was about to reveal before the evening was over.

3

A fter Bannon and his wife resumed mingling with the rest of the crowd, Hannah and I wandered into the main ballroom. At first, most of the assembled groups gave us a wide berth, unsure what to make of the two girls dressed in such revealing costumes. Hannah's latex Batgirl outfit clung to her naked body like a second skin, the shiny fabric accentuating every crease and curve like it was painted on her. And the cutouts on both sides of my leather chaps left little to the imagination, even with the modicum of cover provided by my fake genitals covering my bare mound.

I was glad to have the freedom to mill about the room for a while, surveying the faces and costumes of the high-powered gathering. I recognized a fair number of public figures from the senior ranks of the local political, business, and media fields. The mayor was there with his wife, dressed as Little Red Riding Hood and the Big Bad Wolf, which seemed fitting given the ongoing level of corruption at City Hall. Bannon's business partner and fellow billionaire Kent Schiffer circled the room with a familiar supermodel, outfitted in matching red tights as Mr. Incredible and Elastagirl. And our local news anchorman was paired with his pretty sidekick, dressed as Woody and Bo Peep from the movie Toy Story.

Many of the guests were dressed as famous characters from superhero movies or nursery rhyme stories, with most of the men playing the more dominant role. *Typical display of macho-entitled privilege*, I thought. *Why does it seem every man who achieves a certain degree of power have to lord it over everyone else, thinking they're better than the rest of us?* My cheeky cowboy costume seemed a perfect counterpoint to the heavy dose of testosterone permeating the room, mocking their oversize male egos as I swung my big dick around like I owned it.

As Hannah and I began mingling with the small cliques scattered around the room, I found it amusing that while most of the women praised my cocky outfit, their male partners seemed threatened by it, silently stealing glances at my huge dong while their wives and girlfriends chatted with me comfortably. I wasn't sure if it was because they felt intimidated by my outsize genitals, or because they were secretly fantasizing about fucking me.

As more and more people began gravitating toward us, intrigued by my outrageous costume, Hannah slowly drifted off to the other side of the room. I couldn't blame her, with everyone asking me silly questions like what it felt like to be a woman carrying a man's dick. For a while I amused them, swinging my hips from side to side and playfully grabbing my balls, flaunting my male persona.

But I soon tired of the incessant stares and never-ending quips about my tranny disguise, and began looking for an excuse to break away. Just as I was about to excuse myself to go to the ladies' room, the governor and his wife approached our group and introduced themselves. They were dressed in matching his and hers chef outfits, the only difference being that his wife wore a less poofy hat and a backless apron that showed off her sexy ass and legs.

"That's quite a provocative costume," the governor said, extending his hand to me. "I'm Jack Scanlon and this is my wife, Alicia."

"Pleased to meet you, Mr. Governor," I said, quickly seeing through his thin disguise. "But no less daring than your wife's, which I dare say is even *more* revealing."

"In some respects, possibly," he said. "Except you're revealing both sides of the coin."

"Heads *and* tails, you mean?" I smiled.

"In a manner of speaking," he said, temporarily at a loss for words by my sassy attitude. "Are you here alone tonight?"

I scanned the room and noticed Hannah chatting it up with a hunky guest dressed in a Tarzan outfit.

"It seems my partner is out looking for greener pastures. I guess she felt this one had been fully tilled."

"Oh?" the governor said, glancing at my pendulous prick. "Who's been doing most of the figurative plowing—you, or all these other farm animals?"

"At this point, I'd say everybody's just getting the lay of the land," I said, dragging out the metaphor. "Surveying the landscape, deciding the best place to position their hoes."

"I see what you mean," the governor said, his eyes widening from my double entendre. "You seem to be particularly–*ambidextrous* in that respect."

"I'm just having fun pretending what it might be like to cultivate both sides of the field," I said, running my eyes up and down his wife's sexy body before locking eyes with her. "You never know when a particularly fertile plot might need tending."

"Well put, my lady."

"Please—call me Jade," I said, turning my attention to his wife, who'd been staring at my outfit the entire time. "What about you, Alicia? Have you been enjoying the evening so far?"

"Yes," she said, happy to deflect attention away from her overbearing husband for a moment. "So many interesting people and costumes."

"I find yours very alluring also," I said, staring at her plump breasts pressing against the front of her skimpy apron. "But it seems that all your fun parts are hidden from view, at least while we're talking face-to-face. It's only when you turn around that you reveal your adventurous side."

"I guess you'll just have to catch me when my back is turned then," she said, winking at me sexily.

"I'll definitely be keeping a lookout. Hopefully we can catch up later."

As much as I wanted to continue our playful flirtation, I knew I'd never have a chance for some alone time with her as long as I continued to engage them as a couple. Besides, I was getting tired of her husband's thinly veiled sexist comments.

"Will you excuse me for a moment while I use the restroom?"

"Of course," she said. "But be careful in there. It's not as simple for us ladies to pee standing up as it is for the men."

"Not to worry," I smiled. "Fortunately, this thing is easily removed. Though it might be kind of fun to try it just once."

"Will you be using the men's or the ladies' room?" the governor smirked.

"I'm pretty sure the toilets are unisex in this place," I said, gently admonishing him for another chauvinist remark. "Which will be a refreshing change from the usually cramped ladies' rooms we have to endure in other public places. Enjoy your evening. Perhaps we'll see each other a little later."

"We'll look forward to that," the governor smiled.

As I pulled away from the crowd, I shook my head at the impudent tone of the governor, ignoring his beautiful wife while he shamelessly flirted with me. Little did he know that I was far more impressed with Alicia than by the trappings of his high political office. I felt like I needed to wash myself off after dealing with his sexist attitude and while looking for a place to freshen up, I recognized the familiar red and white uniform of the mayor's wife as she waited outside the closed door of an adjacent anteroom. As I approached her from the side, I admired her shapely legs and full bosom pressing against her tight bodice. Her Little Red Riding Hood costume seemed the perfect outfit to highlight her youthful face and figure.

"You'd think we wouldn't have to wait to use a toilet in this place," I said, sauntering up next to her. "There must be at least twenty washrooms in this mansion."

"No doubt," she laughed. "But even in a place like this, with this many guests, unfortunately we ladies still have to wait to use the lavatory." She glanced down at my faux genitalia and smiled. "It's too bad they don't have his and hers toilets like in most public settings. With that getup, you'd probably get away with slipping into the men's room."

"Maybe," I said. "But I'd still have to pee sitting down. I'm just looking to freshen up anyway. I was hoping for a respite from all the overcharged testosterone out there."

"Tell me about it," she nodded. "I've been dealing with city politics from the other side for almost twenty years now. It's still very much an old-boys network in this business. Women are just treated as chattel, to be trotted out as eye candy whenever there's a public relations opportunity like this."

"That's partly why I wore this outfit," I admitted. "I thought it would be kind of fun to swing my own dick around all these heavy hitters at this posh event."

The washroom door suddenly swung open and a woman wearing a Victorian costume brushed past us, sneering at our haughty outfits.

"Judging by the heft of that thing," she said, "I'd say yours is the biggest one here by a large margin. Do you want to join me while I freshen up inside? It looks like the last thing you need right now is to stand outside alone while everybody wags their tongues at you."

"Thanks," I said. scurrying in behind her as we locked the door, giggling like two schoolgirls. "I'm Jade, by the way," I said stretching out my hand.

"Haley," she said, grasping my hand firmly as she smiled into my eyes.

As we leaned in to the doublewide mirror over the marble vanity to check our lipstick and mascara, I noticed Haley's gaze drifting lower to check out my package.

"You know, if it weren't for the straps holding that apparatus onto your hips, I'd swear that thing was real," she said. "It's so life-like. Even your *testicles* look authentic."

"The whole thing is made out of a special latex engineered to mimic real skin. With all the advances in artificial dolls these days, it's amazing what they can do with sex toys."

"Do you mind if I—*touch* it?" she asked.

"I thought you'd never ask."

As I stepped back from the vanity, Haley turned to face me, reaching her hand down to touch my artificial cock.

"My God," she said, squeezing it firmly. "It even *feels* like a real dick. If only it could get hard, I shudder to think how big it would be angry."

As she reached further down to cup my balls, her face came closer to mine, and we kissed. I pressed my tongue into her mouth and she reached lower still, running her fingers over my moist labia. I purred in pleasure, pressing my crotch harder into her hips. She hiked up her skirt, and I was pleasantly surprised to see that she was completely naked underneath. Recognizing my opportunity to have a little fun, I positioned my hand over my right pistol, gently pumping the trigger. Slowly, my synthetic cock began to fill with air and inflate between her legs.

"What the—" Haley gasped, pulling back to see what was happening. "You've got to be kidding me. You can *animate* that thing?"

"In a manner of speaking," I said. "You want to give it a try?"

"*Hell* yes!" she said. "I'm so horny right now, I could fuck just about anything. But first, let me take a closer look at what I'm working with."

As I smiled at her wickedly, I pumped my trigger harder until my organ rose to a full ten inches of erect flesh. Haley couldn't help herself as she fell to the floor and took my member into her mouth while she proceeded to give me a pretend blowjob. As I watched her stretch her lips around my thick pole, I placed my hands behind her head and imagined fucking her face like a man. Although I was being far gentler than most, it was fun fantasizing being in the man's role for a change, having my way with my muse.

"That's it," I purred. "Suck my big cock, baby. Squeeze my balls while I fuck your pretty face."

Without hesitating, Haley reached underneath me and began

rubbing my balls against my raging clit. The sensation was not unlike what I imagined a real man would be feeling as she stimulated my sex organ.

"Fuck, yes," I panted. "That feels good, Haley. I want to fuck you so bad."

Suddenly, she stood up and smiled at me.

"That makes *two* of us. I'm so turned-on, I could pop off any second."

She reached behind her, placing her hands on top of the vanity and lifted herself up onto the counter, hiking her skirt all the way up. I took one look at her glistening pussy and leaned in to kiss her passionately. She reached down and pointed my hard pecker toward her opening and when I pressed it into her, she gasped.

"Oh God, Jade," she groaned. "Your cock feels so good. Fill me up with your big dick. I want to feel your balls slapping against my pussy."

Her dirty talk got me even more worked up, and as I pressed my hips forward, she moaned loudly. As we began to grind our hips together, our tongues danced in each other's mouths. Haley flapped her thighs against me as I plowed in and out of her, grinding my clit against the underside of my rubbery balls. While we grunted and moaned with abandon, anybody who might have been waiting to use the restroom must have surely known what was going on inside. But neither one of us cared, lost in the moment by the rising feeling of ecstasy engulfing our joined bodies.

Suddenly, Haley wrapped her legs around my ass and pulled me even deeper inside her pussy.

"*Damn*, girl," she panted. "You're going to make me come with that big thumper of yours. Fill me up while I come all over your pretty pussy."

"Yes," I groaned. "I'm close too. I'm going to cum with you. God damn, I like fucking you."

"Here it comes," Haley moaned. "Take me over the edge."

I grabbed Haley's hips by both sides and pulled her strongly toward me, grinding my cock and balls as hard as I could against her while ramming my cock in and out of her sloshing pussy. Suddenly, a wave of passion rolled over me as my clit began pulsating against the underside of my faux balls.

"Oh God, Haley," I groaned. "Cum with me baby. Come all over my big dick."

"Yes!" Haley howled. "I can feel you pounding my G-spot. It feels soooo good!"

Suddenly, I felt Haley spraying all over my balls and mound as her pussy clenched down over my phallus while we ground our hips against one another. We moaned inside each other's mouths as we locked lips in a tight and passionate kiss. After what seemed like a full minute of shaking and convulsing in each other's arms, our breathing finally returned to normal, while we kissed with me still inside her.

"*Ahem*," a woman's voice called impatiently from outside the door, from someone waiting to use the facilities.

"I guess we'll have to vacate the premises," Haley smiled. "Though I could make love to you all night long."

"Same here," I said. "Let's clean up and get out of here. Maybe we can find a more private place to continue our fun."

While Haley pulled down her skirt and reapplied her smudged lipstick, I unfastened my appendage and washed it under the tap before reattaching it to my mound. When we finally got ourselves put back together, we opened the door and walked past a long line of stunned onlookers as their eyes widened in shock ogling my still-dripping, semi-hard cock.

4

It didn't take long after Haley and I returned to the main ballroom for her husband to spot us. While we giggled amongst ourselves about the pretentious costumes of all the men in the room masking their tiny peckers, the mayor approached us with an angry scowl on his face.

"Where've you been?" he barked at Haley, his ruddy, pockmarked face making his wolf costume look all the more ridiculous. "I've been looking all over for you. There are a lot of prominent people I wanted to introduce you to."

"Jade and I were just freshening up. No need to get your knickers in a twist, dear."

"*Freshening up*?" he said, darting his eyes back and forth between Haley's face and my tumescent cock. "How long does that take? You must have been gone for at least a half hour!"

"Well, you know how we women are when we hang out in the ladies' room," she replied with a straight face. "There's no telling how long it might take to get ourselves put together in front of the mirror. You *do* want me to look pretty and proper for all your important friends, don't you?"

"I—suppose so," he stammered, distracted by my glistening

joystick. He grabbed Haley's hand, trying to drag her away from me. "Come, I want you to meet one of my biggest fundraisers, Kent Schiffer."

As he steered Haley toward a gathering in the center of the room, she looked back at me with an apologetic expression, mouthing the words *later*. Soon after, Hannah came up behind me and cupped one of my bare cheeks with her hand.

"What was *that* all about?" she said. "It looked like the Big Bad Wolf was about to bite off his wife's head."

"He might as well have," I huffed. "The way he was acting as if he owned her. All these upper-class snobs seem interested in is congratulating themselves around their buddies while showing off their arm candy."

"He did seem a little distracted by you," Hannah said, noticing Haley peering in my direction with a flushed face. "And he wasn't the *only* one. What kind of trouble did you get into with his wife? You've got a strange glow about you."

"Nothing much," I lied. "We were just freshening up in the ladies' room, looking for an escape from all the overbearing egos in this place."

Hannah looked at me suspiciously, pinching her eyebrows as she peered at my puffy appendage.

"Well, judging by the flush on your chest and the sweat dripping down your ass, I'd say you were up to a little more than just fixing your makeup. If I didn't know better, I'd swear even your *dick* looks more excited than usual."

"We may have been touching up a bit more than just our *faces*," I admitted. "We started admiring each other's costumes and one thing led to another..."

Hannah reached down and squeezed my tumescent dildo, then her eyes widened as her lips curled up into a knowing smile.

"Is it just my imagination, or does it seem a little *bigger* than when we first came in? You better be careful—you could poke somebody's eye out with that thing."

"That's not the only thing it's good for poking," I grinned.

"No way!" she said, stepping back in mock indignation. "You were *fucking* the mayor's wife in the washroom? Did he have any inkling?"

"I don't think so. But judging by how much noise we were making in there, I imagine it won't take long for word to spread around the room."

"Not to worry—just stick with me, girl," Hannah said, moving closer to protect me from everyone's disapproving glares. "If any of these jokers cause you any trouble, I'll give them a batkick to the groin."

"I doubt that'll be necessary," I sighed, catching Hannah's Tarzan friend stealing glances at me from the open bar on the other side of the room. "Most of the men in here seem reluctant to engage me in any kind of conversation, let alone actually approach me in this getup. I don't know if they're more threatened by my provocative outfit or they're just afraid to admit they're attracted to a pretty girl with a big cock."

I noticed Tarzan moving to the other side of the bar to get a clearer look at me. I found it strange that he seemed so focused on me after Hannah had spent so much time with him earlier. Unlike me, I knew she had a preference for men, and I suspected she was hoping to land a wealthy boyfriend at this event.

"What about you?" I said, shifting my position to deflect Tarzan's gaze. "What kind of trouble have you been getting up to around all these society types?"

"Not as much as I'd like," Hannah frowned. "I've found a few interesting candidates, but so far everybody's been politely keeping their dicks in their pants."

"Well, you know how it is. With all their extra ornamentation, it might be kind of hard to just whip it out. Most of these guys seem to have gone to great lengths to gussy themselves up with all this embellishment."

"I know what you mean," Hannah said, pulling her tight latex skin down uncomfortably under her crotch. "I guess I didn't give this costume as much forethought as I should have. I'm sweating like a pig under here. I have to dismantle the whole thing just to go pee."

"Not exactly conducive to pulling off a quickie in this place," I chuckled.

"Not as easily as you," she grumbled. "You don't have to remove a single stitch of clothing to get your freak on. All you have to do is find a willing accomplice and insert your magic wand."

With Hannah's back turned away from the bar, I saw Tarzan adjusting his equipment under the counter. His loincloth had begun pouching in front of his penis, and he seemed to be getting more and more aroused watching me.

"What about that hunky Tarzan character I saw you flirting with earlier?" I said, hoping to redirect his attention. "He seems worthy of a little deconstruction."

"It crossed my mind, believe me," Hannah said. "But he seemed more interested in talking about everyone else in the room. Either he's just here for the people watching, or he's gay. I mean, I'm still a *catch*, right? Who can resist a sexy chick in this tight outfit? I was practically throwing myself at him."

Tarzan turned away from me holding his hands in front of his crotch, trying to keep his rising member from making too obvious an appearance. Then he suddenly stood up and exited through a door next to the bar.

"He's probably just trying to keep up appearances," I said. "It's a pretty snooty affair, you have to admit. People would likely get their nose out of joint if they caught a couple getting too carried away in public."

"That's what *powder rooms* are for, right?" Hannah grinned.

"Speaking of, I gotta go pee for real this time. Catch up with you in a bit?"

"Sure," Hannah said. "Just try not to dip your dick anywhere it doesn't belong this time. There's no telling what kind of hullabaloo it might generate if one of these heavy hitters caught you getting it on again with another one of their wives."

"Don't worry," I smiled. "I'll be staying far away from the ladies this time."

As soon as I left Hannah, a flock of men suddenly converged on her, no longer threatened by the presence of her sexy androgynous partner. But I was happy for the distraction, because there was something about this Tarzan hunk I needed to check out. He was the first man I'd met at the ball who'd demonstrated any genuine interest in me, and I wanted to see which persona he was more attracted to.

I meandered through the crowd making small talk with some of the guests then I ordered a cocktail at the bar and slipped quietly out the same door I'd seen Tarzan use. It led to a large wine cellar, darkened and chilled to a frigid fifty degrees. I looked around the room, catching sight of Tarzan huddled between two kegs with his hand moving suspiciously between his legs.

I strolled over in his direction and smiled when I noticed his predicament. His cock was at full mast, flapping up over his flimsy loincloth, high up against his belly. I nodded when I saw how well hung he was, his organ standing a good eight inches in length and at least two inches thick.

"Aren't you a bit underdressed for this place?" I asked.

"I suppose so," he said in a shaky voice. "But I didn't know where else to go." He looked down at his crotch with a sheepish expression, vainly trying to cover up his erection. "It seems I'm having a bit of a wardrobe malfunction."

"Is *that* what you call it?" I said. "Can I offer some help? Provide a little body heat at least? You're shivering in that skimpy outfit."

"Maybe," he hesitated, peering down at my even bigger cock hanging down over my naked belly. "At least you can provide some cover if anyone else comes in here."

As if on cue, the door on the other side of the wine cellar opened, and a uniformed waiter entered the room, walking in our direction. He appeared to be looking for a particular bottle, but when he caught sight of the two of us, he stopped and did a double-take. Without pausing, I stepped closer to Tarzan and flung my arms around him, pretending to make out. It was just the cover he needed, and this was the perfect excuse to get a little closer. The waiter smiled as he nodded toward us, then collected his items and exited the room.

"Thanks," Tarzan said, pulling away awkwardly. "This is beyond embarrassing. I can't seem to make this thing go down and I have nothing to cover up with."

"I can't imagine why you'd *want* to," I said, running my fingers over his hard chest muscles. "With a body like this, you should be showing off as much of it as you can."

He glanced down at my full breasts pressing up against him in my tight leather vest.

"I hadn't counted on getting quite so—*aroused* at this event," he stuttered. "I thought I'd be able to keep it together around all these stiff necks. This has never happened to me before in a public place..."

"Not to worry," I said. "This little accident will stay between us. But if you don't mind my asking, may I ask what's gotten you so worked up? I saw you looking in my direction, and all of a sudden you wanted to hide."

"I'm sorry," he said, his face flushing like a teenager. "I just couldn't help staring at you. I find you incredibly sexy, and with so much of you hanging out for everyone to see, I guess I just had a visceral reaction."

"I understand," I said, darting my eyes over his handsome face, finding myself getting surprisingly turned by his shy demeanor. "But which *part* of me were you most attracted to? I'm hanging out on both sides."

"Both," he said, without hesitation. "You have a sexy body and you're absolutely stunning. But there's something especially alluring about a woman flaunting a man's genitals overtop their naked body. It's very—*ballsy* of you."

"You like *cocky* women, do you?" I said, leaning in towards him as I brushed my thick cock against his tight balls.

"In a manner of speaking," he huffed.

"Did you want to play with it?"

"May I?" he said. "I've never really touched another penis before..."

"You mean besides your *own*?" I kidded. "Is that what you were doing in here? Stroking it trying to make it go down before you went back into the ballroom?"

"I was so turned on, I didn't think there was any other way to get myself back together."

"Maybe I can help you with that," I smiled, reaching down and grasping his throbbing cock with my left hand. "Is this warming you up a little bit?"

"Yes," he panted, clutching my ass while he rocked his hips toward me, trying to create some much-needed friction against his throbbing hard-on. "But you've got goosebumps too. How can I help warm you up?"

I wasn't sure what he had in mind, but I wasn't interested in him fucking me in the usual manner. I'd long been fascinated seeing gay men play with themselves. I found one of the most erotic things was when they rubbed their erect cocks together. Something about the playful jousting of their erogenous parts always got me turned on.

"Well, we're both equipped with similar equipment," I said, raising an eyebrow. "I've always wondered what it would feel like to rub two cocks together..."

"Oh my God," Tarzan said. "I've fantasized about that too. But you're not exactly *functional* in the way most men are—"

"You might be surprised what this ladyboy is capable of," I grinned. "This little package comes equipped with a few extra features."

As I began stroking his hard-on, I squeezed the trigger of the pistol on my right hip, slowly inflating my rising pecker. Tarzan looked down and widened his eyes, seeing my love muscle inflating to its full ten inches. When it reached its maximum length, I placed it against the underside of his prick and began rocking my hips in tandem with his. Even though he was better endowed than most men, my giant phallus looked like an anaconda slithering up next to his garden snake. As the rubbery veins of my dildo rolled over the sensitive flesh on the tip of his rod, he shuddered and emitted a drop of dew out of his hole.

"Uhnnn," he groaned. "This is incredibly hot. I've always wondered what this would feel like, but to do it with such a sexy woman is a dream come true."

"You've always wanted to get it on with a *tranny*?" I smirked. "Well now you've got your wish."

I reached down and cupped my hands around both of our cocks and began humping him more vigorously. Tarzan groaned as he placed his hands against my chest, squeezing my breasts over my cowboy vest.

"Open it up," I nodded. "See what it's like to fuck a real ladyboy. I want to feel your hard pecs rubbing against my tits."

He didn't need any more encouragement as he fumbled with my buttons until he freed my boobs from their tight enclosure. When he saw my firm breasts bouncing on my chest, he circled them with his hands and pinched my nipples gently while I continued frotting our cocks together in my hands.

"Fucking hell," he said. "You are so hot. You are truly the woman of my dreams."

"And *man* also?" I smiled.

"Yes," he admitted. "I've long fantasized what it would be like to hold another man's penis in my hands."

"Why don't you take the driver's seat then?" I said, acknowledging his bisexual nature. "Let me admire the scenery for a while."

When I removed my hands, he placed his palms around our joined cocks and squeezed them together firmly. More precum oozed out of the head of his pole, and he moaned as he began to pick up the pace of his rocking motion. Neither one of us seemed interested in kissing, fixated on the appearance of our two big cocks frotting in and out of his hands. As he began to moan more loudly, I slapped my sweaty breasts against his hard chest. I could tell he was getting close to the point of no return, and I was eager to watch him cum with our cocks joined together.

"Yes, baby," I purred. "Let it come. Cum all over my big tits. Let me hear Tarzan's call of the wild."

Suddenly, he arched his back and thrust his dick as hard as he could against my organ, pressing his balls tightly against mine. My clit throbbed as he shot one giant geyser after another between my boobs, cumming all over the underside of his chin and face.

"Fuckkkk!" he growled with each spurt. "I'm cumming all over your cock. *Uhn, uhn, uhn!*"

With each throb and spasm, he grunted like a wild animal until he was fully spent. When he finally recovered his strength, he looked up at me with gratitude.

"Thank you," he said. "I needed that. You were even more magnificent than I imagined."

"Glad I could be of service," I said. "Now you should get yourself back in there. Somewhere out there is your *real* Jane, waiting for you to scoop her up and take her away to your jungle."

"What about you?" he said, looking at me confused.

"I'm still looking for my Jane, too," I smiled.

The whole time neither one of us had so much as touched lips. All either one of us wanted was a quickie in the wine cellar, where we could live out one of our mutual boy-on-boy fantasies. As Tarzan tucked his pecker back under his loincloth and staggered out of the cellar, I smiled.

That's one way to get it on with a man, I thought. I wondered what other fantasies awaited me before the night would be over.

5

After Tarzan left the wine cellar, I found a sink nearby and cleaned myself up, removing all the cum that he'd splattered over my dildo and chest. Feeling flushed and sweaty, I decided to catch some fresh air before going back into the main room. A side door from the cellar led onto an expansive terrace overlooking the lake. Standing alone in a corner of the balcony stood the governor's wife Alicia with her back toward me. Her arms rested on the stone railing as she puffed a cigarette, leaning over with her naked ass jutting out behind her backless apron. My pussy fluttered as I admired her shapely figure, feeling the moisture accumulating on my lips tingling in the cool autumn air.

Alicia had one of the most magnificent backsides I'd ever beheld. Her long, slender legs were taut and shapely like a professional dancer's and her ass was as tight and firm as a teenager. The rising moonlight reflecting off Lake Michigan shimmered between the space in her thighs, illuminating the dark pit under her mound. It was almost as if she were daring me to approach her and fuck her from behind.

I surveyed the rest of balcony and seeing that we were alone, I began tiptoeing toward her. It was a calm and cloudless night and the light of the full moon shone brightly over the Bannon estate, revealing the splendor of its manicured gardens. Amidst autumn-speckled trees and perfectly manicured flower beds, lay a geometric hedge maze accented with stone sculptures and a flowing water fountain.

I paused for a moment to breathe in the floral scent of the breeze wafting in from the shore. I couldn't imagine a more romantic setting for a private encounter with my pretty temptress. As I edged closer toward her, I stepped on a small pebble and it went skittering over the stone tiles in Alicia's direction. She cocked her head and turned slightly in my direction, then bent lower on the handrail, taking another puff of her cigarette. Whoever she imagined approaching her from behind only increased the boldness of her seductive pose.

Maybe being the wife of the most powerful figure in the state gave her the confidence to blow off any would-be interlopers. Or maybe she was just bored and looking for an anonymous fling to mix up her dull political life. Whatever the reason, her self-assured nature turned me on even more and as the glistening slit of her pussy came into focus, I felt the wetness from my own sex beginning to run down the insides of my thighs. When I came within a few feet of her, she stood up with her arms extended on the balustrade and blew a stream of smoke high in the air.

"Beautiful night, isn't it?" she said to no one in particular.

"Spectacular," I said. "The view is truly magnificent in this light."

"Mmm," she replied, oblivious to the identity of her midnight paramour. "Were you admiring the landscaping?"

"Among other things," I said, staring at her bald snatch. "Every-thing is so perfectly balanced and neatly trimmed. It really makes you want to pause and appreciate Mother Nature."

Alicia took a step back with one of her legs, arching her ass higher.

"It would be a shame just to *look* at it," she said, "Nature is meant to be immersed in, don't you think?"

"Absolutely," I said, taking a step closer, brushing my bare breasts against her chilly back. "You never know what you might find until you make contact."

"Like the way a woman's nipples pucker when it's cold?"

"Or when they brush against a soft surface," I replied.

"Or her lover's skin," she said

She pressed her ass further toward me and touched my protruding organ, then gasped and turned her head in my direction, checking it before we made eye contact.

"And sometimes—" she mused, recognizing the familiar shape of my leather chaps. "Nature has a way of *surprising* us with her wonderful diversity."

"Do like surprises?" I teased.

"In the right circumstances."

I reached under the front of her apron and squeezed her breasts, pressing my cock harder between her legs. She reached underneath and began stroking my dildo against her wet cleft.

"I particularly like the way nature has a way of adapting to its surroundings—" I said, beginning to inflate my rubber penis with my pistol trigger. "Like the way it expands and contracts to fill the void in any particular situation."

"Yes," Alicia panted, running her hand up and down my giant shaft. "I'd like you to fill *my* void."

By now, my inflatable penis had reached its maximum length and Alicia was busy rubbing the bulbous head against her inflamed clit.

"Fuck me, Jade," she said, dispensing with any further pretense. "I've been fantasizing about you banging me with your beautiful dick all night long."

"As have I," I panted, angling the tip into her dripping opening. I've dreamt of pounding your beautiful ass from the moment we met."

"*Fuck* yes," she grunted, as I pressed myself inside her. "Pound me with your big cowboy dick. Let me feel your balls slapping up against me while you ride me."

As I began to hump her, I marveled at how enthralled all the guests seemed to be with my transgender persona—both male and female. Everyone seemed to want a piece of my girl-cock, no matter how they could get it. While I watched my drumstick pounding in and out of her hole, I had to admit it was kind of fun assuming the male role for a change. There was something strangely empowering about being connected to a man's cock, watching all these strangers bow to my made-up masculinity. As I grasped the sides of her hips and pulled her toward me, she moaned and gyrated her hips, holding on to the rail for support.

"God damn, girl," she hissed. "You feel so good inside me. I've never had a man fill me up quite this way before. I only wish you could cum inside me. I want to hear you get off with me."

There was something about the sight of my big phallus plowing into her tight little ass that was getting me especially worked up. Even though she wasn't providing direct stimulation to my lady parts, I could have come just watching the incredibly sexy scene that was unfolding before my eyes. But I'd been saving up one more special secret. I pressed a button on the inside of my handle and suddenly my balls began vibrating from a battery-operated motor embedded inside. As I pressed my scrotum against her underside, I was instantly taken to a whole new level of excitement.

"Holy shit!" she squealed. "That's *definitely* something no man has ever done to me. Grind your nuts against me, Jade. Trib me with your big fat balls."

"Fuck, yes," I growled, feeling the rising tide of ecstasy building within me.

I couldn't help smiling, acknowledging the multipurpose capability of my male equipment. Not too long ago I was frotting a man with my big firehose, and now I was tribbing a sexy woman with my vibrating balls. For a brief moment, I felt envious of a man's equipment, but as my pussy began throbbing and dripping over my strap-on apparatus, I became acutely aware of my true gender. I leaned forward and rubbed my tits against Alicia's back, pinching and rolling her nipples between my fingers.

"Can you feel my wetness, Alicia?" I panted. "Can you feel how much you're turning me on?"

She reached under my vibrating balls and inserted two fingers inside me, stroking the front of my G-spot.

"Yes," she grunted. "You feel exquisite. You're going to make me come soon. I want to feel you come with me."

"With every part of my body actively engaged in fucking her, I didn't need any further encouragement. Within seconds, a surge of energy coursed through me, as my pussy began clamping down over Alicia's fingers. At the same time, she hunched over and began shaking wildly as she gripped the railing with all her strength.

"Fuck, Jade!" she hissed. "I'm cumming! Pound my ass with your big dick. God, I'm cumming so hard!"

As the two of us grunted and shook in simultaneous orgasm with my buttocks clenching as I pressed my cock deep into her, I suddenly became conscious of the extra light that was being cast onto the terrace from the open windows of the ballroom. When we finally came down from our powerful climax, she turned around and gently kissed me.

"It seems we have an audience," she smiled, directing her eyes toward the adjacent wall.

I peered in the direction of the ballroom and noticed a giant crowd of onlookers staring out the windows with their eyes and mouths agape.

"Good," I said. "It's about time some of these snobs got a taste of the real world outside their sheltered cocoons. "Maybe this will open their minds about the natural order of things."

With that, I lifted Alicia up onto the stone abutment and spread her legs far apart, pressing my still buzzing cock back inside her.

"If they want a show, let's really give them a show."

6

fter Alicia and I came a second time in full view of the crowd, we took a moment to compose ourselves then walked back into the main ballroom as if nothing had happened. Neither one of us seemed to care that virtually everyone was staring at us as they continued gossiping in their little cliques. I didn't even bother to refasten my leather vest or deflate my dildo as my breasts bounced freely on my bare chest in tandem with my turgid hard-on.

The two of us approached the bar and ordered matching margaritas then giggled amongst ourselves about the way everyone was trying not to stare as they talked amongst themselves. In spite of the fact that they pretended to carry on normal conversations, it was obvious that they were still highly aroused by our little tête-a-tête.

"I think Mr. Incredible is regretting his wardrobe choice right about now," Alicia chuckled, motioning toward the billionaire and his supermodel girlfriend.

I stole a glance in their direction and noticed Schiffer had a pronounced erection tenting the front of his tights.

"He's looking more like *Mr. Fantastic* with that cucumber wedged between his legs," I joked.

"And check out our favorite newscaster," she said. "It looks like Woody's popping a little Pinocchio of his own."

I peered at the anchorman and noticed him rearranging the front of his denims as a prominent bulge ran down one side of his pant legs.

"Ha," I chuckled. "I bet he's wishing he wore chaps like me."

I had to admit that I was enjoying the attention of all the powerful people in the room, particularly amongst the men who seemed especially attracted by my naked ladyboy costume.

"I don't know about *Jack* though," she said, furrowing her brow as her husband marched toward us with an angry expression on his face. "I have a feeling that his little willie will be even more shriveled than usual after watching you pound me with your big tool."

The governor stormed up to the bar and grabbed Alicia's hand, trying to ignore the pink pole jutting up from my lap.

"What is it, dear?" Alicia said, feigning surprise at her husband's indignation. "I was just enjoying a quiet drink with my new friend."

"That was hardly *quiet!*" he huffed, dragging her off her barstool. "Come on, it's time for us to go."

"But the party was just getting started," Alicia protested. "I was just starting to get warmed up."

The governor glanced down at my flaring joystick then glared at me.

"It looks like the two of you were getting more than just *warmed up.*"

"Oh, come on, Jack," Alicia said, trying to resist his advance. "We were just having a little fun. You said that you wanted me to get more comfortable around your political friends."

"Not *that* way!" he fumed. "You've made a fool out of me and embarrassed me in front of all my colleagues!"

Alicia tried to protest, but the governor pulled her away from the bar and stormed toward the entrance. After collecting their coats from the butler, they soon disappeared out the front door. Alarmed by the commotion, Hannah joined me at the bar and sat on Alicia's stool, taking a sip of her cocktail.

"Jesus, Jade," she said, slapping my dripping dildo. "You sure know how to rock the boat in these genteel affairs."

"That's not the *only* boat I was rocking around here," I said. "Were you watching the show like everybody else?"

"How could I miss it?" Hannah chuckled. "It only took one person to catch you fucking the governor's wife before the entire room joined in the spectacle. Not like they could have *ignored* it, with all the grunting and groaning the two of you were doing."

"I wasn't paying much attention. I was kind of lost in the moment."

"You sure looked like it," Hannah said. "I have to say, It was an incredible turn-on watching you fuck her from behind. I could actually see your buttocks shaking when you came." She glanced down at my swollen cock and shook her head. "How does that work, exactly? I thought you were kind of detached from that thing."

"Not as much as you might imagine," I smiled. "Touch my balls to see for yourself."

Hannah placed her hand over my rubber scrotum and I switched on the vibrator, then her eyes suddenly flung open.

"Holy shit!" she said. "That thing really *is* fully animated. What else can it do? Spurt out fake cum?"

"As much as I wish it could, no. But these two extra tricks seem to be providing all the entertainment I need."

"I'd say so, judging by how loud the two of you were howling out there on the balcony. I fact, I've got a little girly hard-on of my own thinking what that would feel like inside me. I don't suppose we could find our own private alcove for a little fun, could we? I'm so horny right now, this costume is practically glued onto my body."

I glanced around the room and noticed that everybody was staring at us with disapproving expressions.

"Why not?" I said. "After that last escapade, it looks like all bets are off. There's not much to hide any more at this point."

I took Hannah's hand and began heading in the direction of the wine cellar, but Steve Bannon and his wife stepped in front of us, smiling like Cheshire Cats.

"It appears you've been enjoying my party even more than I could have imagined," he smirked, peering at my dripping dildo. "You seem to have gotten a rise out of more than a few of our guests this evening. I'd have to say you win the prize for the most inventive costume."

"I have to admit, it's been far less of a stuffy affair than I imagined." I glanced at Genevieve, noticing the slit in the side of her dress looking even more pronounced than before, revealing her hip bone above her barely concealed pussy. "I've found the conversation very stimulating."

"So it would seem," he said, staring at my tumescent totem. "Would you like to join my wife and me for a little nightcap in our private lounge? We've been admiring you all night long and would love to continue the conversation."

"Hmm," I said, raising an eyebrow toward Hannah. "Do you mind if I bring my friend along? We were just about to explore some private time of our own."

Bannon leered at Hannah's costume then smiled at her.

"I don't see why not," he said. "What do you think dear? Would you like to bring another partner into our little meeting?"

"The more the merrier," she smiled, jumping at the chance to have some more alone time with me. "Besides, now it'll be more evenly balanced. I'm not sure I could manage the two of you all by myself."

"Come then," Bannon said, leading us to a private elevator at the base of his stairs.

As we crossed the ballroom floor, the entire room followed our movement while my protruding penis waggled playfully between my legs. When we got in the elevator and the doors closed behind us, Bannon pressed button number four and smiled at Hannah and me.

"You've already explored many of the rooms in my house," he said. "But I think you'll find the view particularly appealing from the top floor."

I glanced toward Hannah and saw that her pupils were already dilated in excitement. I didn't know if she was more impressed by the fact that Bannon's mansion had four floors and a personal elevator or that she was about to participate in a private orgy with the richest man in the Midwest.

When the lift stopped and the doors opened, we both gasped at the view. The elevator opened to an enormous bedroom with floor-to-ceiling windows providing a panoramic view of Lake Michigan. As impressed as I'd been with the view from his main floor balcony, from this elevation the lake seemed to stretch out in every direction forever. But the view on the *inside* was even more spectacular. Bannon's bedroom was almost as large as most people's houses, with giant expressionist paintings hanging on the walls, a huge wood-burning fireplace next to the bed, and a separate bar beside the sliding glass windows.

"Would you like something to drink?" he said, lifting a crystal decanter off the table. "Perhaps a glass of brandy? I've got a thirty-year-old bottle of Hennessey that I've been meaning to open for a special event."

As much as I admired his impressive collection of personal effects, I was far more attracted to the elaborate trimmings of his beautiful wife.

"That would be lovely," I said, smiling at Genevieve.

Bannon handed each of us a large goblet filled with cognac, then he pressed a remote control device and the large window panes began to separate, bringing in a gust of cool air.

"Would you like to move to the balcony? The view is even more magical at this time of the night."

"Sure," I said, checking with Hannah to make sure she was still feeling comfortable. She simply peered back at me with wide eyes and nodded silently. We stepped out onto the deck and Bannon motioned to a wicker settee encircling a bubbling Jacuzzi.

"It might be a bit warmer next to the hot tub," he said, extending his hand toward the tub. "Please—make yourselves comfortable."

Hannan and I took a spot next to one another, while Bannon and his wife sat kitty-corner to us, a few feet to our left. The view of the lake was magnificent with the light of the full moon reflecting off the ripples like an evening sunset on a secluded beach. A cool breeze wafted in from the shore, and I pulled my vest over my exposed abdomen.

"Feel free to dip your toes in the water," he said. "Or climb right in if you prefer. It's chillier outside than usual tonight."

"I wouldn't mind getting out of these boots," I said, kicking off my footwear and placing my feet in the churning water.

Then I turned to Hannah and smiled.

"This feels heavenly, Han. Why don't you join me?"

She motioned to her all-in-one ensemble and frowned.

"It's not quite as simple for me as it is for you."

"Don't be concerned about *us*," Bannon grinned. "We're all adults here. Besides, I think we've seen just about everything already tonight. No one's watching this time besides Genevieve and me."

Hannah peered at me for a moment and I nodded. I'd never known her to be shy in these kinds of circumstances and it didn't take long for her to shed her clothes and slide under the bubbling water.

"Mmm," she purred, glancing up at me. "It's lovely. You should come in. These jets are good for massaging more than just your feet."

I looked toward Bannon and his wife and they smiled with a knowing grin.

"You said you wanted to find a private spot to continue your engagement," he said. "Don't let us stop you. We'll just finish our brandies while you two make yourselves comfortable."

He glanced down at my bobbing tool then peered back up at me.

"Is your equipment waterproof?"

"It should be," I said, winking toward Hannah. "Would you like me to keep it on?"

"I think we would," Bannon grinned. "I'd love to see how you use that thing close-up. How about you, dear? Are you interested in watching Jade play with her magic wand again?"

"Absolutely," Genevieve said, staring me directly in the eye. "I'd love to see her make another pretty girl come with her big man-cock."

I pulled off my chaps and vest and squeezed the trigger on my pistol to re-inflate my shaft to its full length then pressed the button on the handle to turn on the vibrator. Bannon and Genevieve squinted at the humming device, and I smiled at them as I slipped under the surface next to Hannah.

She scooted up next to me and lowered her hand under the water, stroking my phallus as she caressed the inside of my thighs. I turned toward her and we embraced in a passionate kiss. I could feel the jets of the Jacuzzi shooting between our breasts as we rubbed our tits together while she lifted her leg, straddling my hips. Within seconds, she lowered herself onto my pole and wrapped her arms around my back. As she began to rock her hips together with mine, I glanced up and made eye contact with Bannon and his wife. I noticed the front of his toga was tenting between his legs and Genevieve's hand was moving up and down as he smiled lasciviously toward us.

"Damn, Jade," Hannah groaned as I embedded my rod deep inside her. "That thing feels amazing. Fuck me with your big cock. Rub your balls on my cunt. I can feel it vibrating."

"Mmm," I sighed, as her tits mashed up against mine in the swirling water. "Squeeze my dick, Hannah. Let's put on a nice show for our hosts."

By now, Bannon had dispensed with any form of modesty, flinging his toga to the side where I could see his throbbing erection standing up between his spread legs. Judging by the size of his wife's hand, he appeared to have a decent-sized hard-on, but nowhere near as large as my own. Genevieve had apparently gotten just worked up watching Hannah and me fucking under the swirling water, and before long she kicked off her heels and hiked up her dress, sitting down over her husband's cock while she faced us. As I darted my eyes between her husband's prick thrusting in and out of her pussy and her dark eyes, our mouths began to open in mutual pleasure.

It was an incredible turn-on watching Genevieve's sexy body squirming over her husband's cock as she watched the two of us writhing in the churning water. Whether she was more excited getting fucked by her husband while two pretty girls watched them get it on or by the sight of Hannan and me enjoying ourselves under-neath the surface, it didn't matter. Before long, all four of us were moaning loudly as we watched each other fuck our partners with abandon.

Hannah was the first to go off, as she started shaking wildly on my hips.

"Oh God, Jade," she groaned. "I'm cumming! Ram it inside me. Let me feel your balls slap up against me. Uhnnnnnn!"

Seeing Hannah having a powerful orgasm on top of me soon put Bannon over the edge as he grunted with his shaft pulsing inside his wife's pussy. Although he was staring at me, I was more interested in watching the expression on Genevieve's face as she returned my gaze with glassy eyes. I could tell that she was close, but needed a little extra stimulation to reach her goal.

As she locked eyes on me, she placed her hand over the front of her mound and began jerking her protruding nub. As her eyes opened progressively wider, I leaned forward and lifted my ass over one of the jets behind me. While the water gushed against my quivering opening, the vibrating balls pressed against my clit, and I felt a surge of pleasure engulfing my body.

"I'm close," I panted, locking eyes with Bannon's wife. "Come for me, Genevieve. Let me watch you come all over my big dick."

Even though she was planted on her husband's cock, we were both thinking the same thing. In that moment of mutual ecstasy, we were both imagining that it was *my* cock embedded in her pussy instead of her husband's.

"Yes, Jade!" she howled. "I'm cumming! I feel you inside me. I want you so bad. Oh *Gawd*..."

While the four of us panted and groaned in simultaneous climax, I glanced at Bannon, noticing him watching me with a wild look in his eye. Locked on me with laser focus, he had a strange, almost animalistic expression. I wasn't sure what he was channeling at that moment, but I could tell it wasn't his wife he was thinking about.

After we all settled down, Genevieve lifted herself off her husband's cock and slid in the water next to Hannah and me. She cuddled up beside me and her hand disappeared under the water, and soon after I felt her caressing my vibrating dildo. As Hannah leaned over to kiss her, Bannon stood up with his penis dripping a string of cum, motioning with his head inside his bed chamber.

"Why don't we all go back inside?" he said. "There'll be more room for us to play and we can watch each other better on the bed. Something tells me there's still a lot of pent-up energy between you girls."

Genevieve stepped up out of the tub first and led me by the hand into the bedroom as Hannah scampered in behind us, shivering. Bannon returned from his washroom and threw each of us a towel. Then he walked over to the bed and sat on the edge, beckoning for the rest of us to join him.

"Come," he said. "Let's share the wealth. There's plenty to go around."

"What did you have in mind?" I said, raising my eyebrows. After the Tarzan episode, I wasn't sure what part of me he was more interested in.

"There's enough parts between us for us to create an interesting *foursome*, don't you think?" he smirked.

As we all lay down on the bed and began exploring each other's bodies, Bannon seemed immediately drawn to my cock. As he sucked on my nipples, he reached down and began stroking my phallus while he masturbated himself with his other hand. While Hannah and Jenny intertwined their legs and began rubbing their pussies together, Bannon lowered himself down my abdomen until his face was directly in front of my giant pole. Suddenly, he stretched his lips around the head and began sucking it while he jerked his hand over his own dripping dick. Within seconds, he began moaning loudly, as he jetted squirts of cum all over his stomach.

Seeing her husband getting off so quickly again, Genevieve sat up and peered at the two of us with a sly smile.

"You seem quite enamored with Jade's cock, dear. I have an idea, if you're game for a little four-way fun. How would you like a *real* cock inside you this time, Hannah?"

Hannah looked at Genevieve then back at her husband, and smiled. There was little doubt that she'd fantasized about being fucked by the hot billionaire for a long time.

"*Definitely*," she said.

"Lie down face up on the bed," Genevieve instructed. "That way we can *both* have access to you. And *Jade*," she purred, with a gleam in her eye. "Why don't you choose whatever outlet looks most enticing to you among the three of us?"

As Genevieve spread her thighs over Hannah's face and lowered her pussy onto her lips, Bannon pulled Hannah's legs apart and straddled her opening with his dripping dick. As I watched them begin to fuck my best friend like she was a piece of meat, something inside me snapped. There was something about the way Bannon thought he could use her any way he wanted that pissed me off.

Just another self-righteous rich asshole, I thought. *This guy needs to be put in his place.*

As I kneeled behind him watching the two of them grinding their bodies against Hannah, Genevieve looked up at me and smiled. She glanced down toward her husband's ass and nodded. It was almost like she was *begging* me to fuck him from behind.

As the sides of my lips slowly curled up in acknowledgement, I brushed my erect dildo over Bannon's cheeks. Instead of flinching, he leaned further forward until I could see his balls waggling above Hannah's pussy. His asshole puckered as he thrust in and out of her, and for the first time in my life, I sensed the attraction of anal sex. There was something incredibly sexy and empowering about fucking a man up the ass. Now I knew why gay men separated into tops and bottoms. Just as with lesbian couples, one had to be the dominant one and one was meant to be the submissive one.

And *this* time, it was *my* turn to be the dominant one. Only in a way I'd never envisioned.

I lifted the tip of my pole, still glistening with Hannah's juices, and pointed it toward Bannon's opening. As I pressed it against his pucker, he grunted and pushed back gently.

So he likes being fucked by a woman? I thought. *It's time to show him who's really in charge here.*

I grabbed the sides of his hips and slowly pressed my cock deeper inside him. It felt strange and titillating at the same time to be fucking a man with my faux hard-on. As my balls pressed back against my clit, I imagined what it would feel like for a man to fuck another man this way. Suddenly, all the times I'd felt used by men who fucked from behind came flooding back. I thrust my dick as far into Bannon's ass as I could and began pounding my hips against his butt cheeks.

As his hole stretched as far as it could go by my coke-can-width hard-on, I found myself enjoying the feeling of thrusting in and out of him. Strangely, Genevieve seemed to be enjoying the show almost as much as me, as she writhed and moaned on Hannah's face while watching the two of us.

"Yes, Jade," she grunted. "Fuck Jack's ass. Make him your bitch. I want to watch him get off while you have your way with him."

Whether it was the sight of her pretty body twisting over Hannah's face or the sense of power I felt fucking her husband, I soon felt the familiar wall of pleasure beginning to overtake me. As I pressed my balls tight against his ass, creating more friction against my clit, I began to moan approaching my peak.

"Damn this is hot," I grunted. "I'm going to come soon. Watch me cum inside your husband's ass, Genevieve."

"Yes," she groaned, suddenly shifting her gaze to her husband's eyes.

I wasn't sure if she was communing with him at that moment or she just enjoyed seeing him at his most vulnerable moment. Either way, the sight of her convulsing over Hannah's mouth as she reached her own orgasm soon opened my floodgates. I pulled Bannon's ass hard toward me as I thrust my cock one last time deep into him, squirting all over my vibrating balls and Hannah's pussy. Within seconds, all four of us were howling in mutual ecstasy as we pounded and quivered atop one another in a mass of sweaty flesh. When we finally collapsed onto the bed in exhaustion, Genevieve leaned over and kissed me, whispering in my ear.

"Thanks for putting my husband in his rightful place," she mewed. "You have no idea how much both of us needed that."

BOOK 17

SWEDISH SAUNA

1

I knew this trip was going to be different as soon as I stepped onto the plane. The flight attendants aboard my SAS flight to Stockholm were drop-dead gorgeous. Not just typical cute-stewardesses pretty, like top supermodel stunning. Every one of them was tall, slim, and *built*. With high cheekbones, full pouty lips, and steel-blue eyes, I felt like was like I was being transported to another *planet*, not another country. One where everybody had natural blonde hair, sexy figures, and movie-star looks.

As I streamed down the aisle with the other passengers, I couldn't stop staring at the crew as they greeted the travelers with perfect smiles and lilting European accents. Instantly smitten, I felt my skin beginning to moisten while I gawked at them like a star-struck colt. When a hunky male attendant in a tight blue uniform offered to help me lift my overstuffed carry-on bag into the overhead storage compartment, I stuttered like an infatuated schoolgirl.

"Can I help you with that madam?" he offered.

"Um, yes," I said, flushing unconsciously. "I guess I overpacked for such a short trip."

As he effortlessly lifted my bag into the bin, I watched his pec muscles bulging under his neatly pressed shirt, with my face mere inches away from his chest.

"How long will you be staying in Sweden?" he asked, flashing me a full set of pearly whites.

With his handsome face and tall muscular build, he looked like a dead-ringer for the Scandinavian actor Alexander Skarsgard.

"Just a couple of weeks," I muttered.

"You can't be too careful at this time of the year," he said. "Winter-time in Sweden can be quite chilly and the nights are very long. It's best to bundle up."

"Thank you," I said, smiling at him warmly.

"Enjoy your stay," he nodded before moving down the aisle to assist another passenger.

When I plopped down into my seat, I suddenly became conscious of how wet my panties had become in the short time I'd been on the plane. A slightly older woman sitting across the aisle from me glanced at the beads of perspiration on my forehead and smiled.

"He had the same effect on me," she grinned. "Do you think *everyone* in Sweden is this beautiful?"

"I don't know," I said, shaking my head. "But if so, this should be one hell of an interesting trip."

I pulled out my phone and pretended to text someone on the screen. I knew it was going to be a long flight overseas, and I didn't want another Chatty-Cathy burning up my ear the entire way. I didn't want to lose another moment soaking up the dazzling flight attendants as they walked up and down the aisle.

When the doors finally closed and the jet began to pull away from the gate, I was happy to have an unobstructed view of the pretty stewardesses from my perch at the back of the forward cabin. As the lead flight attendant provided instructions over the intercom system, her pretty assistant took up position at the front of the aisle and smiled at me. Normally, I ignored these boring safety demonstrations, burying my head in a newspaper or playing games on my phone. But on this flight, virtually every passenger in the first-class compartment sat upright in rapt attention, with all eyes on the model at the front of the room.

While the attendant demonstrated how to properly use the seat-belts and oxygen masks, I squeezed my legs together to quell my throbbing pussy. Beyond her perfect bone structure and pretty updo under her tight bellman's cap, her skin was absolutely flawless. Her creamy alabaster tone radiated a natural blush over her Nordic cheekbones, her ramrod-straight posture reinforcing the impression of watching a model on the catwalk. When she raised her arms to point out the location of the emergency exits, her full breasts pressed against the front of her blouse, showing off her Amazon-perfect physique.

Jesus, I thought, listening to myself audibly panting as I watched her go through the motions. *No wonder men joke about the Swedish Bikini Team as their ultimate fantasy. These people really are as gorgeous as the legend says.*

As I sat in my chair getting more and more turned on watching the sexy flight attendant, I felt like I had a front-row seat at a Paris fashion show. I had the blind fortune of checking out some of the most beautiful people on Earth from in my own personal viewing room. Even my first-class leather chair made it seem like I was sitting in my home studio watching an Ingmar Bergman movie. I was glad the window seat next to me hadn't been filled, as I squirmed between the armrests trying to give my aching clit some much-needed stim-ulation.

But as I began to fantasize about taking the sexy flight attendant into one of the lavatories for a mile-high fling, the demonstration abruptly ended and she took a seat facing me at the front of the cabin in preparation for takeoff. Soon after, the jets began to roar and I felt the pull of gravity push me back against my seat as the plane lifted off the runway. When the attendant made eye contact with me momen-tarily, I fantasized that it was *her* pressing against me instead of the pull of the aircraft.

As she politely glanced around the cabin, I couldn't take my eyes off her. Whenever our eyes met, I looked away, embarrassed at my invasion of her personal space. As the heat between my legs began to build and the dampness in my panties spread, I peered up at the seatbelt sign, impatient to go to the restroom to relieve my pent-up tension. Watching this sexy goddess had gotten me thoroughly worked up and I knew it wouldn't take much to get me off. Even though it wouldn't be as glamorous as the usual in-flight fantasy, I'd have my own fun envisioning the two of us intertwined in the close confines of the tight water closet.

But when the bell chimed signaling that we'd reached cruising altitude and could remove our seatbelts, I found myself wanting to stay in my seat when I saw her getting up to begin the meal service. As she moved down the aisle offering a choice of beverages, I leered at her firm ass whenever she leaned over to hand a glass to one of the passengers. I was happy to be seated in the last row of the first-class cabin, with the relative privacy of the partition separating me from the coach compartment.

While I pretended to flip through the inflight magazine resting on my lap, my right hand began to inch between my legs in desperate need of stimulation for the aching nub underneath my jeans. The closer the cute attendant got to my seat, the more excited I got caressing myself under my magazine. By the time she reached my row, my eyes had already glazed over as I needed all my strength to contain the pleasure beginning to consume my body.

"Champagne?" she said, turning to me with a tray filled with tall goblets.

"Um, yes, thank you," I stammered, gripping the sides of my magazine tightly with two hands.

When she leaned over to hand me the glass, I couldn't help staring at her ample breasts spilling out over the top of her tight vest. A silver name tag dangled from her blouse reading Elsa.

"Can I get you anything else?" she said, smiling at me as I blushed shyly.

"What else are you offering?" I asked, my mind racing ahead with fantasies of her jumping into my lap while I ravished her in my quiet little alcove.

"Coffee, tea, juice," she offered. "Or would you prefer another cocktail?"

There was only *one* kind of tail I was thinking about at this particular moment.

"This will be fine for now, thank you Elsa," I said, biting my lip at the temptation to flirt with her further.

"I'll return in a little while with your meal service," she said. "Would you like the salmon or the filet mignon?"

I smiled, happy that I'd chosen to fly first-class for a change. Not only was the food and service a notch above normal, but I had a far better view of the pretty flight attendants in the smaller confines of the forward cabin.

"I'll have the salmon, thank you," I said, fixing my gaze on her brilliant blue eyes.

When she began walking back to the front of the plane, my eyes locked again on her firm ass.

That's not the only thing I'd like to eat right now, I thought, imagining my face buried between her thighs while she sat facing me on the sink in the lavatory.

While I continued undressing her with my eyes, my clit throbbed painfully under my tight jeans. After a few more minutes of anguished frustration, I finally stood up and bee-lined my way to the washroom. When I opened the door next to Elsa working in the galley, she turned around and glanced down at my midsection. I smiled at her, then closed the door and looked at myself in the mirror in shock.

Was she just checking me out? I thought. *What would be the chances of getting her to join me in here? Maybe if I leave the door slightly ajar...*

I shook my head, realizing the absurdity of my fantasy.

These kinds of things only happen in Penthouse Forum letters. There's no way a professional flight attendant would risk this kind of impropriety while on duty.

As I started unzipping my jeans to free my burning jewel, I noticed they were wet in the front. Peering down in the mirror, I saw that a large wet spot had formed in the crotch.

"*Fuck!*" I cursed out loud. "*That's* why she was looking at me that way."

I blushed in embarrassment at being found out, wondering how many other passengers had used this hiding place for release after watching these vixens go about their work. But at this point, the stain on the front of my pants was the last thing I was worried about. Right now, I just needed to get off, and quickly. I pulled off my jeans and underwear and hung them on the back of the door, then placed my right foot on top of the vanity. My slit stretched open as my flaming clit protruded out of its hood.

Gawd how I'd like to grind my pussy against Elsa's face right now, I thought.

I washed my hands under the sink then thrust two fingers deep into my pussy as I began to fuck myself, watching my reflection in the mirror.

If Elsa could only see me now, I dreamed. I had a pretty good figure for a thirty-six-year-old woman, and my looks were nothing to sneeze at either. Would she be able to resist keeping her hands off me, watching me fuck myself like this mere inches away?

As I began to feel the pleasure rising within me, I started to moan, pretending that Elsa was peering back at me in the mirror instead of my own reflection. I was happy for the background drone of the jet engines so that no one could hear me.

"Fuck me, Elsa," I panted. "Rub your beautiful body against me while we grind our pussies together and enjoy our own inflight entertainment."

While I imagined Elsa moaning in my ear and rubbing her tits against mine, my climax suddenly washed over me like a tidal wave as I grunted and spasmed over the sink. With my fingers embedded deeply in my hole, I jerked my hand up firmly against my mound while I gushed all over my palm. I was glad that I'd had the foresight to remove my jeans completely, because by the time I finished cumming, I'd produced quite a puddle on the floor underneath me.

Damn—I needed that, I panted, nodding at my reflection in the mirror.

I grabbed a few towelettes from the dispenser and wiped the floor, then washed my hands thoroughly and put my clothes back on. Realizing that I'd be revealing the stain on the front of my jeans for the entire cabin to see on my return trip to my seat, I loosened my blouse and draped it over the front of my crotch. Thankfully, it hung just low enough to cover the wet spot without looking too conspicuous. Then I brushed my hair and reapplied my lipstick to make myself presentable and opened the door. Elsa was still working in the galley, and she smiled at me as her eyes drifted down my body.

Had my ruffled blouse given away what I was up to in the lavatory? I wondered. *Or had she heard my moans over the noise of the jet engines?* At this point I hardly cared, and I smiled back at her with a flush in my cheeks as I walked back to my seat.

For the next hour or so, the cabin was fairly busy with the movement of the two first-class flight attendants serving and collecting the main meal service. I made small talk with Elsa whenever she passed by my seat, introducing myself and sharing my plans while I stayed in Sweden. When I told her that I intended to get in some snowboarding during my stay, she told me about the best resorts to visit in the northern part of the country. I was tempted to invite her to join me on my excursion, but my shyness got the better of me.

When things settled down after the meal service, she took a seat for a brief rest in one of the jump seats next to the main door. As she opened a magazine, I took the opportunity to study her body from head to toe. Her legs were crossed while she read the magazine, and the swelling of her calf resting on her knee amplified the sexy curviness of her long legs. I could see her dark leggings running up the underside of her skirt and wondered if they were full-height pantyhose or mid-thigh stockings with garters. It didn't take long for me to begin fantasizing once again about fucking her as she sat quietly reading her magazine.

Only this time I wanted freer access to my pussy, where I could feel my slippery slit directly and rub my burning button without any impediments. I reached up and pressed the overhead call button, and Elsa looked up when she heard the chime. She peered down the aisle and noticing the light illuminated next to my console, she put down her magazine and walked toward me.

Damn, I thought to myself as I watched her glide down the aisle. *She even walks like a supermodel.* With her narrow foot placement down the cramped aisle, her hips swayed from side to side as her calves flexed with each step. I felt sorry disturbing her from her well-earned rest, but I needed one more thing from her.

"Yes, Jade," she said when she reached my seat. "What can I get you?"

"I was wondering if you had a blanket I could use to keep warm?" I said, peering up at her innocently. "It's a bit chilly in the cabin and I didn't bring a shawl in my carry-on bag."

"Yes, of course," she said. "I'll be back in a moment."

Elsa strolled back to the front of the cabin and opened a storage locker, pulling out plastic-covered packet. Then she walked back down the aisle and handed me the folded blanket.

"Was there anything else I can get to make your flight more comfortable?"

I paused for a moment raising an eyebrow, then shook my head.

"This should be fine for now," I said with a knowing smile. "I'm sure this will make the rest of my flight much more relaxing."

Little did she know what I *really* needed the blanket for. I just wanted some cover while I touched myself secretly in the privacy of my corner while I watched her from a distance.

"Just give me a ring if you need anything else," she said.

"I will, thank you Elsa."

As she began walking back up the aisle, I glanced at the woman sitting across the aisle from me and noticing that she had nodded off, I pulled my jeans and panties down below my knees. It felt exhilarating to feel the cool gust of the jet breeze rushing up between my bare thighs. When Elsa returned to her seat, I glanced up at her and smiled, then she picked up her magazine and lowered her head.

Perfect, I thought. *You lose yourself in your little distraction while I lose myself in you as I get distracted doing other things.*

I snaked my right hand under the blanket and moistened the tips of my fingers with my slippery juices, then pulled them up and began circling my throbbing gland. Watching Elsa's pretty face while she read her magazine was the perfect aphrodisiac while I enjoyed myself under my blanket. As I rubbed my hard nub, I looked at her lips covered in clear gloss, imagining what it would feel like to have them surrounding my pearl. It didn't take long for me to start squirming in my seat as the pleasurable feelings began spreading throughout my body. Elsa peered up over the top of her magazine, and I looked away in embarrassment realizing she'd caught me staring at her once again. But when I glanced back at her, I noticed that she was still looking in my direction as she darted her eyes between my face and the bump in the blanket between my legs.

Did she sense what I was doing? I wondered. *Had I been too obvious in my amateur subterfuge?*

Either way, there was no way I was going to stop, because I'd gotten far too worked up to abandon my solo entertainment. As I returned her gaze, I slowly resumed rubbing my clit under the covering. At first, I did it in such a way that she'd have a hard time recognizing any suspicious movement. The last thing I needed was to get arrested for lewd or inappropriate behavior. I knew airlines had a low tolerance for disruptive passengers, and I had nightmares of being carted off the airplane in handcuffs in front of my fellow passengers upon landing.

But far from ignoring me or raising the alarm to her colleagues, Elsa seemed just as interested in what I was doing as I was in her. While she shifted her eyes between the magazine and the other passengers to distract attention from her watching me, I became bolder and bolder in my actions. I spread my legs wider apart and began to move my hand more quickly over my mound.

When it became obvious to Elsa what I was doing under my blanket, she lifted her leg and swung her thigh on top of her other knee. This time, I could see the curvature of her exposed thigh as her skirt hiked half way up her leg. While my hand began to move more forcefully under my blanket, I saw the muscles in Elsa's legs flexing rhythmically as she squeezed her legs together on her chair.

Is she stimulating herself while she watches me get off? I wondered.

Her quiet act of self-pleasure ratcheted up the intensity of my feelings even more, as I moved my other hand under the blanket and began to play with my sopping slit while I rubbed my bean with my other hand. Seeing that I was getting more worked up watching her at the front of the cabin seemed to increase Elsa's courage in lock-step, as the flexing action of her legs increased in speed and intensity. Recognizing that she was stimulating herself in full view of the rest of the cabin was an insane turn-on for me, and I thrust my fingers deep into my snatch, pummeling myself as I watched the flush on Elsa's face begin to spread down her neck onto the top of her chest.

I was aching for release, and when I saw her suddenly hunch over and pretend to cough as her body began to spasm, I gushed all over my hand, cumming hard for the second time during the flight. When she sat back up and glanced in my direction, I was still jerking in my seat with my mouth agape. She tried not to stare at me to avoid drawing attention from the other passengers, but she couldn't help flitting her eyes back toward me until I finally collapsed in my seat in delirious exhaustion.

For the rest of the flight, the two of us pretended like nothing had happened, continuing to carry on casual conversation while she attended to the needs of rest of the passengers. When we began to descend into Arlanda airport, I pulled myself together and collected my belongings in preparation for deplaning.

But by now, the stain in the front of my jeans had spread to the size of a grapefruit from the puddle I'd been sitting on, and I waited for the rest of the first-class passengers to disembark before rising from my seat. Holding my purse strategically over the front of my pants to hide the wet spot, I collected my bag from the overhead bin then made my way to the front exit door. Elsa was standing beside the exit wishing everyone well, and I paused for a moment before heading out onto the jetway.

"Thank you for such a memorable flight," I said, taking her hand and clasping it warmly between mine. "That was the most exceptional customer service I've ever experienced."

"The pleasure was all mine," Elsa smiled, placing her other hand over top of mine. "Enjoy your stay in our lovely country. Perhaps I'll see you on the return leg of your journey."

"I'll look forward to that," I said, realizing that I was holding up the rest of the passengers from exiting the plane. "Bye for now."

As our hands began to separate, Elsa pressed her fingers into the palm of my hand and I felt a strip of paper fall into my palm. I looked at her inquisitively, and she simply smiled and nodded. The moment I got through the jet bridge into the relative privacy of the main terminal, I stopped and unfolded the strip of paper she'd handed me.

Hope you enjoyed your inflight experience, the message read. *Drop me a line when you get settled in Stockholm. Perhaps we can enjoy a few more rides together on the slopes of the interior. Elsaflygirl@gmail.com*

I smiled a silly grin as I pulled my carry-on bag toward the exit door.

That wasn't the *only* kind of riding I had in mind for the remainder of my trip.

2

After I checked into my hotel room, I started up my laptop and opened a new email message. As my hands hovered over the keyboard, I pondered how best to respond to Elsa's invitation. Had she been thinking the same thing I was when she mentioned taking a few more 'rides' together? Was her choice of the words 'slopes of the interior' code for getting undressed and touching each other's naked bodies? Or was she just referring to snowboarding on the mountains of the north country?

Fuck it, I thought as I began to tap the keys. Either way, I wanted to see more of her—any way I could. We'd already shared an undeniably erotic moment together. There'd be plenty of other opportunities to get to know each other better during a few days of snowboarding together.

Hi Elsa, I typed.

Thank you for your lovely note. It was a pleasure meeting you on my flight to Stockholm, even if it was quicker than I hoped. I'd love to have a chance to get to know you better. Do you have some free time to do some snowboarding before your next flight? I'll be in Sweden for a week and I've got an open itinerary. Let me know if you'd like to get together,

Best wishes,

Jade.

For a few moments, I sat in front of my computer hoping she'd reply right away to my message. But after a few minutes, I realized how foolish it was of me to expect her to pause her normal routine just because we'd shared a passing moment on the transatlantic flight. I wondered how many *other* passengers had been equally obsessed by her and made similar passes. Surely, she'd have her choice of the most successful and prettiest travelers if she really wanted to strike up a more serious relationship.

I slammed my laptop shut and got up to distract myself from my single-minded infatuation. After all, I'd come to Sweden for a lot more reasons than just to meet new people. Between exploring the fjords, seeing the northern lights, and shopping the old city of Stockholm, there was plenty to do during my one-week stay. I'd even thought about staying one night at the famous ice hotel in Jukkasjarvi. But mostly I just wanted to recharge my batteries from my boring life in Chicago. I'd been flitting from one shallow relationship to another and needed a change. I figured the further I got away from home, the easier it would be for me to forget about my troubles. I hadn't planned on being gobsmacked by the most beautiful woman I'd seen in a long time.

After I unpacked my clothes and arranged my toiletries, I couldn't help checking my computer for new messages. To my surprise, I had a letter from Elsa marked only a few minutes after I'd sent my note. As I clicked to open the message, my stomach fluttered in excitement wondering what new adventures awaited me.

Jade, her message began.

How nice to hear from you so soon after our flight. I've been thinking of you too, and was wondering if you'd like to join me and a few friends for a little ski trip. My parents have a cabin near the resort town of Are, and I'm traveling there tomorrow with a couple of girls from the airline for a few days of R&R. The easiest way to get there is by train from the central station in Stockholm. There's a departure around 9 p.m. tonight that will get you in to the village early in the morning. If it's not too quick a turnaround for you, I can pick you up when you arrive and we'll all head out to the hill together. You're welcome to stay with us at my parents' place until you're scheduled to leave.

Looking forward to more adventures together,

Elsa

While I read the message, I could feel my heart beating in my chest as I imagined spending more time with the pretty stewardess. But now I'd have to share her with her friends, and I wondered if that would get in the way of our having some more intimate moments together. But she'd already demonstrated that she was attracted to women, and it didn't take long for me to imagine the bunch of us enjoying some quality après-ski time in the cosy confines of her alpine cabin. Besides, if the *girls* she was referring to were the other attendants on the flight from Chicago, the more the merrier. I'd have my very own fantasy bikini team to play with for a few days.

I quickly accepted her invitation, then packed up my things and checked out of the hotel, grabbing a cab to the downtown train station. I was surprised how packed it was for a Saturday evening, and after purchasing my ticket to Are, it took a while to get my bearings and find my way to the right departure track. When the train pulled up, I was impressed at how sleek and clean it looked. So far, I'd found everything about this country to be beautiful, polished, and efficient. Even my round-trip fare for the six-hundred-kilometer trip was thrifty, costing less than a hundred bucks.

When I stepped inside the train, I placed my snowboard gear and travel bag in the overhead rack then settled into a seat next to the window. Everything about the train was first-class, from the spotless upholstery and gleaming handrails to the crystal-clear panoramic windows. Even the *people* on the train looked stylish, dressed in fashionable parkas and fur-lined hats.

When the train began to exit the station, I peered outside the window and watched the passing streetscape flash by. I marveled at the pretty architecture of the multi-colored townhomes and plentiful canals running through the city. Within thirty minutes, the train was hurtling through the snowy forest of the interior, and I soon nodded off with my head resting against the glass.

Three hours later, I woke to the feeling of the chilly window pressing against my head, and I looked outside to see a strange glow moving in the night sky. Realizing this was the fabled northern lights I'd read so much about, I craned my neck to take in the eerie spectacle. The luminous bands swirled and morphed into ever-changing shapes and patterns, like a giant fluorescent ghost dancing in the sky. Now I understood why the indigenous people of the arctic gave such spiritual meaning to this supernatural light show. The swaying bands of color almost looked like a living organism, undulating in perpetual rhythm in the northern atmosphere.

There's another thing I can knock off my bucket list, I thought, staring up at the sky with my eyes agape in wonder.

But as the train continued north, the skies began to fill with clouds, and I checked my watch to see what time it was. The nights were over sixteen hours long at this latitude at this time of year, and I didn't want to arrive at my final destination unprepared. Even though it was approaching 8 a.m., it was still pitch-black outside and the train would be arriving into Are within thirty minutes. I went into the onboard lavatory to check my makeup and have a quick pee, then wrapped a scarf around my neck under my snow jacket, wondering if I'd prepared sufficiently for the cold Nordic weather.

When the train stopped, I gathered up my gear and headed for the station exit. Elsa hadn't been very specific about how we'd find one another at the train station, so when I got outside I stood on top of the steps surveying the parking area. There were a lot of passengers milling about with cars pulling up into the pick-up zone, so I pulled off my woolen cap and began waving in the general area of the logjam.

A few seconds later I heard a car horn beeping and a late-model Volvo SUV pulled up in front of me with the headlights flashing. The passenger window rolled down and a familiar face smiled at me, motioning for me to approach the car. The rear latch swung open and Elsa stepped out of the driver's seat waving back at me. I smiled at her and threw my board over my shoulder as I walked in their direction. When I got to the car, she gave me a big hug and threw my gear in the rear compartment on top of a bunch of other boots and snowboards.

"Did you have any trouble finding your way here?" she asked.

"No," I smiled. "It was pretty uneventful, other than the spectacular pyrotechnics in the evening sky."

"Ah yes," she said. "The aurora borealis. Was that the first time you'd seen the northern lights?"

"Yes—and it was even more beautiful than I imagined."

"We'll have lots more opportunities to view it over the next couple of nights from my cabin."

She opened the rear driver's side door and motioned me inside.

"But first, let's have a bit of fun on the slopes. I think you'll find the *daytime* views can be almost as pretty in this part of the country."

When I stepped inside the vehicle, two familiar-looking blonde girls turned toward me and smiled. I recognized both of them instantly as the other flight attendants on my inbound trip, and dressed in their pastel snowboard outfits they looked even prettier close-up.

"Do you remember Astrid and Inga from the flight?" Elsa said.

"Of course," I said, thinking I'd died and gone to heaven, surrounded by the three gorgeous women. "How could I forget?"

On the way from the station to the ski resort, we made small talk about my plans while in Sweden and what my life was like back in Chicago. The girls said they traveled there frequently, and I immediately returned the invitation, inviting them to stay with me the next time they were in town. But the whole conversation was a blur as I kept flitting my eyes between the three striking Vikings sitting next to me in the car.

When we got to the ski hill, we all carried our gear up to the lodge then went inside for a quick breakfast and coffee. The girls ordered cereal composed of muesli, fermented milk, and strawberries, and I followed along, trying to sample the local cuisine. It wasn't as bad as it sounded, and I soon gobbled down the crunchy yogurt-tasting concoction on my empty stomach. Then we wolfed down some strong coffee and went downstairs to the locker room to change into our snowboard gear. The three girls all seemed quite adapt at getting into their heavy boots, and when they pulled their goggles over their toques in preparation to exit the cabin a couple of minutes ahead of me, I shook my head in wonderment.

"You girls look like you've done this a few times before," I said, gazing up at their pretty two-piece parkas.

Elsa smiled, kneeling down to help me lace up my boots.

"There's not a lot to do during long winters here in the hinter-land," she said. "It's pretty much a choice between hockey or snow skiing. And the airline frowns upon our taking part in contact sports. Something about keeping ourselves in top condition for our guests."

"I can see why," I said, peering at the Swedish beauties. "I wouldn't want to mess with perfection either if I had your looks."

"You know," Elsa said, holding a hand out to help me off the bench. "With your fair skin and light hair, you could easily pass for a Swede too. And I think you're selling yourself short. You're just as pretty as any Scandinavian girl. Speaking of, let's get out there while we still have good light. The rides close in a few hours and it looks like we've had some good powder overnight."

When we got outside, the girls snapped on their boards then shuffled their hips forward as they began to glide to the base of the nearest lift. When we neared the front of the line, we positioned ourselves four abreast and sat down on the wide chair as it swung around to pick us up. As it picked up momentum and lifted us off the ground, my pussy pulsed in excitement feeling the hips of the other girls pressing up against my sides.

"So what brings you to Sweden?" Astrid asked, puffing a cloud of condensed air into the chilly breeze as she spoke.

"Besides the beautiful people and the gorgeous scenery?" I said, peering out over the mountainous landscape. "I guess I was just looking for something new. I was getting kind of bored with my usual routine in Chicago. It's been a while since I've been on a trip outside the country."

"Well if you're looking for something different," Inga said, smiling at the other girls. "Stick with us. We'll be happy to introduce you to some of our more interesting Swedish customs. The après-ski scene can be just as much fun as the daytime opportunities."

Elsa noticed my hands gripping the safety bar in front of me tightly as I shivered under my light snowboard ensemble.

"Are you warm enough?" she said, placing her mittens over mine on the bar. "I noticed you weren't wearing as many layers as the rest of us under that thin parka."

"I'm used to dressing for the mild midwestern winters back home. I guess I wasn't quite ready for the temperatures up here."

"You'll warm up once we get out on the slopes," she said. "All you need is a little exercise to get the blood flowing."

She peered forward as our chair neared the top of the mountain.

"What kind of trails do you like to take? How experienced a snow-boarder are you?"

"I don't get out as often as I'd like," I said, glancing down the steep slope underneath our lift. "I used to be pretty decent when I was younger, but it's been a couple of years since I've hit the slopes. Maybe something intermediate to start?"

"No problem," Elsa said. "Just head to the left when we get off the lift. We can start out on the blue trail. It's wide and gently sloping, with lots of room for us to carve wide unobstructed turns."

When the chair reached the crest of the hill, we all pushed off while I struggled to stay balanced as it thrust me forward. The other girls seemed far more composed and confident, shifting their weight expertly backwards as they dug their edges into the soft corn while I wobbled unsteadily, trying to keep my board from getting away from me.

"Ready?" Elsa said, flashing me a brilliant smile.

"I think so," I hesitated.

Seconds later, the girls pointed their boards down the hill and began carving up the light powder in tight serpentine patterns, three abreast. I watched them for a few moments, marveling at how effort-less they made it seem, but also how pretty their tight asses looked twisting and swaying as they kicked up light sprays of powder, schussing their way down the meandering slope. Not wanting to get left too far behind, I shifted my weight forward and tentatively pointed my board on a diagonal line across the slope.

At first, I was reluctant to commit myself fully into the fall line, but as I began to shift my weight forward and back on my board, I was pleasantly surprised by how easy I could turn in the freshly fallen snow. Before long, I was carving figure eight patterns overtop the trails left by the other girls and smiling with a giant grin as I began to find my groove. About halfway down the hill, I noticed the they'd pulled up on a flat section of the slope and I skidded to a halt a few feet in front of them.

"*Damn*, Jade," Elsa said as I huffed a stream of fog into the cold air, trying to recover my breath. "You know how to *ride*, girl. That's some pretty sweet carving you were doing down the trail. We're going to have to step up our game to keep up with you."

"Hardly," I smiled. "You're the ones making it look easy. I'm already starting to feel the burn in my legs. You might need to give me a couple of days to ease into this, or else I might need a wheelchair to get back onto the plane for the ride back. Something tells me you guys have had a bit more practice at this than me."

"Maybe," Elsa said. "But you sure aren't any slouch. Why don't you go first this time and we'll follow. Show us your best Lindsey Vonn moves."

I thought it ironic that they'd likened me to the pretty American downhill champion who'd recently turned the European circuit on its ear.

"I'm not *that* good," I said. "I'll just be happy if I can make it down the rest of the way without wiping out."

This time I flipped my board forward and headed straight down the fall line, rapidly picking up speed as I arched my body from side to side, reveling in the soft champagne powder of the Swedish resort. When I got to the bottom of the hill and stopped at the base of the lift, the three other girls followed close behind and skidded to a stop beside me.

"It looks like you've found your legs," Elsa said. "You can carve, girl. I was admiring your form all the way down."

"Are you referring to my ski technique or my skimpy little outfit?" I smiled.

"Both. I had a hard time staying on the course with such a pretty distraction in front of me."

"Glad I was able to keep you distracted," I smiled. "I'm hoping there'll be lots of other opportunities to divert your attention over the next couple of days."

The four of us spent the next couple of hours carving the hills, taking increasingly steep and exciting trails before we decided we need a rest. When we stopped near the bottom of one of the trails, Elsa looked over toward me and smiled in a heavy plume of mist.

"Are you ready for some fika?" she said.

Not knowing exactly what that was, but sounding pretty close to fucking, I nodded eagerly, happy to have a different kind of alonetime with the girls.

"Let's head into the lodge," Elsa said. "I don't know about you guys, but I could eat a moose after a hard morning of riding."

"Count me in," Astrid said.

"I could use a warm cup of coffee right about now," Inga nodded.

"Is that what fika is?" I said, pinching my eyebrows in disappointment.

"Yes," Elsa said. "In Sweden, coffeetime is more of a social gathering opportunity than just an excuse to get charged up on caffeine. Let's go inside and rest up for a bit while we get warmed up. We don't want to turn your body into rubber on the first day."

We trudged into the lodge and found an open spot next to a large wood-burning fireplace. As the girls began to take off their heavy parkas and outerwear, I couldn't stop scanning their shapely figures in their tight, form-fitting sweaters. The cute reindeer motifs reminded me of Pippi Longstocking, but their swelling breasts and hourglass figures reminded me more of that other Swedish meme. There was something about the warmth of the roaring fire and the sweat dripping down the back of my neck from the exertion on the slopes that was quickly getting me worked up. As I continued undressing the girls with my eyes, my mind began to wander to the possible après-ski activities that Elsa had mentioned.

"Shall we get a bite to eat?" she said, catching me eyeing up her body.

"Absolutely," I said, trying to quell my churning insides. My stomach wasn't the *only* body part that needed attention right now. I needed a distraction quickly before I peeled off their clothes right then and there and jumped their bodies in my mind's imagination.

As we strolled up to the food line, I once again followed the girls' lead. Everybody was ordering hot pea soup or oven-cooked pancakes with ligonberry jam and maple syrup. But when it came time to order coffee, they all looked at me with a strange expression when I ordered a latte with extra cream and sugar.

"What?" I said, looking at the girls with a puzzled expression. "You guys are looking at me like I just ordered *antifreeze*."

"We don't put all that extra stuff in our coffee in Sweden," Elsa said. "We like to take it straight-up, where we can enjoy its natural goodness."

"Mmm, I get that," I said, glancing at her shapely ass in her tight leggings. "Straight up it is."

When we returned to our table next to the fire, I was surprised how good the pancakes and soup tasted. I was so used to the typical American brunch of bacon and eggs that I'd almost forgotten about the pleasures of a foreign diet. Even the plain coffee tasted unusually good, as I savored the natural flavor of the north African bean.

While we made small talk about our favorite trails at the resort, I couldn't help staring at the girls' shapely figures in their tight sweaters as their chests expanded and contracted while they ate their food. The orange flames from the fireplace cast a warm glow on their faces, accenting their natural beauty. By the time we'd finished our meal, my entire body was burning and flushed in excitement.

"So what do you guys do for fun after playing on the hills all day?" I said, hoping to plant the seeds for some more adventurous après-ski activities.

Elsa looked at her friends for a moment then peered at me with a devilish grin.

"Have you ever participated in a polar bear plunge?" she asked.

"Isn't that where people jump into freezing cold water in the middle of winter?" I said, shaking my head in bewilderment. "Isn't that kind of painful and dangerous?"

"Not the way we do it. We only stay in for a short time then head into the sauna to warm up. It's actually quite refreshing. After a hard day of snowboarding, the cold water actually reduces muscle inflammation and speeds up your recovery time."

"Do you guys wear some kind of special insulation?" I said, not quite buying Elsa's dubious explanation.

"Actually, the best way to do it is in the nude. The less clothing, the better. You don't want any cold clothing clinging to you when you get out of the water. We'll have terrycloth robes ready for you to warm up quickly. But the best part about it is the sauna afterward. Feeling the warm steam all over your newly cleansed skin is absolutely heavenly. It's is a tradition we Swedes have been practicing for centuries."

The idea of seeing the three pretty flight attendants in the buff quickly eliminated my concerns about the discomfort of the procedure. It actually sounded like a lot of fun, and my mind was already racing ahead to all the possibilities once we got in the sauna.

"When in Sweden..." I smiled, cocking my head playfully. "You guys certainly aren't holding back giving me the full immersion experience. I'm eager to learn *all* about your special customs."

"Good," Elsa said, reaching down to lace up her boots. "Let's get back out on the slopes while we've still got some good light. It'll turn dark in a couple of hours and we haven't even tried the most challenging trails."

I smiled nervously, feeling the burn in my thighs when I stood to zip up my jacket.

Hopefully the *rest* of my body will still be able to function by the time these girls are ready to stop torturing me, I thought.

By three o'clock, the shadows were beginning to lengthen over the mountain, and the four of us headed back into the lodge to collect our belongings. I was actually looking forward to the dip in the cold water to help relieve my aching muscles. As we drove through the dense forest on the way to Elsa's cabin, I marveled at the natural beauty of the Scandinavian landscape. Heavy pillows of snow hung over the roofs of quaint chalets nestled among the tall evergreen trees, like icing on gingerbread houses. The woods got thicker and thicker, until we emerged onto a clearing with a small wooden cabin at the edge of an ice-covered lake.

"Here we are," Elsa said, pulling her car up next to a broad porch at the front of the structure. The setting reminded me of a prototypical arctic winter scene, like something out of a Christmas fairy tale.

"Let's go inside and get the fireplace going," she said. "You'll need to get warmed up before taking a dip in the lake."

When we stepped through the front door, I was surprised how cold the cabin was as I rubbed my hands over my shoulders trying to increase the circulation.

"Sorry about the chilly temperature," Elsa said. "We normally keep the furnace set just high enough to keep the pipes from freez-ing." She nodded toward a giant stone fireplace with tall stacks of wood framing the opening. "We prefer to heat our houses the natural way. There's nothing like the sound and smell of freshly cut birch cackling in the open hearth."

She kneeled down in front of the fireplace and rolled some news-paper into little balls then placed some kindling over top of them and struck a match. The material quickly burst into flame, and as she stacked the silver logs over the iron grate, the fire soon began roaring, throwing pretty sparks against the safety screen.

"*That's* what I'm talking about," I said, taking a seat on the mantle next to the fire, rubbing my cold fingers together.

"Can I get you something to drink while you warm up?" Elsa said. "Maybe a hot chocolate or a black coffee?"

"If it's not against the rules trying something a little sweet," I smiled. "A hot chocolate would be lovely."

Elsa disappeared into the kitchen and reemerged a few minutes later with a platter holding four steaming cups. She handed one to each of us, then the girls sat down on heavy armchairs facing me. I could feel my cheeks begin to flush as I gazed at them with the orange glow from the fire dancing over their pretty faces.

"So what do you think of our country so far?" Elsa said.

"It's a little chillier than I imagined," I said, clasping my mug between my palms to warm up my still-tingling hands. "But every-thing about it certainly is beautiful."

"We'll get you warmed up soon enough," she smiled. "Would you like a little tour of my chalet? We've got the place all to ourselves for the next few days, and you'll need to know where to find the water closet and other amenities. Besides, I need to stoke the coals in the sauna to heat it up in preparation for our polar bear plunge."

"Oh yeah," I said, huddling closer to the fire. "I'd almost forgotten about that."

As I followed Elsa through the different rooms of the cabin, I was struck by how small the place was. With only two bedrooms and one washroom, I wondered how four girls would comfortably share the space for more than a few days. But I hesitated asking about the sleeping arrangements, hoping we'd be able to at least double-up in the small space. I was already beginning to plan how I'd nestle up against Elsa on the pretense of getting warm as a prelude to more intimate exploration.

When we reached the back of the cabin, Elsa opened a heavy door and the smoky scent of fresh cedar filled my nostrils as I peered into a large wood-paneled room. Every surface of the interior was lined in reddish-brown planks of wood, with wraparound wooden benches on two levels surrounding a small metal stove topped with gray rocks.

"Wow," I said, inhaling the smoky scent. "This room is even bigger than the bedrooms. You must spend a lot of time in here."

"Having a daily sauna is like a spiritual experience for us Swedes," Elsa nodded. "It's part of our DNA. There's no better way to relax and wind down after a busy day."

She stepped toward the little stove and placed a large ladle into a wooden bucket of water. As she spilled the liquid gently over the glowing rocks, a hot steam began to fill the room with a pleasant eucalyptus aroma.

"That's an interesting way to warm up a room," I said, my heart racing at the thought of soon lying in the heavenly space next to the three beauties.

"Radiant heat is the cleanest type of heat," Elsa nodded. "Plus, the humidity does wonders for cleaning out your lungs and your pores. You'll feel like a new woman after spending a couple of hours in here."

"I can imagine," I said, beginning to feel my pussy perspire at the thought.

"Are you ready for a bracing swim first?" Elsa said, flashing me a sly grin.

"I guess so," I murmured, preferring to stay in the comfortable and aromatic environment of the steam room.

"Let's get changed out of our outerwear," she said, opening an adjacent closet. "I've got some heavy robes to keep you warm before and after the swim."

We all returned to the living room, where the three girls began to disrobe. I hesitated at first, nervous to reveal my naked body among a group of strangers. But as they peeled off their layers showing more and more skin, I slowly began to undress. Their firm breasts bounced on their chests as they pulled off their undershirts and I couldn't help gasping when they finally removed all their clothes. All three of them had creamy pale skin and Playmate-perfect figures. With nary a hair to be found anywhere on their bodies below their flowing blonde locks, my pussy pulsed in excitement as I stared at them unashamedly.

"Jesus," I said, shaking my head in amazement. "Is *everybody* in Sweden in this good shape? You guys all look like somebody straight out of a beer commercial."

"Yeah—we get that Swedish Bikini Team thing all the time," Elsa said, shaking her head. "I'm not sure Budweiser did us any favors creating that image of Scandinavian girls for North American consumption."

She gave my body a quick going over as I pulled off the last of my underclothes.

"But you're no slouch either, Jade. With your blonde locks and athletic figure, you could pass for a Swedish girl any day."

I stood awkwardly facing the three girls, feeling the heat of the nearby fire burning the back my naked body.

"I'm just happy to be mentioned in the same *sentence* with you guys, let alone be thought of as one of your countrymen," I said, hoping to deflect everyone's attention from my naked figure. "Are we going to do this or what?"

"Of course," Elsa said, handing out terrycloth robes and slippers to each of us. "But be careful as you walk down the path toward the water. There's plenty of ice, and the rocks are quite slippery. You might want to hold my hand as you make your way over the flagstones."

We all put on our gowns, then Elsa opened the front door as I felt a rush of cold air enter the cabin.

"Come on, scaredy-cat," she said, holding out her arm for me. "We don't want to let the cabin get cold again. Let's take a dip before you lose your nerve."

I wrinkled my forehead, then took Elsa's hand as the four of us scampered down the frozen flagstone path to a small dock extending out over the water. When we got to the end of pier, I noticed a ten-foot-diameter hole cut into the ice covering of the pond and I looked at Elsa with an incredulous expression.

"You want me to go in *there*?" I said with my eyes agape.

"Just for a few moments," she said. "I promise you'll enjoy it. There's nothing so invigorating as a brief plunge into freezing-cold water to charge up your adrenaline. Are you ready?"

"I don't know..." I said, pulling back on Elsa's hand.

Suddenly, Astrid and Inga threw off their robes and jumped into the black pool, emerging from the frigid surface hollering in delight.

"Come on in, Jade," Inga said, flinging her wet hair behind her head. "The water's lovely. Come experience the crystal-clear water of our natural habitat."

"Natural habitat?" I scoffed. "Maybe for a *polar bear*."

Elsa turned to face me and squeezed my hand.

"Come on Jade, you're just torturing yourself standing out here in the cold air. We'll jump in together and it'll be over before you know it. Then we can all get nice and cozy in the warm sauna."

There was something about the way she said *nice and cozy* that encouraged me to get this over with.

"Ready?" she said, dropping her robe onto the dock.

I looked at her sexy body shining in the bright moonlight and pulled off my frock.

"One–two–THREE!" she shouted, then she leaped off the dock pulling me into the pitch-black lake.

It took a moment to register the feeling of the cold water surrounding my body as my mind was still in shock at the audacity of what we were doing. But within seconds, I could feel the painful burn of the freezing depths as my teeth began to clatter while I treaded water.

"Isn't it *fabulous*?" Elsa said, smiling at me with a big toothy grin.

"Ye-yes," I stuttered, trying to block out the numb feeling rapidly spreading over my body. "That's one thing you could call it."

"Look, up at the sky," she said, peering upward. "The northern lights are even more beautiful this far away from the city."

"It's stunning," I said, recognizing the swirling green clouds. "But I think I could appreciate it better dressed up in a warm sweater from your front porch with a warm cup of coffee resting on my lap."

"Okay," Elsa nodded. "I think we've exposed you long enough to the natural elements for one night. Let's get out of here and warmed up."

She swam to the front of the dock and climbed up a small wooden ladder then held out her hand to me as she bent down over the edge.

"Give me your hand so you don't slip getting up."

As I kicked my way to the ladder and placed my hands on the rungs, I could feel my muscles shaking as I tried to pull myself up. Elsa grabbed one of my hands and lurched me out of the water, then wrapped one of the robes around my shivering body. As she held me close trying to share her body heat, I watched the other two girls emerge from the pool with beads of water running over their sexy figures. Their areolas contracted with deep goose bumps as their hard nipples extended out from their breasts almost a full inch. For a moment, I forgot that I was standing near-naked in subfreezing temperatures soaking wet while I admired their sexy bodies.

"Come on," Elsa said. "Let's get back into the cabin and warm up in the sauna. I think you're ready for a new kind of Swedish experience."

The four of us scurried up the path, then Elsa opened the front door and we scampered over the hardwood floor into the sauna. While Elsa poured three ladles of water over the steaming coals, the room soon filled with the soothing sensation of the humid heat. I sat down next to the stove, with the other three girls sitting on the two levels directly opposite me.

"There," Elsa purred. "Doesn't that feel a little better?"

"Yes," I said. "But not enough to take off my clothes quite yet. I'm still warming up in this nice cozy robe."

"Feel free to keep it on for a little longer," Elsa said. "But we normally like to take our saunas in the nude. Soon you'll begin to sweat and you'll want to give your pores a chance to open up and let your body cleanse yourself."

As if on cue, Astrid and Inga unfastened their belts and pulled their robes open, revealing their glistening breasts.

"Yes," I panted. "I want to experience *everything* here in Sweden the same way you native girls do."

"You know," Elsa smiled. "I kind of like watching you covered up. It reminds me of our little affair on the plane."

"Oh?" I said. "You remember that still?"

"How could I forget?" Elsa grinned. "That was the most interesting flight I've had in a long time."

"You seemed to be enjoying yourself almost as much as I was."

"I have a little secret to confess," she said. "I had a little help of my own while I watched you."

"Really?" I said, pinching my eyebrows together in confusion. "I saw you flexing your thighs, but–"

"There was a little more than that going on. I had something *inside* while I was rubbing myself."

"Inside?"

"Ben-wa balls. Have you ever tried those before?"

"I've heard of them but never tried it. How do they work?"

"You gently rock your hips or squeeze your legs together, and they roll around inside your pussy providing a very erotic sensation. It's quite an exquisite feeling. I have them inside me right now."

"*You do?*" I said, widening my eyes in surprise. "How do you keep them from falling out?"

"It's not hard to keep them in using your Kegel muscles. In fact, it's considered a good way to exercise those muscles to maintain optimal sexual function."

Elsa paused for a moment, as she began to spread her legs apart.

"Can you do me a favor and play with yourself under your robe while I replay our little erotic encounter on the plane?"

"*Hell* yes," I said, happy to see that Elsa and the other girls were just as interested as I was moving our relationship to the next level of intimacy.

As I slipped my hand under my robe, I felt my still cold and clammy skin over the front of my hairless mound. But as I moved my fingers over my slit, I felt my warm natural juices beginning to lubricate my vulva.

"Mmm," I purred, watching Astrid and Inga spread their legs further apart as they watched me. "I *like* seeing you in your natural habitat."

"Yes," Elsa groaned, rocking her hips gently on the wooden bench. "You're very pretty, Jade. I've been dreaming about watching you up close ever since our flight ended."

"I was so happy when I read your note," I smiled. "I've pleasured myself many times replaying that moment over and over."

"As have I," Elsa said, rubbing her thighs together as she opened her robe wider for me to see her juggling tits. "And I wasn't the *only* one who enjoyed that memory," she said motioning to the other girls sitting on the bench beside her.

Astrid and Inga nodded as they moved their hands between their legs and began to circle their nubs.

"You *told* them?" I said, feigning surprise.

"Of course. We share everything together. You're not the *only* one who likes a little play time between girls every now and then."

I smiled at the revelation that they were all bisexual like me.

"It looks like the only person missing from your troop is the hot flight attendant who reminds me of Tarzan," I said

"You mean *Erik*?" Elsa said. "He's quite a dish to be sure, but I think he prefers to bat for the other team as much as we do."

"You mean he's gay?" I said. "What a shame. I was undressing him on the plane almost as much as I was you girls."

"Not to worry," Elsa smiled. "I'm pretty sure between the three of us that we'll be able to keep you properly entertained during your stay."

"I hope so," I panted, watching Astrid and Inga place their fingers inside their pussies while they jilled themselves watching me play with myself.

"Open your robe now," Elsa ordered. "Let me see exactly what you were doing under that blanket on the plane. I want to watch your pretty body while you pleasure yourself. It's just us girls this time and nobody else is watching."

I didn't need any more encouragement as I began to feel the pleasurable sensations spreading throughout my body. The rising steam from the coal stove had increased the room temperature to well over one hundred degrees and I didn't need any more excuses to fully disrobe. I took my gown off my shoulders and threw it on the bench beside me and spread my legs wide apart to let the girls see my glistening lips.

"Yes," Elsa said. "Show us what you were doing with your fingers under that blanket."

By now, I was burning up inside from the rising passion as I watched the three goddesses touching themselves while they watched me. I plunged my middle two fingers into my snatch and pulled my palm against my throbbing button, stroking myself with increasing intensity as the three women writhed on the wooded benches in front of me. Elsa spread her legs further apart, rocking her hips forward and back while she rubbed her clit in tight little circles.

"Yes, Jade," she purred. "Fuck that sweet pussy with your pretty fingers. I want to watch your body heaving and shaking again when you come."

"Damn, Elsa," I said, feeling the wall of pleasure rapidly building inside my body. "This is a feast for my eyes. I'm going to come soon."

"Yes, my pretty American," she said. "Let us watch you satisfy yourself while we pleasure our bodies. I'm close too."

As I watched the three beauties rocking their bodies on the warm planks, I felt my body fall over the precipice as I clamped down over my fingers, hunching over in a series of rhythmic spasms. With the pressure built up inside my pussy from my fingers damming the flow of my juices, I pulled my fingers out of my hole and began spraying long streams of fluid over the steaming wooden floor. Seeing me squirting my juices while racked in pleasure soon pushed the other girls over the edge, and within seconds all four of us were shaking and groaning in the steamy fog of the sauna.

"Now I see why you were covering yourself up when you left the plane," Elsa sighed when she came down from her climax. "That's one part of the experience I definitely missed. You are one talented and sexy lady, Jade."

"Not nearly as sexy as the three of you," I said, catching my breath. "That was the hottest show I've seen in a long time."

"I have to agree," Elsa smiled, peering at her colleagues. "What do you think girls? Is this the sexiest passenger we've ever had on our transatlantic flight?"

"Definitely," Astrid nodded. "I've seen a lot of fuckable passengers in my day, but nobody I've wanted to get down and dirty with as much as this one."

"And we're just getting started," Elsa grinned. "There's so many other ways we can have fun together now that we're free of all the limitations on the plane. What's your ultimate fantasy, Jade? What would you like to do now that you have the three of us all to yourself?"

"Oh my God," I said, realizing all my dreams were about to come true. "My mind is racing with so many possibilities right now. But honestly, I'd just like to watch you three do your thing together. This is the like the ultimate erotic video, watching three gorgeous girls touching each other. I'll be happy to get in on the action soon enough. For now, let me just soak up your fabulous figures a little longer while I watch you get a little more interactive."

Elsa smiled as she peered over at Astrid and Inga.

"What do you say, girls? Shall we indulge our guest in her little fantasy?"

"I thought she'd never ask," Inga smiled, shifting her body closer to Elsa.

"If you're just going to *watch*," Elsa said, pinching a little string between her legs and pulling two glistening chrome balls out of her slit. "Would you like to try my little toy? I think you might find it makes for a more engaging experience."

"Absolutely," I said, raising my eyebrows as I peered at the intriguing balls.

Elsa stood up and walked across the floor then handed me the slippery orbs. I could smell the musk of her scent on the globes and I looked up at her, grinning a broad smile.

"Just be sure to leave some of the string hanging out your opening," she said. "They can get pretty far up inside you in the heat of the moment and you don't want to lose them up there. Once you place them inside, you'll find plenty of ways to stimulate yourself. Enjoy."

Elsa returned to the other side of the room, sitting on the upper bunk while Astrid stood on the lower bench facing her with her back toward me. As she lowered her face toward Elsa's pussy, Inga sat between her legs and tilted her head up as Astrid planted her mound over her chin. Within seconds, all three girls were rolling their hips in a three-way ménage as they began to grunt and moan in unison.

Watching them pleasuring themselves just a few feet in front of me soon got my juices flowing again as I awkwardly pressed the two chrome balls into my slit. They slipped inside easier than I imagined, but it felt unusual to have such a strangely shaped object inside me other than the usual dildos and vibrators I was accustomed to.

But as I began to rock my hips slowly on the bench, I could feel them sliding forward and back against the walls of my pussy, and I soon began to mew and groan along with the other girls. It didn't take long for me to get comfortable with the pleasurable feeling of the slippery balls stroking the walls of my pussy, and when I placed my fingers against my dripping clit, I felt a jolt of electricity running through me.

This is a little different, I thought. *Why haven't I tried this before?*

Now I understood why Elsa brought them with her wherever she flew. With their unobtrusive form factor and concealed placement, no one would be any the wiser as she went about her duties receiving gentle, sensuous stimulation whenever she moved.

As I watched Elsa spread her legs wide apart and Astrid humping Inga's face while they ate each other out, I began to rock my hips faster and faster watching the girls bucking and moaning in front of me. With Inga's legs splayed far apart as she rubbed her bald pussy with her glistening fingers, and seeing the base of her chin planted firmly against Astrid's mound, watching the three girls fucking themselves in the superheated environment of the aromatic sauna was the most erotic thing I'd seen in a long time.

When Elsa placed her hands beside Astrid's head and pulled her face harder against her pussy as she locked eyes on me, I suddenly felt a surge of pleasure engulfing me. With our mouths yawning wider and wider apart in shared ecstasy, I couldn't hold back any longer.

"Oh *fuckkk*," I groaned in pleasure, my body beginning to shake once again in another intense orgasm. I could feel the Ben-wa balls rolling around inside as my pussy walls contracting rhythmically against them, sending me into new paroxysms of pleasure.

Watching me shaking uncontrollably on the steamy wooden planks seemed to bring Elsa to a new level of pleasure, and soon she also began jerking spasmodically as she held Astrid's face tightly against her pussy. Like a chain reaction, Astrid suddenly became weak at the knees as she slumped forward against Inga's chin with her buttocks shaking like a bowl of water. Feeling Astrid coming all over her face, Inga raised her hips off the bench and began flapping her thighs in and out in mutual ecstasy. Realizing that all three girls were coming together took me to another level, and within seconds I was having my third powerful orgasm of the afternoon.

After we all come down from our climaxes, I suddenly became aware of the ache in my quads from my hard day of snowboarding. I'd been so lost in the moment watching the other girls having fun and pleasuring myself that I'd forgotten I'd just had the most intense exercise in months.

I'll have to take it easier on the slopes tomorrow, I thought, *if I'm going to keep up with these girls and enjoy some more off-piste action.* The après-ski experience had been even more exciting and adventurous than the vigorous snowboarding exercise. I wanted to save myself for the next step in my Swedish immersion.

4

Over the course of the next few days, Elsa, Inga, Astrid and I made love many more times between our snowboarding, polar plunge, and sauna escapades. By the end of the week, I'd experienced every erotic entanglement with the three girls that I'd fantasized about on my initial flight to Sweden. When it finally came time to say our goodbyes, I was sad to leave but thrilled to have had the opportunity to spend so much quality time with the three Scandinavian beauties.

As the four of us drove back to Stockholm in preparation for my return flight to Chicago, we talked about reconnecting stateside, but I never expected to see the girls again. We'd had our moment of glory together, and that was enough for me. I'd cherish the experience forever and carry enough memories to keep me entertained for quite some time into the future.

But I still had one last flight with the girls, and I planned to make the best of it. Elsa and I had talked over the last couple of days about how we might be able to arrange a *real* mile-high liaison, and my body was tingling all over in anticipation of the trip. After I passed through airport security and collected my boarding pass, I smiled at Elsa and Astrid as I boarded the plane and took my seat near the back of the first-class cabin. The same woman I'd met on my inbound flight was sitting across the aisle from me again, and I smiled politely before pretending to check my email messages.

While the rest of the passengers shuffled onto the plane, I tried to keep myself distracted reading a magazine while I squirmed uncomfortably in my seat. Watching Elsa do the safety demonstration drove me crazy knowing she was receiving internal stimulation the whole time from her Ben-wa balls. I cursed myself for not remembering to buy some of my own to keep me entertained during the long flight.

But when the demonstration was over and the girls took their seats in preparation for take-off, Elsa winked at me, giving me a sly smile. Within thirty minutes, we reached cruising altitude and Astrid and Elsa began delivering the meal service. It was difficult restraining myself from interacting with the girls in a more familiar manner, but I continued playing the role of naive first-time traveler to maintain their professional demeanor. Besides, I knew that very soon we'd be able to dispense with the charade and have one last chance at resuming our special relationship.

When the meal service was over, Elsa and Astrid seemed more generous than usual offering the passengers their choice of alcoholic beverage. Before long, most of the early-morning travelers had nodded off in their seats from the combined effects of full stomachs and the alcohol-induced sedative. The girls took their seats at the front of the cabin for a brief rest, and after briefly scanning the attentiveness of the passengers, Elsa nodded toward me and tilted her head in the direction of the forward lavatory.

I carefully glanced around the cabin and when I saw that everybody was either sleeping or absorbed in their reading material, I rose from my seat and slowly made my way up the aisle. As I opened the door to the lavatory, I smiled at the two flight attendants and they winked back at me. When I closed the door behind me, my heart began racing a million miles an hour thinking about what we were about to do. Whether it was from the danger of being exposed or from the excitement of soon reconnecting with my Swedish lovers, I wasn't sure. But either way, my panties were already soaked from the rush.

It seemed to take forever for Elsa to join me in the lavatory, and after a few minutes I began to wonder if some of the passengers had woken up or requested additional aid. Not knowing what to do with myself, I began to disrobe and hung my clothes on the peg over the door. Looking at my fully naked body in the mirror, I began to play with myself imagining her touching me in the private cubicle. Just as I was about to come remembering the sight of the three sexy stewardesses in the sauna, suddenly the door swung open and Elsa stepped inside. She looked at me hunched over the sink with my hands between my legs and smiled as she shut the door quietly behind her.

"It looks like you've gotten started without me," she said. "That's my girl. We won't have too much time to do this while Astrid is keeping watch."

She stepped toward me then reached up to the paper towel dispenser above the sink and laid a protective layer of towels over the vanity.

"Get up on the sink and spread your legs for me," she instructed. "I need to fuck you right now. I've been dreaming about this ever since I saw you."

"That makes *two* of us," I sighed, turning around to face her while I lifted myself up onto the sink, splaying my knees against my naked breasts.

Elsa took one look at my glistening pussy and hiked up her skirt, revealing her bald pussy framed between black garter stockings.

"I *knew* you were naked under there," I smiled, feeling my juices beginning to run over my perineum all the way down to my throbbing rosebud.

"Would I have it any other way?" she said, pressing her mound against mine as she locked lips with me and pressed my back against the cold glass mirror.

"Mmm," I hummed, feeling her wetness touching mine. "Fuck me, Elsa. I've been waiting for this a long time."

Elsa lifted her knee and extended her right leg, placing her foot against the mirror beside me. Her legs were separated like a pair of open scissors, with our pussies grinding together as we moaned in each other's mouths. For a moment, my mind reeled at the audacity of what we were doing, but it didn't take long for me to begin feeling the rising tide of pleasure spreading throughout my body. Elsa had already revealed her incredible flexibility to me in our prior erotic encounters, but this new technique with her fucking me in a perfect split took me to a whole new level of sexual intensity.

"*Oh God*," I panted as I listened to our wet labia smacking together while we ground our pussies against one another. "Are you still carrying those love balls inside you?"

"You tell *me*," Elsa grunted as I felt her buttock muscles contract against my sweaty palms.

Suddenly, I felt the slippery balls pass out of her pussy into mine as her pussy began contracting in the initial stages of orgasm.

"Come with me, Jade," she panted. "I want to feel you spray all over me like you did in the sauna."

"*Fuck* yes," I hissed, feeling my climax suddenly overtake me from the feeling of Elsa's balls swirling around inside me. "I'm cumming, Elsa!" I groaned. "I'm cumming so hard!"

As my walls contracted tightly over the steel balls and I began squirting all over Elsa's pussy, the balls suddenly spurt back out as we grunted in unison from the feeling of the slippery orbs rubbing between our slits. We tried to remain as quiet as I could in the narrow confines of the lavatory, but it was difficult to stifle our screams of mutual ecstasy as we ground our hips together on the shaking vanity.

When the two of us came down from our powerful climaxes, I peered down, noticing that I'd soaked Elsa's black stockings with my juices.

"Sorry, sweetie," I said, shaking my head. "But I couldn't help myself. When you passed me the balls, I had the hardest climax I've had in a long time."

"Not to worry, babe," Elsa smiled, reaching into her purse beside the counter. "We flight attendants come prepared for every emergency."

As she began to pull out a new pair of stockings, we heard a tap on the door. Fearing we'd be caught by a passenger wanting to use the lavatory, my heart began thumping wildly as my eyes widened in fright. Elsa held a finger to her lips then tapped back twice on our side of the door, and the person on the other side tapped back quickly three times in succession. She smiled back at me then opened the door as Astrid squeezed in next to us.

"*What the...?*" I said, pinching my eyebrows in surprise. "Who'll be our lookout in case another passenger needs to use the washroom?"

"Everybody's completely passed out and sleeping peacefully," Astrid said. "We've got a few more minutes to have a little fun. I couldn't resist. Listening to you guys has gotten me all worked up."

"We were *that* obvious?" I asked.

"Only if you were standing next to the door. The sound of the jet engines drowned out most of the noise."

"Okay," Elsa said. "But we'll have to act fast. Let's let Jade take the driver's seat this time. I'll listen for any passenger pings next to the door."

Astrid hiked up her skirt and leaned back against the sink, pulling me toward her, rubbing her mound against my slippery pubis.

"Who's wearing the balls *this* time?" she smiled, peering toward Elsa.

Elsa passed Astrid the glistening balls and she slipped them inside her pussy, then she pulled me closer and began kissing me hard on the lips. Although we were standing in an upright missionary position this time, we were able to angle our hips just enough to touch our clits as we ground our pussies together. As I began to feel my pleasure rapidly escalating, thinking our little tryst couldn't possibly get any more erotic, suddenly Elsa stepped behind me and thrust her fingers into my snatch as she began finger-fucking me from behind.

"*Yes, Jade!*" Astrid panted, feeling Elsa rocking our hips together. "I want to feel you cream all over me when you cum. Fuck me with your pretty American pussy."

Feeling Astrid's pussy grinding against mine with Elsa finger-fucking me from behind as she squeezed my tits was a sensory over-load. Within seconds, I began climaxing once again as I squirted a stream of powerful jets inside Astrid's hole while we moaned into each other's mouths, gripping each other tightly. Elsa pressed her own mound hard against my quivering buttocks as the three of us groaned in simultaneous ecstasy with the cabin full of passengers just outside the door seeming a million miles away.

When we all recovered from our climaxes and realized what a mess we'd made, the girls quickly changed stockings while I cleaned up the room. When we finally collected ourselves and prepared to leave, Elsa placed her ear to the door and nodded.

"I'll go first to make sure the way is clear," she said. "If everything looks good, I'll tap twice then you can both come out."

Astrid and I nodded, then Elsa opened the door and closed it quickly behind us. Within a few seconds, we heard a soft double-tap and the two of us exited the washroom as I made my way back to my seat past the still-sleeping passengers. But when I got to my chair, I peered over at the woman sitting next to me and she opened one eyelid, smiling at me.

Fuck, I thought. *We've been made.*

But seeing that she wasn't overly perturbed by the incident, I settled back into my seat, feeling the dampness of Astrid's and Elsa's juices clinging to my pussy pressing up against my moist panties. I glanced toward the front of the cabin and saw the girls sitting quietly beside one another in their jump seats with a sexy glow still on their cheeks. I smiled at them and mouthed the words *Thank You*, blowing each of them a kiss.

Seconds later, the woman sitting next to me pressed her call button and when Astrid walked down the aisle to attend to her, she asked for a blanket. When Astrid returned with the cover, the woman placed it over her lap and moments later I noticed her hand slip underneath it as she began to stroke herself between her legs. Sitting in the middle row of seats, she wasn't able to make direct eye contact with Astrid or Elsa, so she turned her head and smiled at me. As I saw her eyes begin to glaze over in self pleasure, I smiled back at her with our shared secret.

It looked like I wasn't going to be the *only* one enjoying a little mile-high thrill on our trip back from Sweden.

BOOK 18

THE THERAPIST

1

"Every time I see you, I want to tell one of those bad gynecologist jokes," I said to my sex therapist friend Hannah at our weekly luncheon.

Hannah rolled her eyes as she took another bite of her salad. Her practice seemed to be the never-ending butt of jokes among our friends, but she'd learned to take the digs with good humor.

"Well you know I'm a far cry from a gynecologist, but I could use a little laugh today, so if you really need to get it out of your system, lay it on me."

"Ok, so this old lady goes to see her dentist," I started. "When her appointment is called, she sits in the chair, lowers her underpants, and raises her legs..."

"Uh huh," Hannah murmured, lifting a glass of soda water to her lips to signal her disinterest.

"So the dentist says," I continued, 'Excuse me, but I'm not a gyne-cologist.'"

I paused long enough for Hannah to begin swallowing her water. "'I know,' said the old lady. 'I want you to take my husband's teeth out.'"

Hannah lurched forward, spewing her soda water all over her salad as she raised her hand to her mouth, coughing loudly.

"Are you okay?" I said, glancing at the surrounding restaurant patrons alarmed by the sudden commotion at our table.

"Y–yeah," Hannah gagged. "The water just went down the wrong way. I wasn't expecting that punchline."

"Pretty good, right?" I smiled.

"Better than most, I'll grant you," she nodded. "But I don't know why you guys always make fun of my practice. *Someone* has to help all the sexually dysfunctional people out there."

"I know," I said, frowning sheepishly. "It's just hard to imagine what goes on in your office when people talk candidly about their sex lives."

"You'd be surprised," Hannah said, taking another swig of water to clear her throat. "In fact, I was thinking of inviting you to one of my sessions sometime."

I pinched my eyebrows and shook my head, surprised at her offer.

"As a *patient* or as an observer?"

"You don't need any help with your sex life," she said. "You're already miles ahead of me with all your wild escapades and adventures. I'd like to present you as more of a role model for what a healthy, sexually uninhibited person looks like."

"What would you have me *do* exactly? Don't you have to protect patient-doctor privilege? I thought you guys had to keep everything at arms-length, so to speak."

"I've been experimenting with some different strategies lately," Hannah smiled. "Let's just say I've been trying out some more *active* therapeutic techniques."

"No way!" I said, widening my eyes as I rested my cocktail on the table so as not to spill it. "Isn't that against the rules? I thought you had to maintain a certain degree of professional distance or risk losing your license."

"I still do. The only difference is now I encourage them to practice some of the prescribed self-empowerment techniques in my *office* instead of at home, so I can coach and guide them more actively. Besides, everybody signs a waiver before we take it to the next level."

"Holy shit!" I said, shaking my glass incredulously. "While you *watch* them touch themselves intimately?"

"Sometimes," Hannah nodded. "But most patients prefer to be concealed behind a protective screen when they first start the process."

"So you basically guide them through a facilitated *masturbation* session?"

"In a manner of speaking, yes. I find most patients need a little more active engagement to get them over the hump becoming comfortable enjoying sex with another person. You'd be surprised how many sexually dysfunctional women there are out there."

"So most of your patients are women?"

"Yes–I find them much more interesting to work with."

"Oh my God," I panted, beginning to feel my panties moisten under my tight jeans. "I'd love to be a fly on the wall in one of these sessions. How do you manage to stay focused when things start to heat up? Don't you get aroused while these women pleasure themselves?"

Hannah shifted uncomfortably in her chair, signaling for the waiter to bring her another cocktail.

"I do. At first, I just kind of squirmed in my chair and squeezed my legs together in frustration. But I've discovered a more animated way to keep myself stimulated while I watch my patients enjoying themselves."

My eyes flew open as the fluid in my cocktail glass began to tremble.

"You stick a *vibrator* down your pants?!" I said. "Isn't that kind of noisy? How do you hide that from your patients?"

"It's not just *any* vibrator," Hannah said with a crooked grin. "Our friend Cheryl from the local Babeland store introduced me to a new kind of toy. It's designed by a woman to mimic the touch and movement of real fingers and lips. It doesn't buzz so much as *hum* as it undulates both inside and on the outside of your vulva."

"Jesus!" I squealed, furrowing my brow in frustration. "Just when I thought I had the full collection of the latest toys. What does this thing look like?"

Hannah opened up her purse and passed me a large finger-shaped device attached to a hollow cone at the base.

"I just happen to carry one with me wherever I go," she said. "See for yourself."

I peered at the strange-looking object, stroking the soft silicone surface gently.

"It sure doesn't look like anything I've seen before. How does it work if it doesn't vibrate?"

"The long finger-shaped appendage goes inside you and bends in a series of come-hither motions against your G-spot. Give it a try by tapping the control button on the base one time."

I pressed the button and the finger began waving toward me like some kind of animatronic alien finger.

"*What the fuck?*" I said. "That's insane! It moves just like a real finger. And it hardly makes a sound."

"That the best part. You can use it anywhere. Even in a crowded restaurant. You should give it a try. Pretend that you're reclining on a couch in my office."

I glanced around the table to make sure no one else had seen the strange device that I was fondling at the table.

"It's tempting," I said, peering into the orifice at the top of the cone. "But what's with this little hole near the bottom of the device? What goes on there?"

"See for yourself," Hannah smiled. "Tap the button a second time. You might be in for a bit of a surprise."

I tapped the button again and a long, tongue-shaped object pushed up out of the hole and began undulating like a hypnotic snake against my palm.

My eyes grew wide as saucers as Hannah nodded at me with a huge smirk.

"Like I said," she grinned. "It's not a vibrator so much as a *replicator*. Doesn't it remind you of a real finger and tongue?"

"In a weird, perverted, *ET* kind of way–yeah."

Hannah lowered her gaze and nodded toward my midsection.

"You've got to feel it down there to really appreciate it. Go ahead–give it a try. No one needs to know besides us girls."

"Seriously?" I said. "Right here?!"

"Why not? There's a long skirt surrounding the table. You can loosen your pants and insert it inside you without anyone knowing. Let me have a little bit of fun watching you pleasure yourself for a change. We haven't been together that way in quite a while."

"I have to admit," I huffed. "I *am* insanely horny right now. I'm dying to try this thing out. But what are you going to do while I amuse myself?"

"I'm going to eat my salad like we're having a normal luncheon. This is all about *you* girl, don't worry about me. Knock yourself out."

"I can't believe I'm thinking about doing this," I said, watching the tongue slither back into its hole as I turned the toy off temporarily.

"It should be pretty easy to insert it if you're already properly worked up," Hannah said, lifting her glass to her lips.

I glanced to both sides of our table to make sure nobody else was watching, then reached under the tablecloth and unzipped my jeans, pulling them down to the floor. I could feel my juices already pooling on the wooden chair between my legs as I lowered the device under the table.

"Just be sure to position it so the hole is over your clit," Hannah whispered.

"I'm all over that," I nodded, slowly inserting the bulbous tip into my opening.

It slipped inside my slit smoothly, and I gasped as I pushed it all the way up inside me.

"It's not like just *any* old finger, is it?" Hannah grinned.

"No," I panted. "It's longer and fatter than most."

"It's designed with the ideal shape and form to stimulate your G-spot. If you've got it pressed all the way inside, turn it on to see what it feels like when it's animated."

I glanced around me nervously, watching the other restaurant patrons lost in conversation with their partners.

"Are you sure I'm going to be able to control myself in full view of all these customers? What if I break out into a Meg Ryan in front of all these people?"

"That'll be up to you to keep things under control as much as you can. But if not, what's the worst that can happen? Just like in the movie, everybody will want to know what you ordered that made you so happy."

"Very funny," I said, fumbling to find the control button on the base of the unit resting over my mound.

I pressed the button and began squirming in my chair as the long pointed finger began caressing me like no lover I ever had.

"Uhnn," I groaned, feeling the unusual stimulation inside my pussy.

"Not too bad, is it?" Hannah smiled. "Imagine all that going on while you're watching one of my patients pleasuring themselves."

"Is that really *possible*?" I said, getting even more turned on at the thought of watching one of her clients playing with herself in Hannah's private office.

"I've been thinking about it for a while," Hannah nodded. "It's the logical next step in the process of learning to become fully functional in a paired relationship. I've already had a few of my patients suggest they'd like me to guide them through their first encounter with another partner."

"You know how I like to *watch*," I groaned, as my eyes began to glaze over from the delicate sensation of the long finger rubbing up against my G-spot.

Hannah crossed her legs under the table and began to bob up and down as she flexed her buttocks and thighs together watching me get off.

"I do," she said, lifting her cocktail glass off the table and sliding her tongue around the rim suggestively. "Try the tongue action now."

"You're such a tease," I hissed, reaching under the tablecloth and tapping the control button one more time.

When I felt the flexible appendage push out of the hole and begin rolling over my hard clit, I bent over my place setting, grasping the handles of my chair tightly.

"That's it, babe," Hannah purred. "Feel the rhythm. Close your eyes and imagine it's your fantasy partner licking your pussy. Surrender to the feeling..."

"Is this how you do it with your clients?" I panted. "Talking to them all sexy while they play with themselves?"

"Sometimes," Hannah smiled. "Or sometimes I just let them do most of the vocalization while they tell me what they're doing behind the screen."

I spread my knees further apart imagining myself in one of her sessions.

"Do they ever get to the point where they're comfortable letting you watch them?"

"That's the ultimate goal. I've had a number of clients reach that level already. But I'd like to try taking it one step further. That's where you come in–"

"Tell me, Han," I moaned, beginning to lose myself in the fantasy. "Tell me what you want me to do with your sexy patients."

"We'll start out slowly at first," she instructed. "We'll just have you listen to them moan and purr as they begin the process of self-discovery behind the safety of their protective screen. But you'll have to be quiet at first to not distract their self-focus."

"At *this* point," I said, beginning to feel the pleasure spreading over my entire body. "That might be enough. With this amazing device doing its thing, I could probably get off listening to the sound of running water."

"That's the intent," Hannah laughed. "At least for my clients. But in order for them to become truly uninhibited and be able to function competently, the next step would be for the two of you to emerge from your hiding places and become comfortable watching each other in a face-to-face setting."

"*Fuck, yes*," I panted. "If I can help another soul learn to enjoy the full pleasures of lesbian sex, count me in!"

"I know *you* won't have any trouble participating in this next phase of the process," Hannah smiled. "Just try to keep some of your more extreme methods in check for a while so you don't scare away my customers."

"I promise to keep my big dildos at home if you insist," I smirked.

"Once we get them feeling comfortable touching themselves and achieving climax in this voyeur scenario, the last step will be for the two of you to join together on the same couch and explore each other with more direct contact."

"Can I break out some of my favorite moves then?"

"If you find your partner is responding appropriately. Just be careful to always be gentle and focused on her needs. If you get to the point where she feels comfortable getting more inventive, by all means–"

"Oh, I've got the *means* alright," I moaned, imaging myself strad-dling one of her patients with her legs splayed wide apart as we ground our pussies together and I watched her come all over me. "How soon can we set this up?"

"I've got a certain patient in mind. She's young and never been with another woman before. She's had some unfulfilling experiences with men and confided that she's always fantasized about being with a woman. We'll just have to ease her into it carefully. Are you up for the opportunity, assuming she's game?"

"You know I am," I grunted, pressing harder down against the artificial tongue. "But first, tell me more about this girl..."

"She's nineteen, a sophomore in college, with a cheerleader's body–"

"She's athletic then?"

"Oh yes," Hannah smiled. "Tight ass, firm tits, and legs that could wrap all the way around you while you tribbed her virgin pussy–"

"Oh God, Han," I moaned. "I can't take it any longer. Sign me up– I want to taste her sweet pussy in my mouth..."

"Yes, Jade," Hannah purred. "Let it go, hun. Surrender to the feeling–"

As I imagined the co-ed writhing in ecstasy sitting on my face, the pleasure generated by the lifelike sex toy suddenly peaked, and I bit my lip as I began convulsing in my chair. I'd never fought so hard to remain quiet during a powerful orgasm in my entire life. There was something about the experience of cumming surrounded by scores of oblivious restaurant patrons that made the experience all the more erotic. While I twisted and squirmed in my chair, Hannah smiled as she raised her glass in toast to me.

"Congratulations, Jade," she said. "You've just passed the first test with flying colors."

2

With every passing day after our luncheon, I grew increasingly excited about the idea of participating in one of Hannah's guided therapy sessions. When she finally called me back, I almost dropped my phone fumbling to answer it.

"Han?" I answered the phone expectantly.

"Are you sure you're up for this?" Hannah asked.

"Are you kidding me?" I said. "It's all I've been thinking about since I last saw you."

"I've got another session scheduled with my target client for this Thursday at eleven a.m. Are you available?"

"With the young co-ed?"

"Yes."

"Absolutely!" I gushed.

"Ok," Hannah said. "We're going to have to set this up carefully. I don't want to put too much pressure on either one of you during this initial encounter. I think it's better if she doesn't even know you're there at first. I'll talk to her while she begins to explore her body behind the safety of the protective screen, then broach the subject of introducing a potential partner at the next session."

"Okay," I said. "But where will you hide me?"

"As strange as it may sound, I think the only safe place to be sure you're not discovered is in my closet. You can open the door a crack and listen if you promise to be absolutely quiet the entire time. That way, I can protect her identity in the event she doesn't wish to escalate things to the next level."

I shook my head at the idea of spying on her like a peeping Tom, but the dampness in my panties betrayed my true feelings.

"I'll feel like a bit of a lech hiding in the closet, but if that's what it'll take to make sure she's comfortable, I can work with that."

"Okay then," Hannah said. "Meet me at my office at 10:45 and I'll get you situated. And remember–not even a peep."

"I promise to be on my best behavior," I smiled. "If I can stay silent surrounded by a hundred restaurant customers, I think I can handle one uptight schoolgirl."

"And don't bring any toys either. I don't want to take the chance she'll hear anything other than my soothing voice."

"Not even your special vibrator that doesn't make any noise?"

"I'm not sure I can trust you with that thing. Besides, it's already going to be put to good use while you're in the closet."

"No fair!" I protested. "*You'll* be the one having all the fun!"

"I'm sure you can find other ways to amuse yourself," Hannah said. "You'll have plenty of chances to get more actively engaged during the next session. Just don't trip over anything in there when things start to heat up."

As soon as Hannah hung up, I rushed into my bedroom and positioned my dressing room mirror in front of my clothes closet. Then I opened the door a crack and imagined it was the schoolgirl I was watching while I jilled myself to a quick orgasm.

This should be interesting, I thought, quivering in the darkness. *I just hope her patient will find it as erotic as I do, knowing someone else is on the other side of the curtain.*

O n the day of the scheduled session, I arrived fifteen minutes early as requested, while Hannah reiterated the ground rules and gave me final instructions. She made me promise that I wouldn't open the door until her client was safely behind the protective screen. She knew she was already pushing the boundary of professional ethics, and she wanted to make sure that her patient's identity would be protected until the girl felt comfortable introducing another person into the mix.

When I got into the closet, I pushed the coats to one side to produce an open space for me, then I peered through the louvers as I heard a soft tap on Hannah's office door. The slats were angled downward, so I could only see the floor a few feet ahead of me, but that was enough to get my heart racing in excitement already.

"Good morning, Haley," I heard Hannah say as two shadows crossed the floor in front of me. "Can I get you a coffee or tea? It's a bit chilly out there today, and you probably need to warm up."

"I'm fine, thank you," a young woman's voice spoke softly. "I'm pretty nervous about today's session and I don't think I should be holding any hot beverages in my trembling hands."

"There's no need to worry," Hannah assured the girl. "We're going to take things slowly, at your own pace. May I take your coat?"

"Yes, thank you," the girl said.

I heard the rustling of clothes then the sound of footfalls moving toward the closet. The door on the opposite side of the closet opened and Hannah reached in to fetch an open hanger, then she hung the girl's coat over the crossbar. I could smell her perfume on the garment, and my pussy twitched when I realized how close she was to me on the other side of the door. But neither Hannah nor I so much as made eye contact, to protect the secrecy of our little ruse.

"Have a seat, please," Hannah said, and I heard the sound of the girl reclining on the office divan.

"If you remember from our last session," Hannah continued, "we talked about trying something a little different today. You shared your discomfort about touching yourself intimately based on your prior family history, and that you thought it might be helpful to have me coach you through a private session. Are you still feeling comfortable taking it to this next level?"

"I think so," Haley said. "But you mentioned the possibility of my having a bit more privacy. I'm not sure I'm ready to have you watch me just yet."

"Of course," Hannah said. "It'll be easier for you to concentrate on exploring your body and focus on what you're feeling without any outside distractions. I can move the linen screen between the two of us to protect your privacy, but I'd also like to place this long dressing mirror in front of your couch so you can watch yourself and begin to get more comfortable with your body. Will that work for you?"

"I suppose so," Haley said, hesitating. "Do you have any expectations for today's session? I mean, in terms of achieving climax or anything like that?"

"None whatsoever," Hannah said. "This is all about you becoming comfortable in your own skin and beginning the process of self-exploration. The only desire I have is that you learn to relax and accept the beauty of your own body. This is a journey, not a destination. You need to learn how to love *yourself* before you can begin to think about loving someone else."

Oh, she's good, I thought. If only every girl could have this kind of advice when they're first experiencing the strange feelings of puberty and early adulthood. Far too many parents make their kids think sex is dirty and that enjoying any kind of carnal pleasure before marriage is sinful. For a moment, I reflected back on my own awkward attempts at sex with my first husband, realizing how much time and pleasure I'd forsaken until I learned to explore my sexuality on my own and with other like-minded women.

I listened to the sound of furniture moving across the floor as Hannah positioned the mirror in front of Haley's settee then placed the curtain between their two chairs.

"Does that make you feel more comfortable?" Hannah asked the girl.

"Yes, thank you," Haley said.

"Good. Now first, I just want you to look at yourself fully clothed in the mirror. Look at your pretty face and the curves of your figure and recognize that you're a beautiful woman who was designed to enjoy the natural pleasures of your body. And that this is also part of the natural process of pairing with a partner and enjoying the shared union that is part of the human experience."

"Okay..." Haley said with a hesitating lilt.

As I listened to her soft voice, my mind raced imagining what she looked like lying on the divan, watching herself in the mirror.

"But first you need to get fully comfortable in your own skin," Hannah said. "And begin to experience the pleasures that you've been naturally endowed with as a healthy young woman. Unfortunately, our society has learned to cover up our bodies as if they're a shameful thing we should hide. I want you to see your body as a beautiful thing and recognize the pleasures it can deliver to you, both when you're alone and with a partner."

Damn straight, I thought, feeling the blood rushing to my pussy as I reflected back on my own first tentative explorations of my young body that led to my first climax.

"Now I want you to take off your blouse and your bra,""Hannah continued. "And lie back against the chair as you examine your body and begin to explore some of your erogenous areas."

I heard the sound of soft rustling behind the screen, followed by awkward silence.

"Can you see your naked torso in the mirror in front of you?" Hannah asked.

"Yes..." Haley said softly.

"Look at your breasts and examine their shape. Did you know that every woman has her own unique shape? Some have large breasts, some have small breasts, some have pointy breasts, and some have floppy breasts. It's all part of the female expression and what makes you unique."

More awkward silence.

"Do you like the shape of your breasts, Haley?" Hannah said.

"I suppose so..."

"I want you to cup them in your hands and feel how soft and pleasant they feel to be held and coddled. A woman's breasts are a beautiful thing, and they serve many purposes. Besides feeding a newborn child, their shape is meant to attract other partners whose bodies you can likewise enjoy and appreciate. And of course, your breasts can be a source of intense internal pleasure for yourself. Did you know that some women can climax just from the feeling of their babies suckling on their teats?"

"I had no idea," Haley said.

While Hannah talked the girl through the process of self-examination, I mimicked her movements and gestures, trying to imagine how she felt and how her body was responding. I unbuttoned my blouse and opened my bra, feeling an electric charge race through my body as I felt the fullness of my breasts in my hands.

"Now I want you to pinch your nipples gently between your thumbs and forefingers as you cup your breasts and roll them between your fingers, telling me what you feel."

"It tingles a little bit," Haley confessed.

"In a good way?"

"Yes–I think so."

"Do you notice any changes to the size and shape of your nipples?"

"Yes," Haley said. "They're growing larger and firmer."

"That's another one of the amazing reactions our bodies experience when our erogenous zones are properly stimulated. Do you like the feeling when you touch your breasts in this way, Haley?"

"Yes," she panted softly.

The girl's visceral reaction to touching herself sent a chill down my spine as I felt myself getting wetter and wetter by the moment.

"Look at your body in the mirror as you touch yourself. Do you see your chest flushing and your breasts subtly changing shape?"

"Yes."

"That's from your blood rushing to the area to provide more oxygen and nutrients to feed the increased stimulation. Isn't it wonderful how our bodies naturally respond when we stimulate it in a pleasant way?"

"Mmm," Haley purred.

"Now I want you to bend your head down and lift one of your breasts toward your mouth. You've been blessed with larger breasts than most, and if you can suck and lick your nipples, I want you to tell me how it feels."

Soon after, I heard the sound of liquid sloshing and the smacking of lips. I knew that Haley was sucking her plump nipples, and the thought of it sent rivers of fluid running down the inside of my legs. I was glad that I'd chosen to wear a dress instead of jeans so I'd have freer access to my pussy in the tight confines of Hannah's closet.

"How does that feel?" Hannah asked.

"Heavenly," Haley sighed. "I've never really explored my body in this way before."

"You'll be amazed at all the ways you and your partner can create exciting sensations like these using different techniques and body parts to explore the different areas of your body. Look up at your nipples in the mirror every now and then, but don't let me stop you from continuing your exploration."

I could hear the sloshing and smacking sounds increasing in frequency and pitch, along with Haley's moans and sighs. I had to bite my lip to keep from moaning myself, as I imagined what she must have been feeling at this moment.

"What do you see and feel?" Hannah asked.

"The dark ring around my nipples is getting smaller and my nipples are getting harder the more I lick and suck them."

"Mmm, that's good," Hannah said.

I could tell Hannah was getting just as turned on as I was from the exchange, and I wondered if she'd turned on her vibrator yet.

"Mix up the way you stimulate your nipples," she said. "Try circling your tongue around the perimeter and flicking it over the ends of your nipples every now and then. Most of the pleasure in exploring our bodies is discovered from the many different ways we can stimulate ourselves and others. Squeeze your breasts with your hands, pinch your nipples, suck and play with them as you lose yourself in the moment."

"It feels good," Haley panted. "I think I'm ready to try some of those other new techniques you mentioned now."

I smiled when I realized Haley was losing herself in the process and beginning to surrender to the pleasurable feelings flooding her body.

"Let's get comfortable seeing your *entire* body in the nude then," Hannah continued. "I want you to take off the rest of your clothes and throw them to the side. There are so many other ways to give yourself pleasure."

I heard some more rustling of clothes, this time more urgent-sounding, and the telltale sound of clothes dropping to the floor. It was obvious to me that Haley was getting more and more worked up and that she no longer cared if her clothes got a little wrinkled or dirty.

After the rustling sound stopped, Hannah paused for a moment to let the silence in the room escalate the sexual tension. Her professional technique was working for more than just her client, as I froze with my hand still as a statue against my dripping pussy while I imagined the pretty schoolgirl looking at her naked body on the chaise lounge chair.

"Are you fully naked now, Haley?" Hannah asked.

"Yes," the girl said.

"Examine the curve of your profile for a moment. See the way your waist tapers and the swelling of your hips above your long, shapely legs. Do you think you're beautiful, Haley?"

"Yes," she said. "I feel good all over."

"Good," Hannah said. "Now I want you to spread your legs and knees apart a little bit so you can examine your private area. Can you see your skin glistening on your vulva and on the inside of your thighs?"

"Yes," Haley panted.

"That means your body is enjoying the stimulation you've provided so far and that you're feeling aroused viewing your own body. Can you see the slit between your legs?"

"Yes–"

"I want you to run your hands gently down the front of your torso, feeling the softness of the skin on your abdomen..."

"My tummy is trembling," Haley said.

"That's a natural reaction to the excitement you feel as you caress yourself and move closer to your magical place."

"Magical place?"

"You'll see what I mean soon enough. Can you see the natural hairs covering your private area?"

"Yes," Haley said.

Both Hannah and I guessed that a girl this young and innocent wouldn't have learned yet to trim her pubic hair in the manner of the modern custom.

"I want you to run your fingers through your bush and tell me what you feel."

For a moment I envied the virgin schoolgirl with her natural muff. It had been a long time since I'd felt the wonderful feeling of my pubic hairs being caressed and stroked in this way. By way of consolation, I raised my slippery fingers up from my crotch and spread my juices over my bare mound.

"It feels kind of ticklish," Haley said from behind the screen. "But in a good way. I feel all warm and tingly inside."

"That's your body's way of saying it's enjoying the sensation of being touched this way. Now the blood is rushing to an entirely different area of your body. Can you feel yourself becoming wetter and wetter around your opening?"

"Yes," Haley said. "It's a good thing you put a blanket down over your chair. Otherwise, I'd be making a mess of your pretty office."

"That's perfect," Hannah said. "I'd like nothing more than for you to make a mess of my office. That just means that you're enjoying the experience and that your body is reacting the way it was meant to."

"I can feel things beginning to heat up down there," Haley grunted. "And there's other changes too–"

"Spread your legs further apart now and tell me what changes you see. And what you *feel*."

"I can see my lips are getting wetter and darker. And my little bean is getting plumper and harder. I feel like I'm tingling all over now..."

"Move your hands between your thighs and feel the slippery wetness as you caress the sides of your labia. How does that feel?"

"It feels *good*," Haley panted. "It's so warm and wet. I'm feeling some other sensations now..."

"Isn't it wonderful how good you can make yourself feel just by gently exploring your body and appreciating your natural beauty?"

"Yes, Dr. Marshall."

"Please, call me Hannah. At this point, we don't need to stay so informal, plus it will make it easier for you to vocalize what you're feeling. Now, I want you to explore a very special place on your body. Trace your fingers up along the edges of your labia until they meet at the top, then touch your little nub and tell me what you feel."

"*Huh!*" Haley gasped. "Oh, that feels–different. It's a much more intense type of tingling now."

By now I was rubbing my button furiously as I imagined Haley playing with her clit for the first time. As I peered through the slats trying desperately to catch any sight of her shadow or movement on the reflective floor, I could hear the soft sound of my own juices as I became more and more excited by the sensory deprivation of being locked in the closet.

"Yes," Hannah said, encouraging Haley on. "We women are lucky to be endowed with the most sensitive organ on the human body. Our clitorises are bestowed with more than eight thousand nerve endings–more per square inch than even on the end of a man's penis. Rub your fingers softly over your jewel and close your eyes as you savor the feeling."

"Oh God," Haley moaned. "That feels so good. I had no idea I could make myself feel this way."

"We're just getting started exploring all the possibilities," Hannah said, her own voice starting to become ragged. "Run your fingers over your clit, trying different movements. Sometimes it's nice to pinch it gently between your fingers, and sometimes it feels good to rub your fingers in circles over your button. Can you see anything *else* changing in your vulva as you rub yourself this way?"

"Yes," Haley groaned. "My lips are getting puffier, and they're beginning to separate a bit."

"*Fuck me*," I groaned under my breath, wishing I could be looking into the same mirror that Haley was viewing at this precise moment. *How I'd love to fuck her sweet little pussy right now.*

"That's perfectly normal and healthy," Hannah purred. "That's just your body's way of saying that it's ready to accept another partner into the equation. Do you think you'd like to try that someday soon?"

"Maybe," Haley said. "But right now I'm having too much fun all by myself. I'm beginning to feel some different feelings now. The tingling is getting much more intense. It almost feels like I have to pee or something..."

"That means you're getting closer to reaching the apex of your pleasure," Hannah said, shifting in her chair. "Close your eyes now and focus on your body as you surrender to the pleasure. Don't worry if things start to get pretty intense. Just lose yourself in the process..."

"Yes, doc–I mean Hannah," Haley squeaked. "I feel it now. It feels like a wave is falling over me. A big, beautiful wall of pleasure engulfing me..."

"Yes, Haley," Hannah mewed. "Let it consume you. Surrender to the passion inside your body."

"Oh God! Oh God!" Haley whimpered. "It feels so good. Something is happening. I feel it coming over me–. Uhnnn! Uhnnn! Uhnnn!"

As I listened to Haley having her first powerful orgasm, I lost all control and began squirting over the floor of Hannah's closet as my pussy clamped together in multiple contractions while I leaned against the wall to steady myself. I'd never heard anything so erotic in my entire life, and my whole body was trembling at the thought of meeting her face-to-face at our next session.

When Haley finally stopped moaning and silence filled the room, I could hear Hannah shifting again in her chair. I wondered if she'd been unable to control herself and had had a powerful orgasm of her own listening to Haley. With that lifelike sex toy embedded in her pussy, I couldn't imagine how she'd able to hold back.

"How does it feel to experience the natural pleasures of being a woman, Haley?" she said.

"Oh my God," Haley panted. "I had no idea I had this inside of me. I want more–"

"There's so much more for you to experience, young lady. I encourage you to experiment with more self-exploration before our next session. Of course, the ultimate pleasure of being a woman happens when you get to *share* this pleasure with another partner. Do you think you might be ready to try this at our next meeting?"

"Um–maybe. But how will that work? I don't think I'm quite ready to jump right into an intimate relationship with a complete stranger."

"With your permission," Hannah said, "I'd like to invite another patient to the session who's expressed similar feelings about being with another woman. We can start slowly at first with the two of you just watching and talking to one another before we consider taking it to the next stage. You should always feel completely comfortable with your partner before agreeing to share this kind of intimacy."

"That does sound interesting," Haley said. "Would we be separated by protective screens again?"

"Only if you both want it that way. But something tells me you're ready to discover for yourself how much higher it can elevate the experience watching another woman pleasuring herself with you at the same time."

"Yes," Haley said. "I think I might like that."

"Let me know before your next session if you'd like to meet this new girl. Because she's definitely ready to meet you."

No shit, I muttered under my breath as my pussy continued spasming over my fingers firmly embedded inside my hole.

I had no idea know how I'd be able to keep it together for a whole week before I met this girl again. I smiled as my juices streamed down the insides of my thighs.

I'll just have to practice as much as I can in the meantime to get ready.

3

The intervening week before Haley's next scheduled session felt like the longest week of my life. I couldn't stop thinking about what she looked like and how she'd react to watching me respond to Hannah's instruction the way she had. I spent long hours lying on my couch with my dressing mirror propped up in front of me, fantasizing that it was Haley watching me instead of myself.

I must have cum a hundred times contorting myself into different positions trying to make myself look as sexy and alluring as possible. I didn't want to take any chance that she wouldn't respond positively to me in this shared therapy session. Beyond my desire for her to enjoy the experience to the fullest extent possible, I didn't want anything getting in the way of her moving on to the final step in her journey of sexual awakening. Every time I thought about actually touching her, my pussy throbbed and I had to tear my clothes off once again to quell the yearning desire within me.

When the appointment day finally arrived, I spent most of the morning trying on different outfits I thought might strike the right balance between sexually enticing and emotionally guarded. After all, Hannah was presenting me as another repressed patient who'd reached out for help overcoming her fear of intimacy with other women. I finally decided on a pleated mid-length skirt with inch-high pumps and a creamy silk blouse that hugged my breasts just enough to highlight the fullness of my bosom.

Hannah had asked me to arrive at her office five minutes after the hour so she could prep Haley first and confirm that she still wished to proceed as intended. The plan was for her to send me a quick text with either a smiling or frowning emoji to signal her readiness. When I still hadn't heard anything by 11:15, I shifted uncomfortably in her waiting room, wondering if Haley had gotten cold feet.

I couldn't blame her if she had. This whole idea was highly irregular and must have been kind of frightening for her. It was a far cry from meeting someone the natural way, getting to know them over a period of time before deciding to initiate intimate relations. But if she was too afraid to approach another woman the traditional way, I had every intention of making this experience as comfortable and uplifting as possible.

When my phone pinged and I saw the smiley-face symbol in my message thread, I stood up and nervously smoothed out the wrinkles in my blouse. I chuckled at the realization that I was just as anxious as the young schoolgirl at the prospect of our chaperoned playdate. Hannah stuck her head out her office door motioning me inside, and I straightened myself out and walked confidently into her office.

The girl was standing a few feet to Hannah's side, smiling nervously at me when our eyes met. I was surprised how young she looked in her skinny jeans, tight t-shirt, and Keds sneakers. She had long blonde hair, big bright eyes, and the plump skin of an adolescent who hadn't lost any of her youthful collagen. I must have looked ancient almost fifteen years older than her, as I pulled my shoulders back trying to lift my chest and press my breasts against my tight blouse.

Hannah turned toward the girl, arcing her arm toward me.

"Haley," she said. "This is Jade. In spite of your difference in age, I think you'll find you actually have a lot in common. I've brought the two of you together today to share some of your mutual experiences and learn to become more comfortable expressing your intimacy in the presence of another woman."

Hannah peered at the two of us and smiled.

"Would you like a drink before we get started?"

"Have you got some *tequila* behind your bar?" I joked.

"That might not be such a bad idea to help you both loosen up," Hannah chuckled. "But unfortunately, all I have to offer is coffee or tea."

"I'll have a coffee with a bit of cream and sugar then," I said.

"Tea is fine," Haley nodded.

"Cream and sugar also?" Hannah asked.

"Yes, thank you."

As Hannah turned to prepare our drinks, I moved closer toward Haley and extended my hand. She looked even prettier up close, with thick natural eyebrows and long dark lashes.

"Pleased to meet you, Haley," I said. "Hannah's told me so much about you. You're even more beautiful than she described."

Haley reached out and clasped my hand softly, and I could feel the nervous dampness in her palm as we touched for the first time.

"Thank you," she said. "You're very pretty also."

Her eyes blinked as she stole a glance down my body, peering at the cleavage formed by my push-up bra peeking out of my loosely unbuttoned blouse. My breasts were at least full size larger than hers, and I stood three or four inches taller in my elevated pumps.

"You remind me a little of Marilyn Monroe in that white blouse and skirt," she said.

"That's very kind," I smiled. "I could never hold a candle to her, though I feel a certain affinity given my own little seven-year-itch. It took me at least that long to break free of the oppressive bonds of my first marriage."

"Have you married again?"

"No–I guess I'm still discovering myself. I've kind of been looking

for a change of pace lately. I never felt fully satisfied in my relationships with men."

"I've never felt comfortable approaching *either* gender, actually.
My parents were pretty strict about the whole dating thing when I
was growing up–"

Hannah returned from her kitchen and handed each of us a
steaming mug.

"I see you two are beginning to get more comfortable," she said.
"I'm glad to see you hitting it off so quickly. Would you like to get
more comfortable?"

Haley and I turned to see two long chaise lounge chairs facing
one another about ten feet apart, angled slightly toward Hannah's
armchair positioned at the apex of the triangle. I smiled when I realized she'd done this intentionally to facilitate her own enhanced
viewing of the two of us once we got loosened up.

We walked toward the settees and I paused, motioning for Haley
to take the one on the left side. Both chairs were covered in a long
throw blanket, and I kicked off my shoes before sitting back against
the curved backrest, crossing my ankles on the end nearest Haley. It
felt awkward holding my coffee in this semi-reclined position, and
when I leaned over to rest it on the floor beside me, Haley did the
same.

"How are you both feeling today?" Hannah said as she sat in her
chair in front of us, crossing her legs sexily with her pointed pumps
bouncing gently in our direction.

I had little doubt she was wearing her special sex toy under her
prim business suit, and I envied her for a moment, knowing she'd
have a leg up on the two of us for the rest of the session.

"Good," Haley said, with a gentle lilt.

"Better *now*," I said, smiling toward Haley.

"You've both expressed interest in exploring a same-sex relationship, but also about your reservations initiating the process given
your previous experiences."

I nodded, realizing there was more than a hint of truth in her statement, even though I'd long since resolved my reticence about being with other women.

"The purpose of this session is to give you both an opportunity to become more comfortable in the presence of another woman, and to the extent you feel ready, to begin to explore the boundaries of your sexuality in the safe confines of my office. Is this still something you both feel comfortable proceeding with?"

I looked at Haley and she peered back at me, as we both nodded gently.

"Okay," Hannah said. "At first, I'd just like the two of you to gaze into each other's eyes for a moment and pause as you take a moment to acknowledge each other as willing partners and make a silent connection..."

I smiled at Haley and saw a soft flush spread over her cheeks as her pupils began to widen while she peered back at me. Even though neither of us said a thing, the longer I looked at her the more excited I got as my chest began rising and falling from my elevated respiration rate.

"Now, I want each of you to take a minute to look over each other's bodies without making any judgements or feeling self-conscious that you're checking each other out. Take a moment to appreciate the different shapes of your respective figures, and listen to how your body is reacting as you soak each other up."

I was happy to be given free license to leer at Haley's youthful figure, and as my eyes drifted down her body, I could feel my panties begin to moisten in excitement seeing the girl of my dreams reclining directly in front of me. Her breasts looked like they were painted on her body, sitting high and firm under her tight t-shirt. She had a narrow waist and slim but shapely hips, tapering to slender hourglass-shaped legs, looking all the more toned resting gently on the firm surface of her settee.

She in turn ran her gaze all over my body, pausing to stare at my full breasts pushing up against the flimsy silk fabric of my blouse. For a moment, I wished I'd decided to go braless, so she could see how she was turning me on as my nipples pressed against the soft fabric of my lace bra. After a few seconds of lingering, her eyes traced a line further down my body, pausing at the bottom of my skirt's hemline, as if hoping to catch a glimpse into the shadow between my closed legs. When her gaze reached the bottom of my feet, I wiggled my toes playfully, and she did the same with her cute sneakers. Even though we hadn't said a thing to each other for several minutes, I felt like we were already beginning to bond over our strange circumstances.

"Take a moment to revel in the beauty and diversity of the female form," Hannah whispered. "Recognize that everyone is built differently, and that these differences contribute to making each of us all the more interesting and alluring. Can you see the natural beauty within each of your own bodies and in those of your partner?"

"Yes," Haley nodded, tracing her gaze once again up to my pointed breasts.

"Absolutely," I enthused.

"Let's take this to the next level then," Hannah said. "If you feel comfortable, I'd like each of you to remove your tops and lie back in your chair while you admire one another in your undergarments."

As I slowly began unbuttoning my blouse, Haley leaned forward, pulling her t-shirt over her shoulders. When she lifted it over her head, her blonde locks fell down over the front of her cream-colored sports bra. I was a little disappointed to see her covered up so tightly, but her bra only seemed to accentuate the firmness of her perky tits.

When I unfastened the last button on my blouse, I pulled my arms out one side at a time then leaned back against the soft backrest. It felt electrifying to rest there in my lacy bra as Haley ran her eyes lustily over my exposed chest and abdomen. My brassiere was low-cut enough that she could see the tops of my dark areolas, and they puckered slightly as my hard nipples began to lift the fabric away from my skin.

"Now look at each other's bodies more closely," Hannah intoned. "Examine the shape of each other's breasts, the curvature of your waists, and the smoothness of your stomachs. What do you see that appeals to your feminine senses?"

"I like the fullness of Jade's breasts," Haley purred. "And the way the top edge of her bra angles sexily down toward her cleavage."

"Yes," Hannah said, stretching the S out the end of the word. "Being a sensual woman means we can dress up in different ways to tease and excite our partners as a precursor to more intimate relations. What do you see in Haley's body that you find most attractive, Jade?"

I paused for a moment, examining her tight belly and the subtle striations in her stomach.

"I like the line running down the middle of her abdomen from the bottom of her bra to her belly button. I wish I could be that lean and sexy once again."

"That's the beauty we share as women of different generations. Some women are more lean and chiseled, while others are more full-bodied and curvy. It's all part of the magnificent palette of the human form and what makes it so interesting for each of us to experience. Are you beginning to imagine what lies further underneath?"

"Yes..." Haley said, her cheeks flushing a crimson red.

"Oh, very definitely yes," I sighed, wishing I could jump out of my seat and tear Haley's sports bra off with my own hands.

"If you're ready then, you may remove your brassieres and begin to get more comfortable being naked in the presence of one another."

Haley hesitated for a moment, looking at me to make the first move. Fortunately, the bra I'd chosen to wear had the closure at the front, and as I pressed my fingers together unhinging the clasp and spreading the cups apart to reveal my naked breasts, I heard Haley gasp a few feet away. Her reaction only excited me more as I peered down at my tits, seeing that my nipples had already hardened and extended to their full extent. I pulled my bra off my back and threw it on the floor, and my whole body started buzzing as Haley stared at my torso with wide eyes.

Within a few seconds, she felt emboldened enough to remove her own sports bra as she pinched her thumbs under the lower band and pulled it over her head in one swift movement. Her breasts jiggled softly on her chest and I marveled at how perfectly round and symmetrical they were. They looked bigger than I imagined when I saw her fully clothed, and I began to salivate as I leered at her creamy skin and her light-colored areolas. They'd already begun to bunch up in excitement, protruding like two erasers on the end of a pencil.

Hannah paused just long moment to give each of us a chance to soak up each other's bodies. I could see Haley's eyes darting excitedly between my points as a light dew formed at the top of her chest between her breasts. This just accentuated the youthful look of her glistening skin, glowing like a sexy goddess. As my mouth watered at the thought of taking her moist nipples into my mouth, another part of me began to grow rapidly wetter.

"What are you feeling as you look each other's naked bodies?" Hannah said, interrupting our thoughts.

"I'm thinking how much I want to touch Haley right now," I confessed.

"There'll be plenty of time for that soon enough," Hannah said, admonishing me gently. "What are you feeling at this moment, Haley?"

"I'm just..." Haley panted, her moist lips parting slightly. "I'm just amazed at how gorgeous Jade's tits–I mean *breasts* are. She's looks like a supermodel to me."

"It's okay to use informal terms to describe each other's bodies," Hannah nodded. "It helps to desensitize the experience and lose yourself more readily in the feelings of arousal that you're experiencing. Are you beginning to recognize how each of you are responding to the sight of watching one another in this manner?"

"Yes," Haley said as she locked her eyes on my tingling teats.

"You have *no* idea," I smiled, peering at Haley's quivering tummy.

"I'm happy you're both responding so positively. That means you're attracted to one another and that you're becoming more comfortable with the idea of exploring a different kind of union. Are you ready to take it to the next level?"

"I think so..." Haley hesitated.

"*God* yes," I panted, feeling the wetness in my panties beginning to run down the crack of my ass.

"Why don't you both take off your lower garments now, but keep your panties on for the moment? Part of the attraction with foreplay is taking our time to build the desire and teasing our partners by withholding those things we most crave. Take a moment to look at your naked bodies, but not completely undressed yet."

I leaned forward and unclasped the latch at the back of my skirt, then lowered the zipper and pulled my skirt down the front of my legs, throwing it playfully on the floor. Haley locked eyes on me as she unfastened the front of her jeans, wiggling sexily on her divan while she pulled her pants down, then flipping off her sneakers and throwing everything on the floor beside her.

She was wearing plain white low-cut panties that stretched at least four inches below her navel. I could see the dark outline of her bush under the thin fabric, and my pussy twitched knowing I'd soon get to see her completely naked. She leaned back and fixed her gaze on my crotch while I teasingly separated my feet a few inches. I was wearing matching lace panties and the light color must have shown the giant wet spot that had formed in the fabric. But I couldn't yet see any sign of wetness in Haley's underwear, since she still had her legs closed in a protective posture.

"How does it feel to view another woman like this, nearly naked?" Hannah asked. "Are you noticing any new reactions in your body as you watch your partner disrobe?"

"Yes," Haley panted. "I'm beginning to feel that same tingling sensation I experienced at our last session. It feels like my whole body is on fire..."

"How about you, Jade?" Hannah said, smiling at me. "How do you feel sitting in front of Haley almost naked?"

"Very sexy," I said. "I'm feeling things I haven't felt in a long time."

"So it would appear," she said, glancing at the wet spot between my legs. "Now I want each of you to spread your legs a little further apart to witness the effect you're having on one another. Take a moment to recognize the reaction each of you are experiencing as you become more and more aroused looking at one another's bodies."

As I spread my legs further apart, Haley pulled her feet up a few inches, then angled her knees down onto the divan to reveal the white swath of fabric running between her legs. I could see the indentation of her slit in the tight cotton and the telltale darkness of a small wet spot in the middle of her panties. Seeing her reveal this little slice of her private anatomy raised my excitement level even higher as the wet spot in my own panties slowly spread all the way from one side to the other.

While Haley stared at the widening dark spot between my legs, I noticed her chest begin to rise and fall as she started breathing more heavily. It took every ounce of my willpower to stay seated in my settee and not sprint over to her side and take her for myself. Hannah was right about one thing. All this slow buildup was driving me more crazy with desire and just increasing my longing to touch her.

"Can you see how each of you are responding to one another the more you reveal of yourselves?" Hannah said. "Are you beginning to become more comfortable with the idea of watching another woman being intimate and moving closer to a more formal connection?"

"Yes," Haley sighed.

"*Fuck*, yes," I gushed.

"Let's remove our remaining entrapments then and revel in the naked glory of the female body. You may both remove your last vestiges of clothing if you feel comfortable. Take a moment to soak up one another's bodies and connect with your feelings. A healthy sexual relationship starts with feeling comfortable in both your and your partner's nakedness."

I raised my hips, practically tearing my panties off as I pulled them down my legs and tossing them on the floor. While I kept my legs slightly parted, Haley wriggled out of her little white panties and dropped them sexily on the floor beside her. This time, she parted her legs the same distance as mine as we both stared at each other's wet slits shining in the bright overhead lights of Hannah's office. Haley's light pubic patch formed a perfect triangle over her mound and I clenched the fabric on the divan beside me trying to keep my hands from straying any further.

"There now," Hannah purred. "That wasn't so bad, was it?"

"No," Haley said. "It was actually easier than I imagined."

"How about you, Jade? How do you feel seeing your partner fully naked in front of you?"

"I'd hardly call it *easy*," I groaned. "The hardest part is remaining still on my sofa. My hands want to wander all over the place right now."

"If that's what you feel like doing, don't let me stop you from enjoying the process. I encourage each of you to begin touching yourselves while you verbalize how you're feeling. Communication and openness are the first two essential ingredients in any healthy relationship."

As I watched Haley separate her legs further apart, I lifted my hand to my breast and squeezed it tightly while I lowered my other hand to my crotch and began to circle my button. Normally I'd take more time to tease myself, but at this point I was so horny I needed to get right down to business.

Watching me touch myself and begin to moan softly seemed to encourage Haley, as she moved her hand to the inside of her thighs and began to flutter her fingers over her button. While we both began to moan and roll our hips over our divans, Hannah began to bob her foot more forcefully over her knee and cleared her throat.

"Yes," she mewed. "It's a beautiful thing watching another woman pleasuring herself. Focus on one another as you listen to the reaction of your own body and that of your partner. The biggest turn-on is seeing your partner respond excitedly to your touch."

I wasn't sure if she was talking more about what *she* was feeling at this precise moment, or referring to what we were experiencing. It must have been even more exciting for her watching two sexy women touching their naked bodies only a few feet in front of her. With her special sex toy working its wonders underneath her business suit, I imagined she'd have experienced multiple climaxes facilitating these sessions.

"Don't forget to communicate how you feel," she said. "Tell your partner what she's doing to you right now."

"I'm so excited watching Jade touch herself," Haley said. "I never thought a woman could look this sexy and beautiful before. The feelings inside are even more intense than last time–"

"And *you*, Jade?" Hannah said. "How is your body responding seeing Haley get excited watching you?"

"Oh my God," I groaned. "I want her so bad. I want to touch her and taste her and feel her trembling in my arms."

"Soon enough," Hannah smiled. "For now, I just want you both to learn how to satisfy one another at a distance without the added pressure of direct engagement. Focus on what you're feeling, and surrender to the pleasure engulfing your bodies. As before, feel free to experiment with different forms of stimulation. You can begin learning from one another even before you come together."

I spread my legs further apart and inserted two fingers from my other hand into my hole as I began to rub my clit more quickly.

"Mmm, yes," I panted. "You're so beautiful, Haley. I'm imagining you touching me..."

"Yes, Jade," Haley said. "I want to touch you and feel your wetness. You're making me so hot right now."

Haley mimicked my technique, awkwardly inserting the middle finger of her left hand into her slit while she pumped it in and out as she began jilling herself more rapidly. Our hips began to slowly lift off our divans and our mouths opened in pleasure as we moved inexorably closer to orgasm.

"Yes, baby," I purred. "I want to watch you let it go. Imagine me sucking your jewel as you come in my mouth–"

"Oh God," Haley squealed as she arched her hips higher in the air. "It's *coming*! Suck my pussy, Jade!"

Suddenly, Haley fell back onto the surface of the divan and she hunched over, jerking her body back and forth while she pressed her fingers deeper inside her pussy. Seeing her come just inches away from me was more than I could take. I suddenly flipped over on all fours and pounded my cunt as my tits wobbled excitedly over my chest. Within seconds, my orgasm washed over me like a tidal wave as I began squirting long streams in Haley's direction. While I peered at her between my legs, I saw her mouth gape wider apart as she watched me writhing uncontrollably on the chair in front of her.

I glanced over at Hannah for a moment and saw her slumping rhythmically in her own chair as she watched the two of us cumming with our fingers deeply embedded in our pussies. I smiled, knowing she had her *own* special finger stimulating her G-spot as she surrendered to an entirely different kind of lover.

4

After we all came down from our highs at Hannah's therapy session, she asked Haley and me if we were ready to proceed to the next stage in our intimacy journey. Knowing this meant we'd be allowed to touch each other, we both quickly agreed, but since we'd used up all the allotted time in the day's session, Hannah scheduled our next meeting for the following week. When we parted, Haley and I kissed each other on the cheek, but that was enough to keep me going until we met next time.

In the intervening week, I ran through all kinds of scenarios imagining how I'd like to touch and caress her. It was kind of fun not using any toys for a change, since I knew those would be off base during our next encounter. Hannah didn't want any artificial stimulation getting in the way of Haley learning to enjoy sex in the natural manner. That was easy for *her* to say, I thought, remembering how she'd responded watching Haley and me writhing on our divans while she let her special sex toy do all the work for her. But I knew she was right, and as I lay on my sofa dreaming of all the ways I could stimulate Haley, I came many times remembering what she'd said to me when she experienced her first orgasm in the presence of another woman.

This time, I thought, *she won't need to pretend that I'm touching her when she comes next to me.*

On the day of our next scheduled session, we arrived at Hannah's office a few minutes early, which gave her a chance to prep us and set the ground rules. The most important thing, she said, was to go slow and make sure our partner felt comfortable before pushing any further.

I looked around her office and noticed that the two settees had been pushed to the side, and I looked at her inquisitively.

"Where did you want us to relax?" I asked.

Hannah smiled as she led us into another room with a four-poster bed. The drapes had been pulled and a series of candles were lit around the room to set the mood. I could smell a hint of lemongrass from some burning incense on the night table, and I nodded at Hannah's preparation.

"I thought you might like something a little more comfortable to relax on this time," she said. "Plus, I suspect you'll need a little more room to maneuver as you begin to explore each other's bodies. I wanted to make sure you felt as cozy as possible before proceeding to the next step. Why don't you give it a try and see what you think?"

I strolled up to the bed and ran my fingers over the linens. The high thread count made the bedding feel like silk, and I got goose-bumps imagining what it would feel like to lie next to Haley on the sumptuous surface.

"What do you think, Haley?" I said. "Do you think this will be suitable for our purposes?"

Haley stepped forward and ran her hands over the sheets, then turned toward Hannah and smiled.

"It feels like I'm in a five-star hotel," she said. "I've never experienced anything so luxurious in my entire life."

"I wanted you to feel completely relaxed in preparation for the next step in your journey of sexual awakening."

"What about *you*?" Haley asked. "Where will you be while Jade and I are resting on the bed?"

Hannah turned to a reclining chair resting in the corner of the room.

"I'll be sitting in the shadows not too far away. I want there to be minimum distraction while you and Jade explore each other's bodies."

"So you'll be with us for the remainder of the session then?"

"If that's what you prefer."

"You were very helpful last time," Haley nodded. "Plus, it somehow seems more erotic knowing you'll be watching us."

Hannah paused as she peered at the two of us with a sly smile.

"I'll try to be less involved this time while I give each of you a chance to experiment with what turns you on. But I assure you that I'll be enjoying the process almost as much as you will."

She walked to the other side of the room and lay down in her chair, crossing her legs.

"To get you in the mood, sometimes it can be more exciting to let your partner take your clothes off before you lie down. Who'd like to begin?"

Haley and I peered at one another, and a blush fell over her cheeks. It was obvious that she wanted me to make the first move, which was fine with me since I'd been undressing her with my eyes from the moment we came in the door. She'd chosen to wear a more formal outfit today, with a collared blouse, wool pants, and suede loafers. Whether she was trying to mimic me or she was trying to project the image of more sophisticated woman, was unclear. Either way, I liked the look, and I felt my heart beating faster as I imagined unbuttoning her blouse.

I stepped forward and reached out my hand to her, and she met mine with her opposite hand, squeezing my fingers gently. I tilted my head down, and she closed her eyes, anticipating my kiss. Pausing an inch from her mouth, I felt her cool breath on my skin, and my pussy twitched when I realized I was about to touch her intimately for the first time.

When our lips touched, she puckered them like they used to in old-time movies. I smiled, realizing that this might have been the first romantic contact she'd ever experienced and that she still hadn't learned the art of erotic kissing. I lifted my hand and cupped her face as I moved closer, pressing my body against hers. She unconsciously tilted her pelvis, pressing her hips against mine. I parted my mouth and nibbled her flesh, feeling the fullness of her lips.

She sighed as we pressed our breasts together, and I circled my arm around her, caressing the indentation of her lower back. I was dying to plunge my tongue into her, but I remembered Hannah's admonition about going slowly, and instead I turned around and sat down on the bed with my knees straddling her hips. While Haley peered down at me, I began to loosen the buttons of her blouse from the top. As I began to spread the panels apart, I smiled when I noticed that she was wearing a lacy bra like the one I'd worn at our last session.

I leaned in and kissed her exposed belly with my moist lips, reaching up to cup her breasts as I squeezed them gently. She began to moan and reached behind my head to run her fingers through my hair. I'd almost forgotten how to properly make love a woman with all my recent escapades, and suddenly I was happy that I'd agree to participate in Hannah's guided session.

Maybe I'd needed this as much as Haley did.

As she pulled my head tighter against her belly, I reached behind her and unfastened the clasp at the back of her bra, pulling it gently over her shoulders. Her brassiere fell below her breasts, and I lifted myself up, licking her pointy tips. Her nipples were hard and warm, and as I sucked them into my mouth one at a time, she gasped, pulling my head harder against her body. As I began to roll my tongue over her tips, I moved my hands to the front of her chest and squeezed her breasts more tightly. They felt full and firm in my palms, and for the first time since I'd entered the office, I became conscious of the warm feeling in my pussy. My juices had been flowing for some time now, and the feeling of wetness between my legs made my nipples harden.

Haley was running her fingers through my hair more wildly now, and I took this to mean that she was ready for me to take it to the next step. I traced my hands down the front of her belly, unclasping the button at the top of her pants, then I slowly pulled the zipper down to reveal a pair of black lace panties. Seeing her wearing sexy lingerie got me even more turned on, and I slipped my fingers over the waist of her pants and began to pull them down over her hips.

My heart pounded as I felt them tighten up when they reached the widest part of her hips, realizing just how curvy and tight her ass must have been. As I pulled them further down her thighs, Haley lifted her feet and kicked off her loafers, stepping out of her jeans. I pulled her blouse off her back, and her brassiere fell softly onto the floor. Now she stood inches away from me, almost naked and quivering in excitement.

Hannah must have sensed Haley's trepidation, as I heard her shift in her chair for the first time and clear her throat.

"Sometimes it's even more erotic to have your partner remove her clothes while you *watch*," she said. "Would you like to undress Jade yourself Haley, or watch her do so herself?"

"I've been dreaming of seeing her naked again this whole week," Haley said. "But I'm not as experienced as Jade in the art of undressing another woman..."

Taking Haley's cue, I stood up off the bed and stepped back a few paces to give her a chance to take in my full figure. I smiled at her as I began to slowly unbutton my blouse. I'd decided to go braless for today's session, and as it became apparent to Haley that I was naked under my shirt, I saw her eyes widening in excitement. After I unclasped the fourth button, I let the silky fabric fall on top of my breasts while I breathed in and out deeply. As my nipples began to harden, pressing against the soft fabric, Haley's lips begin to separate.

I teased her for a moment longer, bringing my hands together and pushing my tits closer together. She panted looking at my cleavage, and I felt my pussy getting wetter seeing her rising excitement. When I undid the last button and threw my blouse on the bed beside me, I watched the flickering light casting sexy shadows over Haley's mounds. I wanted to step forward and trib her pointed nipples with my own, but I reminded myself that this session was all about her.

The more slowly I could build her desire, the more I knew she'd enjoy the moment when we finally came together.

Damn, I thought. It had been a long time since I'd been this patient in seducing another woman. Apparently I needed Hannah's guided lessons just as much as Haley.

As we stood facing each other in the hypnotic shadows, Haley glanced down my midsection and a small curl formed on the side of her lips. For the same reason she'd chosen to dress more maturely, I'd chosen to wear jeans so she'd feel more comfortable seeing me as a peer. But the problem with the tight jeans was that they revealed the widening wet spot between my legs far more easily than when I wore my skirt.

"It looks like you're getting just as excited as me," Haley smiled, locking her eyes on my dark stain.

"Sorry," I shrugged. "I guess I lubricate a little more easily than most women."

"Mmm, I like that," Haley purred. "I can't wait to feel you. I'm beginning to get wet too."

I glanced down at Haley's legs and saw the shimmering slickness on the inside of her thighs.

"Perhaps it's time for the two of you to get more comfortable on the bed," Hannah interrupted from the darkness.

I'd almost forgotten she was there, but far from finding her intrusions irritating, I was glad she knew when we needed a little prompt. I slipped off my jeans, then lay down on the bed with my arm cocked sexily against the side of my head in a come-hither look to Haley. She didn't hesitate to join me on the other side of the bed, and we quickly melted into each other's arms. As I felt her press her body against mine, I kissed her with an open mouth, and this time she parted her lips and allowed my tongue to probe her cavity. Our breasts mashed together, and as we intertwined our legs, we both began to moan passionately. I pulled my leg up, pressing it against her pussy, and she responded by grinding her hips against my thigh.

By now, she'd joined me in thrusting her tongue into my mouth, and as we writhed together on the bed, I grabbed her ass and pulled her closer. The passion with which she was tongue-fucking me made me think she was ready for different kind of tongue lashing, and after a few minutes I disengaged and began nibbling my way down the front of her body. The only sound I could hear from the other sound of the room now was the soft rusting of Hannah shifting in her chair and the occasional soft sigh. I wondered if Haley sensed how much she was enjoying herself watching us, but at this point my only concern was satisfying the pretty girl lying beside me.

As I nibbled on Haley's teats and swirled my tongue over her areolas, she arched her back and pressed herself more firmly against me. It was apparent to me that she'd lost all of her inhibitions about being with another woman, and I hummed my approval as her body responded to my touch. I traced the little indentation running down the center of her tummy with my tongue, and her stomach quivered the closer I got to her private area as she began to roll her hips in anticipation of my touch.

When I reached her panties, I pulled them over her hips while she lifted her ass off the bed. Her bush felt as soft as fur and I rolled my cheeks over it, reveling in it's sexy scent and plush thickness. Beads of lubrication rested on her muff like morning dew on a spider web, and I paused to suck them into my mouth, tasting her sweet honey.

The further down I lowered myself, the further she spread her legs apart, until my shoulders were comfortably nestled between her legs. For a moment, I paused with my head cocked above her clit as I closed my eyes and inhaled her sweet, perfumy scent. After a few moments, she began to shimmy her hips impatiently, eager to feel my touch in her special place. Instead, I dribbled some saliva out of my mouth and let it fall on top of her inflamed jewel. When she felt the unexpected moisture on her button, she groaned and lifted her hips closer to my face.

"Oh God, Jade," she whined. "You're driving me crazy. I want to feel your touch so bad. Take me into your mouth like you said you would last time. Suck my pussy with your pretty mouth."

Her dirty talk just turned me on all the more, and I lowered my head to encircle her burning clit.

"Oh God–Oh God," Haley panted. "That feels so good. Lick my little man with your lips and make me feel like you did when I watched you last time."

Little man, I chuckled to myself. I hadn't heard that expression used by a woman before to describe her clit, and I wondered if this was a euphemism her parents had used when she was younger. But it didn't matter to me–I was just thrilled that she was expressing her desire for me and telling me how much I was turning her on.

As I hummed in delight, I began circling her button with the tip of my tongue, and she began groaning more loudly. While I mixed up my technique between sucking and licking her pearl, she placed her hands behind my head once again and pulled me harder into her crotch. As her breathing began to get more ragged and accelerated, I knew that she was getting close to the point of no return. I was tempted to pull back for a few seconds to prolong her torment, but then I realized there'd be plenty more time to tease and play with her after she released her pent-up sexual tension. She began to lift her hips off the bed as her body became rigid in a tight lock, and I slipped my fingers inside her and began to stroke her tenting G-spot.

"Oh God, Jade," she hissed. "Don't stop. I'm going to cum. *Yes!*" she grunted. "I'm cumming in your mouth!"

Suddenly, I felt the walls of her pussy clamping down on my fingers in rhythmic contractions as she humped her hips against my face while holding me tightly against her. I paused for a moment to feel her body spasming as I peered up and watched her pretty face contorting into paroxysms of pleasure. After what seemed like a full minute of tensing her body in a prolonged and powerful orgasm, she finally dropped her hips down onto the bed, panting loudly to catch her breath.

With the room suddenly quiet, I heard gentle squeaks coming from the other side of the room as Hannah shifted rhythmically in her chair. It was obvious to both of us what was going on in the dark, and we smiled at one another as I pulled myself back up to look into Haley's steamy eyes.

"That was beautiful, Jade," she sighed. "Thank you for making me feel like a woman for the first time in my life. I can't believe how skilled a lover you are. I'm afraid that I'll never be able to meet your expectations–"

"Remember that there are no expectations or targets in this first direct encounter between the two of you," Hannah breathed deeply, collecting herself. "Jade–why don't you show Haley how she can satisfy you. Sometimes it's more fun for the *receiver* to take the lead."

I knew immediately what Hannah meant, and as I lifted myself up off the bed, I looked into Haley's eyes and nodded.

"Why don't you lie there for a little longer and let me do most of the work?" I said.

I raised myself up on all fours and straddled her face with my knees on either side of her head, and she looked up at me with wide eyes and smiled. As I ran my fingers gently through her silky hair, I began to lower myself until my dripping pussy hovered inches over her pouty lips. She flicked her tongue out awkwardly trying to bat my clit, and I cupped her cheeks, lowering myself a little further until my nub pressed against her lips.

"Just open your mouth a little bit and nibble on me for a moment," I said. "Sometimes when you're making love to a woman, less is more. Let me ease into it while I watch your pretty face."

Haley did as she was told, and as she sucked my hard nub into her mouth, I closed my eyes and groaned.

"Yes, baby," I purred. "Just like that. Suck my button and roll it around in your mouth. I like the feeling of your mouth on my body."

As Haley began to roll her tongue over my bulb in a similar manner to the way I'd kissed her earlier, I smiled. She was a quick study, and I felt myself growing closer to her with every passing moment.

"Yes, Haley," I encouraged her. "Just like that. Feel my hard clit in your mouth. I'm making love to your mouth while I watch you. I'm going to cum for you soon."

Haley's head nodded excitedly, and her eyes began to widen as I pressed my pussy harder down onto her face. I could feel the passion rising within me but I didn't want to drown her in another torrent if I came too hard, so as my orgasm began to take hold of me, I lifted my hips and pointed my pussy over her tits while I squirted my juices all over her heaving chest. As she peered down at me between my legs, I saw her face twist into another silent orgasm. Apparently, I'd excited her so much with my waterworks that she hadn't needed any direct stimulation to come once again.

As we both groaned and shook our bodies together on the bed, I heard the sound of gentle sloshing coming from the direction of Hannah's chair. I peered over at her and noticed that her pants were unbuttoned while she rubbed her hands sensuously over her naked mound.

"That was very good, ladies," she sighed. "You're making excellent progress. It's time for the last step in your pair bonding. Now I want you to touch each other at the same time and experience the joy of coming together. Jade, I'm guessing you have a bit more experience in this area."

"Perhaps just a little," I smiled, as I shimmied my hips over Haley's slippery torso toward her quivering pussy. I paused for a moment when I reached her bush once again and tilted my pelvis back and forth over top of her bush, feeling the soft hairs tickling my clit and wet opening.

"Would you like me to make love to you now, Haley?" I purred.

"Isn't that what we've been doing all this time?" she said.

"Not quite *this* way," I smiled. "I think you might find this brings us even closer together and feels even more amazing. Lift your knees up higher and spread your legs for me."

Haley looked at me confused for a moment, and I nodded reassuringly. When she pulled her knees almost up to her chest, I pushed her thighs apart and peered at her inflamed gland, poking its head out of its hood. I kneeled over top of her and slowly lowered my body until the bottom of our thighs rested on one another. Her eyes widened when she realized what I intended to do, and a sly smile formed on my mouth as our clits touched for the first time. As I began to grind our hips together providing direct stimulation to our most sensitive areas, she threw her head back and groaned . I didn't know if she'd even conceived of two women touching themselves this way, but the look of pleasure on her face indicated that she was quickly losing herself in the process.

As I shifted my weight forward and back, stroking her hard clit and rubbing our sopping pussies together, she began to whimper and toss her head from side to side. Seeing her enjoying the tribbing action so much just made me want to fuck her harder. I transferred more of my weight onto her thighs, and she began to rock her hips in concert with mine. The feeling of our nubs rolling over one another as our slits smacked against one another was the most exciting feeling either one of us had experienced. Before long, she began moaning more urgently, and I saw a flush begin to spread over her chest as her nipples contracted even more firmly.

"Yes, Haley," I groaned, seeing the look of ecstasy roll over her face. "Let it go baby. Let me feel you cum with me while I make love to you."

"Yes, Jade," Haley grunted. "I feel it coming. I'm going to cum so hard against your pussy. Fuck me harder."

That was all I needed to hear as I pressed my hips harder down onto her vulva and began humping her more forcefully. When I heard her pussy begin to make sexy gassy sounds, I knew she was cumming again, but this time I stayed connected to her while my own orgasm took hold of me. The sound of my juices spraying onto her gaping hole as she moaned in euphoria was the sexiest thing I'd ever heard. As we came together listening to the sound of our pussies spasming in the height of ecstasy, I leaned forward and kissed her passionately. Haley had come a long way since her first awkward guided session with Hannah, and as our pussies continued twitching against one another, we both sighed in contentment.

Soon after, we heard Hannah moaning softly in her chair, and we turned our heads to see that she'd pulled her pants down all the way and was ramming her long dildo in and out of her pussy.

"I'd have to say you've both graduated with flying colors," she panted as her body jerked softly in her chair.

Haley and I looked at each for a moment with the same thought, nodding our heads in Hannah's direction.

"I think maybe Hannah needs a little therapy session of her *own* now," I smiled.

BOOK 19

ELEVATOR SHAFT

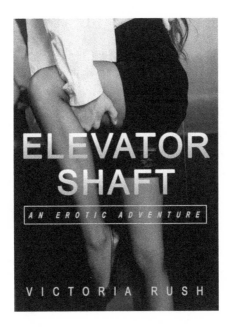

1

I breathed a sigh of relief as I stepped into the elevator just after 5 p.m. on the day before Thanksgiving. My meeting with the creative director of Ogilvy & Mather Advertising had gone better than expected, and I felt elated at the prospect of working with the prestigious agency. We'd taken longer than anticipated to discuss the particulars of their Disney Studios campaign, but at the end of the day he'd awarded me exclusive rights to design all their new movie posters.

The view from their penthouse suite atop the Willis Tower was breathtaking. Chicago had been enjoying an unusually mild November, and I could see all the way across Lake Michigan on the clear autumn day. They'd feted me with a late luncheon in the Skydeck Restaurant on the 103rd floor and although I felt fully sated, I was looking forward to the annual feast with my family over the long weekend.

Ogilvy's offices had cleared out early in advance of the weekend crush, and I nodded toward the two lone elevator occupants as the door slid closed behind us. They were both dressed in expensive suits and looked to be about my age. The man standing to my right had thick ruffled hair, dark eyes, and broad shoulders that curved nicely in his tight wool suit.

But it was the woman standing on the other side of the elevator that caught my attention. Standing almost six feet tall in her Louboutin pumps, her perfectly manicured brows arched over aquamarine-colored eyes and red pouty lips. Like the handsome hunk on the opposite side of the elevator, her busty figure left little to the imagination in her form-fitting skirt and blazer. My pussy twitched as I glanced downward, eyeing her long and shapely legs. Given how far they were standing apart and how hard they were working to avoid eye contact, I quickly surmised that they didn't know each other.

Funny how perfect strangers always find the quickest way to separate themselves in close quarters, I thought.

I glanced at the elevator console to confirm the ground floor button was selected, then I stepped to the back of the lift to get a closer look at the two passengers. They looked even sexier from behind, as I shamelessly ran my eyes over their figures. The man had a nice round bump lifting the back of his blazer, and I could make out the muscular curve of his thighs filling in his tight-fitting pants.

I bet that guy doesn't have much trouble getting his share of the action, I thought, suddenly feeling warm under my form-fitting suit.

But the woman's suit was even tighter, displaying every curve and valley of her sexy figure. As I stared at the globes of her firm ass clearly delineated in her snug skirt, my panties began to moisten thinking about how much I'd like to lick my way up her long legs all the way from her pretty feet to her steamy pussy.

Normally I tried to respect everyone's desire for privacy while traveling on elevators, but whether it was the after-effects of my three-martini lunch or my giddiness from landing the prestigious account, for some reason I felt the need to break the awkward silence in the lift.

I hope you guys have as good a reason as I did to work this late on Thanksgiving weekend," I said.

"Par for the course," the man said, turning his head halfway around and smiling half-heartedly in my direction. "Goes with the territory, unfortunately."

"Mmm," the lady grunted, staring impassively toward the front of the elevator. "No rest for the wicked in the urban jungle."

I peered back and forth between the two strangers, sensing some tension between them. Were they ex-lovers or disgruntled co-workers? Maybe they'd just been working late on a problem account and were exhausted after another long day at the office.

"Do you both work at Ogil–" I said, hoping to make some new introductions at the firm.

But as the pressure increased in my ears from the rapid descent of the elevator, suddenly the lights went out and the lift screeched to an abrupt halt.

"What the–" the woman said, breathing heavily.

"Oh my God!" I said, clutching my briefcase next to me as I quivered in the darkness. "What's going on?"

"It's probably just a power failure," the man said. "Everybody's been gearing up for the holidays and the little heat wave has been drawing a lot of power from the grid lately. I'm sure ComEd will have us back on track in no time."

"Are we safe, stuck so far off the ground?" I said nervously. "This is my worst nightmare – being stuck in an elevator suspended hundreds of feet in the air."

"Not to worry," the man reassured. "Modern elevators are equipped with multiple fail-safe mechanisms. An emergency brake automatically engages in the event of a power failure, so there's no way it can drop any further."

"What about the *cables*?" I asked, still petrified at the thought of losing control over the elevator. "Is there a chance they might fatigue or snap if this goes on for a while?"

"No way," he said. "There's more than one cable holding us up and each one is rated for much higher loads than our current weight. As strange as it may sound, this might be one of the safest places to be in the middle of a blackout. I hate to think how crazy it might be on the *streets* right now with all the traffic lights out."

"That's a small consolation," I said, beginning to breathe a little more normally. "I'd rather take my chances out there in broad daylight instead of being cooped up in this claustrophobic death trap."

In the pitch blackness, I could hear the sound of the woman's hands sliding frantically over the blacked-out console.

"What do we do now?" she said. "Can we communicate with somebody while we're locked up in here? I can't find the emergency call button in the dark–"

Suddenly, the screen of the man's cell phone illuminated and I saw his fingers tapping the surface. A flashlight lit up on the back side, and he pointed it toward the elevator control panel.

"This should help a bit," he said.

We could see a red button near the bottom of the console, and the woman slammed her palm against it repeatedly.

"Can anyone hear me?" she screamed. "We're stuck in an elevator near the top floor of the Willis Tower. Somebody help us, please!"

"The coms are probably down too," the man said calmly. "None of the electronic systems will be working as long as the power is down. I think we just need to wait it out until power is restored or the building's maintenance crew comes to retrieve us."

"Our phones," the woman said, turning her head in the direction of the man's glowing screen. "There are other ways we can call for help."

The two of us pulled our phones out of our purses and tapped 911. A message filled the screen indicating that the mobile network was temporarily unavailable.

"What the fuck?" the woman said. "The *phones* aren't working either?"

As the man lifted his phone to examine his screen, the backlight illuminated his handsome face.

"There's no bars. The power failure has probably disabled the cell towers too."

"Doesn't the phone company have back-up generators or something?" the woman said.

"Yes, but it will likely take some time for their systems to come online. But even if they do, every person in Chicago will likely be calling their family or emergency services to make sure everything is okay. I don't expect we'll be able to make any calls for at least a couple of hours."

"A couple of *hours*?!" the woman exclaimed. "How are we going to survive in this cramped elevator that long? What about air? Won't we run out of oxygen before then?"

"We're going to be fine, Elle," the man said. "There's plenty of ventilation ducts in the compartment, and with fifty floors above and below us, there's enough oxygen in the elevator shaft to support us for quite a long time."

So they do know each other, I smiled.

"You seem to know a lot about elevators for a guy wearing such an expensive suit," I said.

"Working on the hundred and fifth floor of the tallest building in the Midwest will do that to a guy. I'm a little claustrophobic too, so I did a little bit of research before I took this job. We'd *starve* to death long before any malfunction of the elevator would kill us."

"So we just stand here twiddling our thumbs while we wait for someone to come save us?" I said.

"It looks that way. But I'm guessing the emergency response people have their hands full dealing with a city full of panicked citizens. Plus, there's lots of other elevators in this building, so it's likely to be at least a few hours before anyone comes to our rescue. You might want to sit down and relax to make the wait a little more comfortable."

The man squatted toward the floor then leaned back against the wall and straightened his legs out in front of him. Recognizing that we might be in this for a long haul, I followed his cue and sat down kitty-corner to him against the back wall. Peering up at the woman, I saw that she was still tapping the surface of her phone, trying to make an outside connection.

"Why don't you make yourself more comfortable, Elle?" I said, trying to ease her distress. "My name's Jade. I didn't catch your name–"

"West," the man said. "The least we can do is try to get to know one another better while we're stuck in here. Make the best of an uncomfortable situation."

"It's either that or play Candy Crush on our phones until the power comes back on," I joked.

Elle exhaled a sigh of resignation as I watched her phone slide down the wall to my right while she plopped down on the floor.

"Why not?" she said. "I can't think of a better inmate to spend my time with while I'm locked up in here.".

"You two know one another then," I said. "Do you work together, or do you have some kind of *other* relationship?"

"Hardly," Elle huffed. "Not in a million years."

"We work together at Ogilvy," West said. "We handle two of the firm's largest accounts. I guess there's been a bit of a competition of sorts to see who would make partner first–"

"Not likely, with that lame-ass automotive account you've been handed. Can't you see that's a dying business with more and more people switching to foreign cars these days?"

"Maybe, but at least it's *reliable*. Not like that new tech account of yours–"

Suddenly, our conversation was interrupted with the sound of banging coming from inside the elevator shaft.

"What's that noise?" Elle said.

We paused to listen as the clanging sound grew louder and more frenetic.

"Could it be the maintenance technicians trying to open the doors above us?" I said.

"Unlikely," West said. "I can't imagine they'd be able to respond this fast. Most of them are probably stuck in traffic on their way home already."

"What is it then?" Elle asked. "Are the cables about to snap?"

The clanging noises suddenly changed to a rhythmic pattern of short and long taps.

"It sounds like an SOS signal. Probably from another group of people trapped in an elevator above or below us."

"That's not a bad idea," Elle said, pounding her fist against the wall beside her. "At least we know we've got some company."

"Not that it's likely to do us much good," West said. "There's not much either of us can do from our current locations."

Elle tilted her phone up, scanning the ceiling with her flashlight.

"If you're so clever Mr. Smartypants, maybe you can figure out how to get the lid off this thing and find a nearby exit?"

West chuckled softly in the darkness.

"There's a reason these things aren't designed to be evacuated from the inside," he said. "It takes a special key to open the lid from the outside. It wouldn't be safe for us to exit that way even if we could. Who knows when the elevator might start up again and pin us against the walls?"

"With all the time you spend in the gym," Elle huffed, "I would have thought you could jimmy up the cables to the nearest door."

"Yeah," West said. "I'm sure it's that simple. I'll get right on it."

It was obvious there was a lot more going on between these two than a competitive rivalry. Their little digs sounded more like a high school crush than a workplace disagreement.

"Is it getting hot in here, or is it just me?" I said, trying to break the tension.

I'd begun to perspire under my suit, and I was pretty sure it wasn't because I was afraid of plummeting to my death anymore.

"I feel it too," West said. "The air conditioning systems would have gone offline along with the power. And the radiant heat from outside the building is slowly creeping into the elevator shaft."

"Oh great," Elle said. "So now we're going to *boil* to death while we wait for help?"

"It shouldn't get much hotter than the temperature outside. I expect it will begin to cool as the sun goes down. You can always loosen your clothes to get more comfortable."

"That's the best pick-up line I've heard in a while," I chuckled.

"You have *no* idea," Elle sneered. "He's full of them."

"I guess it wouldn't hurt to take off my jacket and loosen my shirt," I said. "It's not like we can *see* anything in the pitch dark anyway, right?"

"I wouldn't put it past him to flash his phone you least expect it," Elle said. "We still have a few fleeting sources of power while we're waiting."

"Not for long," West said, peering at the glowing surface of his phone. "I'm already in the yellow zone for power. How about you guys?"

"I'm showing ten percent," I said.

"I'm down to *two* percent," Elle cursed. "I knew I should have replaced my battery during the last upgrade cycle. I can barely get through a full day at the best of times."

"We're consuming a lot of extra juice with our screens and flashlights on full strength," West said. "It's probably best to turn them off or at least switch to sleep mode to save them for when we really need them."

"Awesome," Elle said. "What do we do in the meantime?"

"Why don't we do what people used to do before the advent of modern technology and *talk* to one another," I said. "It sounds like you guys could use some more open lines of communication anyhow."

"What did you want to talk about?" she said sarcastically. "Our favorite hobbies and the unusual weather we've had lately?"

"Well it's probably best to steer clear of work," I suggested. "Tell us something personal about yourself, something nobody else would know. I mean, I'll probably never see you guys again once we get out of this predicament. Who else is gonna know?"

The compartment suddenly fell quiet as each of us pondered what to say.

"You know, it's strange," West said, breaking the silence. "I've always wondered what it would be like be in a situation like this. It's kind of *exciting* in a way, being left to our own devices without any outside stimulation."

"Kind of like being trapped on a deserted island," Elle chuckled.

"In a way, I guess. Makes you wonder what you'd do to pass the time, so far removed from modern conveniences."

"What do you think *you'd* do to amuse yourself on this deserted island, West?" I said, eager to steer the conversation in a different direction.

"Depends on who I was stranded with."

"What if it were just *you*?"

"I guess I'd have to scrape by on my memories. Or spend my time fantasizing about how to get off the island."

"And if you couldn't?" Elle said. "What would you fantasize about then?

"The usual macho stuff, I suppose. "That I was stranded in paradise with a supermodel—"

"Or two?" I joked.

"The more the merrier," West said.

"You men are always fantasizing about doing it with multiple women at the same time," Elle said.

"What about you then, Elle?" I asked, deflecting the attention away from West temporarily. "What would be *your* ultimate fantasy if you were stranded on a deserted island?"

"I'd probably go stir crazy all by myself after a while. I suppose I wouldn't be much different from West, dreaming about being stuck there with David Beckham or Brad Pitt..."

"Only *men*?" I said, fishing for more details.

"I dunno. I've never tried it with women before. But I suppose if we were stuck on a deserted island long enough, one thing might lead to another..."

"What about you, Jade?" West said, sensing a theme developing.

"I lean more toward women, myself. Although if I didn't have any other choice, I might be tempted to dabble a bit—"

"It *is* getting hot in here," West said as the sound of rustling clothes filled the compartment.

"Hotter than your deserted island fantasy?" I asked.

"It's getting there. All this talk about mixing it up with different partners is making me hot under the collar."

"Don't let us stop you from acting out your fantasy, West," Elle said. "It's just us girls in here. We won't tell if you don't."

"What exactly did you have in mind?" West asked.

"Something tells me you're getting uncomfortable in those heavy clothes for more than one reason," she said. "If you need to free the beast, don't let us stop you from getting your freak on."

"Um..." West paused, unsure if we were thinking the same thing.

"I think maybe West needs a little extra encouragement, Elle," I said. "Why don't you scooch up a little closer to me so he can exercise his fantasy more vividly?"

"This little adventure is getting more interesting by the moment," Elle purred, shimmying her hips across the floor to sit next to me. "I suppose there's more than *one* way to relieve the boredom when you're stuck in an elevator."

2

"So, West..." I said, hoping to capitalize on the rapidly developing heat in the room. "Tell us more about your little fantasy. Maybe it'll help keep our minds off this unpleasant situation we find ourselves in."

"Um, well," he said, happy to have a distraction to mask his real desires. "I guess I'd have to get to know these supermodels a bit better before we got down to business. I'd have to loosen them up a little before they thought about having sex with me, let alone with each other."

"Oh?" I said, playing along. "What would you want to know about us – I mean *them* – in order to get them in the mood?"

"I dunno, something about their families, I suppose. Maybe their relationship status. I'd need to make sure they were unattached before I proposed any kind of physical engagement. They might be kind of shy about wanting to try anything if they were already in a committed relationship."

"Let's pretend *we're* your fantasy supermodels for a moment," I said, nudging Elle's thigh playfully. "Let's see just how good your pick-up lines really are."

West shifted uncomfortably on the elevator floor and cleared his throat, imagining himself in a bar wedged between two women.

"Okay..." he said. "Well, first, of course, I'd ask them their names."

"I'm Jade," I purred.

"Elle," my partner-in-crime giggled.

"I'm West. Bit of a pickle we've gotten ourselves into. I suppose the first thing we need to do is make sure we have enough food and water to get us through this unfortunate turn of events. We don't know how long this situation might last."

"I've got a candy bar in my purse," I said, pretending to ruffle through my belongings.

"And I've got some bottled water," Elle said.

"That won't get us very far," West said. "But we might be able to catch some fish and create a pit to store fresh water when it rains. I guess our next order of business is to figure out how to send a signal to a passing ship so someone knows we're here. Do either of you carry a lighter?"

"I'm afraid I don't smoke," I said.

"Neither do I," Elle said.

"That's funny," West chuckled. "I always said that would be a deal-breaker whenever I met a pretty girl, but in this case we're going to have to find a workaround..."

"Are you saying you think we're *pretty*?" I teased.

"Well I don't want to swell your heads, but if I have to be stuck on this island for an extended period of time, I can't imagine two people I'd rather be with."

He's not bad, I whispered in Elle's ear.

He's got his moments, she nudged.

"So how are we going to let anyone know we're here then?" I said.

West rustled through his suit jacket and I heard a soft tinkling sound.

"I should be able to use my reading glasses as a magnifying lens to start a fire. Then we just need to find some fresh foliage or wet logs to create enough smoke..."

"You seem to know a lot about survival techniques for a guy who works in an office all day long," Elle huffed.

"Maybe I watch a little too much of that show Man vs. Wild."

"Well if you think you can get us out of this situation, we'd be willing to do just about anything you asked," she purred.

"Including eating bugs and drinking your own urine?"

"I'm pretty sure we can find something a little more palatable to eat between the three of us," I said, squeezing Elle's thigh.

"It's too bad we've gotten ourselves into this predicament so close to the holiday," West said. "You both must have been looking forward to enjoying a proper Thanksgiving meal with your families."

"I was just going to have an informal get-together with a few of my siblings at my mother's place," I said.

"What about you, Elle?" West said, fishing for more details about his colleague. "What did you have planned for the holidays?"

"I was on my way to the airport to visit my folks in LA when we got stuck in here. I hope they don't worry too much when they don't hear from me."

"Is there anyone *else* who'll be concerned about your whereabouts?"

Smooth, I nudged Elle. *He's looking to see if you're unattached.*

It was becoming increasingly obvious that West had more than just a working interest in her.

"Other than my *boss*, you mean?" Elle kidded. "Unfortunately, my job doesn't afford much free time for extra-curricular activities. What about you?" she said, turning back to West. "Who were *you* planning to spend some quality time with over the holidays?"

I smiled in the darkness, happy to hear the walls breaking down between the two co-workers.

"Other than my roommate and a few buddies on our house-league hockey team? We were just going to order a pizza and sit down to watch some football over the long weekend."

"You sound like a dyed-in-the-wool bachelor," Elle mused. "I didn't picture you sharing a flat with a buddy."

"Chicago's an expensive city for a single guy. Besides, sometimes it helps to have a wingman to navigate the social jungle. Speaking of living arrangements, it might be a good idea to start looking for a comfortable spot to spend the night–"

"We've already got plenty of shelter in our little corner under the palm trees," I kidded. I shifted my weight, feigning discomfort. "Although it *is* a little hard. I could use a pillow about now..."

West folded up his jacket and passed it toward me in the dark, and I placed it under Elle's knees, nodding appreciatively.

He's a gentleman too, I whispered, trying to encourage their reluctant courtship.

"So you're a *player*, then," she said, still unconvinced. "Where do you and your buddy bring your conquests when you want to have a little fun? Isn't it a bit cramped in your two-bedroom apartment? Or do you two create your own fun with each other?"

"Uh, *no*," West said. "I don't swing that way. What about you two? What are two pretty girls like you doing still single? I might say the same thing about you."

"Oh I like *men* alright," Elle said. "I just haven't found one yet worthy of my attention."

"What kind of man are you looking for?" West probed.

"The strong silent type, I suppose. Someone who knows how to treat a woman like a lady and is good with his hands..."

"Like someone who could get you out of a jam like this?"

"Possibly. But someone who's also a good lover and provider. He'd have to have a stable job and a good build..."

"Fair enough," West said, looking to bring me back into the fold. "How about you Jade? What are you looking for in a potential partner?"

"Someone with long slender legs who can wrap herself around my hips while I fuck her madly–"

"Jesus," West said, adjusting his equipment in the dark. "I've always wondered how you women do that exactly. How you make love without a–"

"*Penis*? Don't tell me you haven't watched your fair share of girl-on-girl porn? We can do pretty much everything a man can do, just without all the mess."

"What about–*penetration*? Don't you ever miss that?"

"We have lots of ways to get that when we're in the mood. Between strap-on cocks, double-sided dildos and all the special sex toys on the market, we can find plenty of ways to stimulate ourselves on both the inside and the outside. In fact, I'm carrying one in my purse right now. You never know when you might feel the need..."

"Really?" West said, his voice taking on a new sense of urgency. "Where do you use it? Isn't it kind of noisy?"

"Not this one. A friend of mine introduced me to it recently. It's called the Osé, designed by a woman. It doesn't vibrate so much as *throb*. It's incredibly lifelike, with a long undulating wand and an opening at the base that provides stimulation remarkably similar to a tongue–"

"*Holy shit!*" Elle interrupted. "Can I see this thing? I've never heard of a woman's vibrator like that."

"Of course," I said, happy to see that see her rapidly warming up.

I opened my purse and handed her the soft silicone instrument. She ran her hands over the long finger-shaped extension, then pressed her hand into the little hole.

"How does it work exactly?" she said. "It's not shaped like any vibrator I've ever seen."

"Feel for a little notch near the bottom of the base. There's two modes, each of which is activated with a press of the button."

Elle ran her fingers over the base of the object in the dark, then I heard her gasp.

"My God," she said. "It's *moving*. Like a real finger!"

"Exactly," I nodded. "It's designed to simulate the movement and feel of a real person. The curvature of the wand is perfect for stimulating your G-spot. Press the button again and see what *else* it can do."

I heard another click and Elle's body suddenly lurched next to mine.

"What the *fuck*?!" she exclaimed. "That feels just like a–"

"Tongue?" I said. "You won't believe how lifelike it is until you try it for real. Why don't you see for yourself?"

"Right here?!"

"Why not?" I said. "We're all getting pretty worked up with all this talk of sex with different partners. Besides, it's not like any of us can see anything in the pitch dark. If ever there was a safe place to try something like this, this is the time."

"I don't know," Elle hesitated. "It is intriguing, but I hardly know you guys..."

"Come on," I said. "I know you want it. I can feel your hips squirming next to me. Why don't you just slip it under your skirt for a moment? I think you'll get the idea pretty quickly what it's capable of."

Elle paused for a moment, then slowly began to spread her thighs apart. I could feel her hand rustling between her legs, then she gasped.

"Right?" I said. "Not like anything you've ever tried before, is it?"

"No," she panted, spreading her thighs further apart. "It feels more like a–"

"Real person?"

"Mmm," she purred.

"It might not be quite as good as the real thing, but you'll never know until you feel it against your naked flesh. Why don't you take your clothes off? We can place West's jacket under your hips if you're worried about the dirty floor. You don't mind do you, West?"

"Definitely not," he said, unbuckling his belt.

"Maybe for just a few seconds," Elle said. "But no peeking."

"Our phones are turned off, remember? No one will have any idea what you're doing unless you tell us."

"Okay, but no comments from the peanut gallery while I try this thing out. I'm self-conscious enough without you guys taunting me in the dark..."

"Maybe if we *all* took off our clothes together, it would make everybody feel more comfortable. That way, we could each explore our own bodies to the extent we feel comfortable. What do you think, West?"

"Way ahead of you," he said, pulling his pants down across the floor.

"Just go slow as you explore the device's capabilities," I said to Elle. "We'll be enjoying ourselves along with you."

"That does sound pretty hot actually," she said. "I'm getting hornier by the moment."

I lifted my hips off the floor, then pulled my skirt down over my legs and placed it underneath me. Then I grabbed Elle's hand and pulled it over my bare thigh, inches from my steaming pussy.

"That makes two of us," I said.

"Damn, Jade," she said. "Your skin is so warm."

"That's not the *only* part of me that's warm right now," I said. "Go ahead, let yourself loose."

Elle paused for a second, then unzipped the back of her skirt and shimmied it down over her ankles. Then she lifted her hips and pulled her panties off her legs.

"There," I said. "Doesn't that feel better? Now give our little friend a try against your bare skin."

Elle paused with the vibrator poised inches from her twitching pussy.

"Do you prefer to use the finger or the tongue?" she hesitated.

"Both, depending on my mood. Why don't you start by letting the finger caress you around your opening?"

Elle turned her hand and positioned the Osé so the finger bent toward her in rhythmic motions.

"It feels–*strange*," she said. "Like I'm being touched by a robot."

"But a very *sexy* robot, yes? Just pretend it's Brad Pitt's or David Beckham's or someone *else's* finger caressing you..."

"Mmm," she sighed, tilting her head back against the wall of the elevator. "That does feel better."

"You might want to tease yourself for a while until you get fully warmed up. When you're ready, feel free to insert it inside to experience the full capability of the toy."

"Oh, I'm getting *warmed up* alright," she panted. "How about you guys?"

I spread my legs further apart and rested my thigh overtop Elle's as I began to circle my hand over my clit. With the two of us sitting so close together, she must have felt the movement of my arm against her side as I began to stimulate myself manually.

"I'm burning up inside," I panted as the sound of my fingers rubbing against my wet labia filled the compartment. "How are you doing over there, West?"

"I'm thoroughly enjoying this fantasy," he panted. "I haven't been this hard in ages."

"I'm guessing there's something *else* hard in this room," I said, flapping my thigh against Elle's. "Why don't you put that wand inside you so you can fantasize along with us?"

I could feel Elle's arms tense up for a moment as she held the tip of the undulating finger against her opening, then she groaned, sliding down the wall. As I listened to the sound of the long appendage slipping inside her dripping pussy, I slid the fingers of my right hand inside me at the same time.

"Uhnn," she groaned, pressing the device firmer against her vulva.

"Do you *still* need Brad Pitt on your deserted island?" I said.

"Not with this thing by my side," she purred. "This is better than any man. At least it knows the right places to caress."

"Feels heavenly, doesn't it?" I said, curling my fingers inside my own hole to rub the front side of my G-spot. "Have you turned the tongue on yet?"

"Not yet," Elle panted. "I'm just enjoying the feeling of being stroked inside right now."

"Mmm," I said, feeling my juices beginning to run down the crack of my ass. I was thrilled that Elle had loosened up enough to feel comfortable sharing what she was experiencing. "Take your time, baby. We've got all the time in the world."

"That's what worries me," she grunted. "That we might be stuck in this elevator all weekend."

"I'm sure we can find plenty of other ways to keep ourselves amused if it comes to that," I said. "But don't worry about any of that right now. Just pretend you're stranded in paradise with your ultimate lover. What would you like him to do next?"

"I'd like her to lick me," she slipped. "I mean *him*. I mean whoever."

I reached between Elle's slippery legs and tapped the button on the underside of her vibrator one more time. She pressed the device harder against her body and squealed with a guttural moan.

"Oh my God," she groaned. "That feels incredible. I feel it's tongue. It's so lifelike..."

"Yes, Elle," I purred. "Imagine it's your fantasy lover worshipping your body. You're so hot right now."

"Is this how you do it?" she said. "I mean when you're with other women? This doesn't feel like any *man* I've ever been with..."

"Like I said, the toy is designed by a woman to provide feminine stimulation in the most erotic manner. But you'll never know what it really feels like to make love to another woman until you try–"

"*Fuck*, Jade," Elle growled. "I want to feel you against my body. This feels so good."

"Yes, baby," I whispered, lifting my hand to her chin and turning her face to meet my lips. As we began to kiss passionately, I pulled my hand out of my pussy and slipped it under her blouse, cupping her breasts and pinching her erect nipples. "Imagine it's *me* licking your clit right now."

"*Oh fuck, oh fuck*," she gasped. "I can feel it coming..."

"Yes," I purred, rolling my tongue around the inside of her mouth. "Come inside my mouth, Elle. I want to feel you twitching as I suck your button."

"Oh God!" she wailed. "I cumming, Jade! I cumming so hard. Suck my pussy!"

As we face-fucked each other imagining we were joined at the hips instead of the mouth, I heard West groan on the other side of the elevator as Elle began shaking uncontrollably against my body. Even though I hadn't touched her anywhere near her pussy, with our tongues intertwined and my hand squeezing her shaking tits, I felt incredibly connected to her. As she groaned into my mouth in the throes of a powerful climax, I suddenly gushed out of my opening, spraying my juices all over her bare legs while we quivered together in the darkness.

Something told me this was going to be just the start of our little fantasy adventure...

3

For the longest time after we came, nobody said anything, as awkward silence filled the compartment. All we could hear was the sound of quiet breathing while we all recovered from our powerful climaxes. There wasn't even any rustling of clothes while we lay there in the dark, completely naked. There was something incredibly erotic about knowing each of us sat inches away from each other, with our exposed genitals still throbbing in excitement.

After a few minutes, I heard Elle reach between her legs and pull the Osé out of her wet pussy with a distinct plop.

"Thanks for letting me share your little toy," she said, handing it to me in the darkness. "I'm sorry that I've made such a mess of it..."

"Mmm," I said, placing the tip of the wand in my mouth and sucking it loudly. "Don't give it a second thought. I like it that way. You taste exquisite. I only wish I could have felt you twitching in my mouth for real."

"With that vibrator's tongue doing its action between my legs and you kissing me at the same time, it was like you were actually there," she said. "I haven't been this turned on in a long time."

"What about you, West?" I said, trying to bring our silent partner into the loop. "Did you enjoy our little fantasy role play? Do you think your supermodels are getting sufficiently warmed up?"

"Damn near," he panted. "That was the most erotic thing I've ever heard. My only regret is that nobody was actually *touching* each other."

"Oh, there was plenty of touching going on, believe me," I said. "And from the sounds of things on the other side of the elevator, you seemed to be enjoying yourself plenty enough."

"Well, yes," he said. "But it's not quite the same as–"

"Having someone *else* touch you? What do you think, Elle? Are you ready to take it to the next level?"

"Maybe," she said, hesitating. "What did you have in mind?"

"Between the three of us, with so many different, um–*tools*–to work with, there's an almost infinite number of ways we can engage. We could pair up to start, then maybe swap partners before the three of us get together. What's your pleasure?"

Elle paused for a minute as she pondered the possibilities. I sensed the walls were beginning to break down between her and West, but there was also no denying her attraction to me.

"I've always wondered what it would be like to make love to another woman," she said. "With you being so much more experienced in that area, maybe you could teach me how to do it properly..."

I grinned at Elle's feeble attempt to mask her real desires. She had no idea what she was in for.

"I can work with that," I said. "How about you, West? Do you think you can hold on a little longer while Elle and I have a bit more fun?"

"Oh, I'll be *holding on*, alright. I'm hard as a rock again knowing I'm about to realize one of my ultimate fantasies."

"Well you go right ahead and enjoy yourself over there while Elle and I get to know each other a little better."

I turned to Elle and squeezed her hand gently.

"Do you want to be the top or the bottom?"

"What do you mean?" she said. "I thought that only applied to men–"

"When two women get together, usually one takes the submissive role while the other takes a more dominant role. It's the same with lesbians as with gay men."

"Okay..." she said. "I guess since I'm the neophyte here, I should assume the more submissive role–"

"Not necessarily," I said. "If you were to take a more active role, you could proceed at your own pace and explore things as they strike your fancy."

"I kind of like the sound of that. How should we position ourselves to start?"

I paused for a moment to think about the best way to give her optimal freedom of movement while still allowing me to touch her freely.

"Why don't you kneel overtop of me while I sit against the wall? That way we can kiss each other while we press our bodies together–"

"Yes," she said. "That sounds perfect. And it will be easier for you to tell me what to do next."

"Possibly. But something tells me you'll pretty soon figure out what to do entirely on your own. But first, take off the rest of your clothes so I can feel *all* of you up next to me."

"Mmm, yes," she purred. "I want to feel every square inch of your body next to me."

While the two of us peeled off our tops and shoes, I could hear West pulling his pants off his ankles and spreading his legs in a wide 'V' on the floor of the elevator. This time, he didn't want anything getting in the way of his enjoying himself while he imagined the two of us making love in the dark.

"Okay," I said, when I heard the last piece of clothing drop to the floor. "Come over here and sit on my lap. I want to feel your wet pussy rubbing up against me."

"Fuck, yes," she growled, swinging her legs over my hips and lowering herself on top of my thighs.

She leaned forward, pressing her tits against mine, and we locked lips as our tongues danced in each other's mouths.

"Mmm," she moaned, twisting her hips on my lap.

I could feel her mound rubbing against abdomen as a trickle of liquid ran down the front of my stomach. I lifted my hands and squeezed her tits, plunging my tongue deeper into her mouth. Elle wriggled her hips over the space between my thighs, trying vainly to get direct stimulation to her burning clit. I reached under her ass and slipped three fingers inside her pussy, and she began to hop up and down on me like a kangaroo.

"Yes, Jade," she panted. "Fuck me with your hand. I want to feel *every* part of you..."

As I listened to the sound of her sopping pussy ramming against my hand, I angled my wrist and pinched her clit between my other two fingers. She pressed her hips harder against my mound and I began to roll her hard button between my fingers.

"*Oh fuck*, Jade," she hissed. "That feels so good. Rub my clit while I fuck your fingers. You're going to make me come very soon..."

Although I wanted to stimulate myself while she rubbed her body against me, with my legs held closed by her vice-grip of my thighs, I decided to give all of my dedicated attention to her.

"Yes, Elle," I purred, slipping down the wall a few inches so I could suck on her tits while she writhed against my dripping hand. "Come for me, baby. I want to feel your pussy squeezing my fingers when you let it loose."

As I sucked on her hard teats, burying my face between her plump tits, Elle suddenly arched her body and wailed at the top of her lungs.

"I'm cumming, Jade!" she screamed. "Suck my tits while I cum all over your sweet pussy!'

The walls of her pussy tightened, contracting over my fingers, and much to my delight and surprise, she began squirting out of her hole all over my mound. With her juices suddenly spraying over my clit, I lurched my body forward as a powerful orgasm suddenly washed over me. While we mashed our tits together and sucked on each other's tongues, I heard West groaning on the other side of the elevator as he flapped his hand wildly against his raging hard-on.

Moments later, the sound of clanging metal began emanating from far beneath us in the elevator shaft. But this time, the banging didn't have any rhythm to it, sounding more like the noise revelers make when they celebrate a new year by thumping pots together. Apparently, our fellow captives had heard the sounds of ecstasy echoing through the shaft and were signaling their approval of our little distraction.

4

Elle remained seated on my lap for many more minutes while we continued kissing and I caressed her wet labia with the tips of my fingers. It felt wonderful to have given her such a satisfying first lesbian experience, and I reveled in the feeling of her dripping pussy pressed against mine as our sweaty bodies rested against one another.

After a while, she pulled back a few inches and peered at me in the darkness.

"Thank you for making love to me so tenderly," she said. "I never imagined it could be this good. But what about you? This whole time you were focused on me. I want to touch you in the same places and make you feel as good as you did to me."

I smiled, running my fingers through her hair softly.

"I enjoyed that as much as you did Elle, don't you worry. When two women make love, it's more about the journey than the destination. We don't always have to get off to enjoy the experience of loving one another."

"I can see that," Elle said, lowering her head down the front of my chest. "But I've never felt a woman that way and I want this as much as you. Don't you want to feel my lips touching *you* now?"

I grabbed Elle's hair, holding her gently against my stomach.

"I do," I said, imagining her joined with me in a different way. "But not *that* way just yet. I want to feel your lips touching me in a different place."

"A different place?"

"I want to *fuck* you this time instead of making love to you. I want to feel your pussy rubbing against mine when we come together."

"Oh my God," Elle panted. "Yes, Jade. That sounds unbelievably sexy. What's the best way–"

I smiled as a devious thought crossed my mind. Up to this point, I'd felt a little guilty leaving West to his own devices, and I knew he and Elle were just waiting for an excuse to come closer together.

"I want you to get on all fours, facing away from me," I said. "I'll turn the other way around while we rub our asses together."

"But how–"

"Just trust me on this," I said. "I think you're going to like this. We won't just be rubbing our *asses* together."

"Oh," she said, quickly lifting herself off me and positioning herself a few feet away from me in West's direction.

I just hoped he hadn't spent himself entirely listening us making love the last time.

"How are you doing over there, West?" I said. "Do you think you can keep yourself amused a little longer while Elle and I try something a little different?"

"Knock yourselves out," he grinned. "I could do this all day and all night if necessary. I haven't been this hard for this long in ages."

"Don't lose that thought," I said. "We might be able to find some use for a *real* cock soon enough. Save a bit for us when the time comes."

"I'm not going anywhere," he said. "And neither is my dick."

I smiled as I positioned our clothes beneath the two of us, placing my hands and the balls of my feet on the floor, facing away from Elle. Then I shifted my weight backward until our cheeks touched.

"Mmm," Elle purred as she swiveled her buttocks playfully against mine. "I like the feel of your ass touching mine."

"That's not the *only* thing you're going to feel," I said, tilting my hips downward as my wet pussy caressed the inside of her thighs.

"Fuck, yes," Elle panted as she lifted her ass to press her vulva against mine. "This is so hot. I can feel your lips touching mine. Fuck me with your pussy. I want to feel you gushing against me again."

"Mmm," I said, mashing our cunts together. With our vulvas coated in slippery juices, as we slid our pussies against one another, a different kind of slopping sound filled the compartment.

"Fuck *me*..." West groaned, inches away from Elle's face with her body positioned near the base of his legs.

I could only imagine what was going through his mind as he listened to Elle and me fucking each other, and I smiled at how prescient his words were about to be.

Soon enough, West, I grinned.

As Elle and I gnashed our pussies together feeling our wet labia sliding over each other, I pressed myself harder against her clit, sliding her further in West's direction. Even though I was lost in the moment fucking her so hard, I had a second agenda for pushing her across the floor. I estimated that she was now only a few inches away from West's throbbing hard-on.

"Look between your legs, Elle," I said. "Even though we can't see each other in the dark, imagine you're watching our pussies rub together and seeing my tits shaking while I make love to you."

"Yes–" she said, then suddenly stopped, with our labia locked in a slippery kiss.

I sensed she'd felt something *else* in the darkness, and I knew her mind was racing about what to do next. But it didn't take long to begin hearing the sound of slurping noises coming from West's side of the elevator, as he began to groan excitedly.

"Oh God, Elle," he hissed. "That feels incredible. I've wanted you for so long..."

As he began thrusting his hips rhythmically into Elle's eager mouth, she hummed in pleasure while I resumed grinding against her pussy.

Knowing that the three of us were joined together in an erotic daisy chain ratcheted my passion to a higher level. As we all began to moan and whine in tandem, my body suddenly tensed up and I squirted hard between Elle's legs, spraying my juices all over her tits and her face impaled on West's pole. She groaned loudly with West's dick in her mouth, then I felt her buttocks spasming against mine as her body quivered in the throes of another powerful climax. At the same time, West began grunting in rhythmic sequence, jetting his cum deep inside Elle's mouth. The sound of the three of us moaning in mutual pleasure must have been music to the ears of the listening gallery a few floors beneath us, and I wondered if they might soon get the same idea that we had.

Suddenly I no longer cared if anyone came to our rescue for the next few hours. We were having way too much fun finding ways to pass the time on our own little fantasy island.

For a few moments, we all remained still while we listened to the sound of the three of us panting in the darkness. This time there was no fanfare from others locked in the elevator shaft, now lost in their own distractions. Elle lifted herself off West's dripping cock and shuffled her body back over the floor, resting her back on the wall next to me. I reached out my hand and we interlocked our fingers, squeezing our hands together in acknowledgement of what had just happened.

Nobody wanted to say anything, embarrassed in the way lovers sometimes are the morning after an impassioned night of drunken partying. After all, we didn't really know each other very well, we were simply victims of the strange circumstance we'd found ourselves in.

It's funny the way a crisis brings people together, I thought.

I was about to break the silence when the sound of a distant voice suddenly perked our ears. As we lay still in the darkened elevator, the unmistakable sound of a woman moaning wafted into our chamber. But this time, the noise had a distinct cadence to it, like two bodies slamming up against a metal wall.

"Yes, yes!" the woman said. "Fuck me hard, Chase!"

I smiled, realizing we'd aroused the interest of more than our little group.

"It seems that we've started a chain reaction," West chuckled from the other side of the elevator.

"What else are people going do when they're locked up in close quarters for such a long period of time?" I said.

"It *is* kind of exciting," Elle mused. "Being stuck in the darkness, feeling our way around with a bunch of strangers..."

"I'd hardly say we qualify as *strangers* anymore," West said.

The woman's voice suddenly grew louder and more forceful.

"Oh God, Chase!" she hollered. "Pound my ass!"

"That's certainly *one* way to get to know each other better," I laughed.

"I can't believe I'm admitting this," Elle said. "But I'm actually getting turned on listening to all this sex in the darkness."

The woman's voice reached a crescendo as the banging noises echoed through the shaft.

"I'm coming baby!" she wailed. "Uhn! Uhn! Uhn!"

"Me too," I said. "What about you West? Do you think you have any ammunition left in your cartridge?"

I could hear the shuffling of clothes, as West reached for something to clean himself up with.

"I don't know what it is about this situation," he said, "but I haven't been this turned on since I was a teenager. It's like I'm thirteen years old again. My cock hasn't been this resilient in twenty years!"

"We shouldn't let all that energy go to waste," I said. "What do you think, Elle? Are you ready for some more fun and games?"

"I'm so horny, I could fuck a billy-goat right about now," she said.

I smiled, sensing the opportunity to bring the two colleagues closer together.

"I suspect you've got something a little better endowed on the other side of the elevator. I can feel the sexual energy between you two. If you don't fuck each other soon, there's liable to be a short-circuit in here before long."

"You're probably right," Elle said. "But what about you? What will you do to keep yourself distracted?"

"I'll let my fantasies wander for a little while," I said. I picked up the Osé vibrator resting on top of my skirt and slid it across the inside of Elle's thighs. "I've got my little friend here to keep me amused. You two go get yourselves better acquainted. I'll be just fine for a little while."

"Okay," she said. "But don't get too attached to that thing. I'm looking forward to tasting you with my *own* tongue when I'm finished with West."

"I'll be waiting patiently," I smiled. "Dreaming of all the ways we can pleasure one another."

"Mmm," she said. "Save that thought. I'll be back soon."

"Don't rush things too much," I said. "I'll be enjoying myself just as much as the two of you."

Elle kissed me sweetly on the lips, then skittered over to West's side of the elevator. Moments later, I heard the sound of wet lips kissing and two voices moaning. From the rustling sounds, I guessed that West had remained seated while Elle had assumed the superior position, sitting on his lap.

This time, she won't have to fish around for something to stimulate her pussy, I smirked in the darkness. As I imagined her sinking down over West's pole, I plunged the Osé vibrator into my pussy and began rocking my hips back and forth.

"Ohh," Elle moaned as the sound of rhythmic thumping emanated from the other side of the elevator.

"Elle," West panted. "I've wanted this for so long. You feel so good."

"I've been watching you for quite some time," she sighed. "I had no idea you were so well equipped."

"Uhnn," West groaned, slapping his balls against Elle's ass.

"Fuck me with your big dick, West," Elle grunted. "Let's give Jade something to think about."

"Oh, I'm *thinking* about it, alright," I said, tapping the button on the bottom of the Osé, activating it's tongue action. "I'm already fantasizing about what I want to do with the two of you when you're done over there."

"Do you want a piece of West's cock too?" Elle said.

"Maybe," I teased. "It depends on whether I'll have a pretty girl to play with at the same time."

"Mmm, yes," Elle said. "Do you think you might *like* that, West? Having your way with both of us at the same time?"

"*Fuck*, Elle," he panted. "I'm trying to keep it together. Don't make me pop off too soon. That's the last thing I need floating around the office when we get back to work. That I couldn't even last long enough to satisfy you–"

"Don't worry, West," Elle purred. "Your secret will be safe with me. Just imagine sliding your cock between our pussies while we rub our bodies together..."

"Oh God..." West groaned as his mind began to wander.

"Yes, baby," Elle said. "Come inside me as you imagine the two of us tribbing your big cock between our wet lips..."

I smiled at Elle's torment of poor West. But I sensed she was trying to excite someone *else* in the room, and it was working. As I squirmed against the pulsing wand and the slippery tongue caressing my pussy, I couldn't resist getting in on the action.

"Fuck, yes," I hissed. "I want to feel some *real* meat between my legs next time, Elle. I want to feel his pole trembling as he comes all over the two of us–"

"*Damn*," West groaned, as Elle pressed her ass down over his balls. "I can't stop it–"

"Yes, baby," Elle purred. "I feel you cumming inside me. Let it go while you dream about your fantasy supermodels. It's about to happen for real."

"Ohh!" I groaned, pressing the Osé toy harder against me as I began cumming in unison with West. "I feel it too. My cock is twitching inside me too. I'm cumming imagining it's *your* cock fucking me right now, West. Come with me, baby."

"*Uhnn, uhnn, uhnn*," West grunted, as Elle's pussy squeezed his pulsating dick.

By the time he finished moaning, I'd soaked the wet floor and clothes in front of me.

"Holy shit!" I sighed, sliding down the wall in contentment. "That was fucking hot! You two sure know how to drive a girl crazy."

"We're just getting started," Elle said, squeezing West's throbbing cock with the walls of her pussy. "I can feel that West is up for some more fun. It's time the three of us finally came together. Why don't you come over here and join us, Jade?"

"I thought you'd never ask," I said, sliding my body over to their side of the elevator.

I reached my hands out to find them in the dark and felt Elle's back as she sat straddled West's hips with his back against the elevator wall. I spread my knees over his legs and shimmied my body against them, pressing my breasts against Elle's sweaty back.

"Mmm," she purred. "You're so warm."

"And wet," West said, feeling my juices running over the top of his thighs.

"All the better to *fuck* you with," I said, reaching behind my ass to squeeze his balls. "Are you still hard? Because we're not done with you yet."

Elle turned her head to kiss me as she flexed her buttocks, gripping West's pole.

"Oh he's hard alright. But I want to get my hands on you before he gets any ideas. I've been dying to taste you since the moment I laid eyes on you."

"Really?" I said. "I thought you were just into men?"

"So did I until I saw you. There was something about the way you looked at us with that gleam in your eye. I knew I couldn't let you get away the moment the elevator doors closed."

"I guess the power failure happened at a fortuitous time then," I chuckled.

"It's the best thing that could have happened to us," West nodded.

I reached around Elle's back and squeezed her tits gently.

"So how do you want to do this? We better act fast before West loses that loving feeling."

"If you *really* want a piece of him," she said. "I suppose I can let you have first dibs–"

I smiled at Elle's offer, but I had other ideas for West's tool.

"I think we can find a way for him to get in on the action while we still have our way with each other."

"Really?" Elle said. "I'm not picturing it. How can we–"

"Never fear," I said. "I've had a bit more practice with these situations. Get back on the floor on all fours."

"But West has already–"

"Don't you worry about him. He's about to have the experience of his life. I'll lie underneath you in a sixty-nine position so we can lick each other at the same time."

"But I thought you said–" West protested.

"There's plenty in it for you *too*, West" I said. "Get behind Elle's ass and play with her from behind. That way, we can both have access to your boy parts."

Elle lifted herself off West's staff and positioned herself over top of our jumble of clothes. I slithered underneath her, grabbing the sides of her thighs, pulling my head between her splayed knees. West patted the floor with his hands trying to locate us and when he felt Elle's ass turned up in the air, he positioned himself behind her.

I reached up feeling for his dick and when I grasped his manhood, I gasped. It was bigger than I imagined, at least eight inches in length and six inches around. As I stroked my fingers toward its apex, I smiled when I felt his slippery head. He was still coated in Elle's juices and I plopped it into my mouth, savoring her delicious scent.

"Hmm," I hummed, swirling my tongue around his corona.

Elle could feel my breath blowing out of my nostrils toward her exposed pussy and she lowered herself toward my face, desperate to feel my touch. I pulled West's cock out of my mouth and rubbed the tip against her clit, licking his shaft from the base of his balls all the way to the tip, slathering my tongue over both of their glans.

"Oh God," West panted in delirious pleasure, feeling two women's bodies caressing his sensitive organ for the first time.

"Lick my clit, Jade," Elle growled, elated to feel my mouth against her sex finally. "Make West cum all over my pussy."

"I'd rather feel you come on my tongue," I cooed. "I've got other ideas for West."

I grabbed his shaft and angled the tip toward Elle's hole, and he eagerly sank his manhood into her tunnel. While they both groaned feeling my breath on their genitals, Elle spread her thighs further apart, lowering her vulva closer to my face. I pressed my hands outward against the inside of her knees until her flaming clit touched my lips. As I sucked her nub into my mouth and swirled my tongue over her shaft, she buckled under the weight.

"Oh my God, Jade," she hissed. "That feels incredible. Suck my clit while West fucks my pussy. I've never felt anything this good..."

As West rammed his cock in and out of Elle's hole, I felt his balls swinging against my forehead and I raised my hands to cup his sac, stroking the space in front of his anus.

"Fuckkk!" he squealed, hardly believing he was the lucky recipient of both our attention.

He leaned forward and grabbed Elle's tits from behind, pressing her face closer toward my steaming pussy. Smelling my box inches from her lips, she placed her head between my legs and began licking me like a puppy. As West began pounding her faster, I swung my arms around her hips and pulled her harder into my crotch. The thrusting motion accentuated the stimulation of my clit, as her tongue slapped back and forth against my inflamed nub.

"Mmm," I moaned, feeling Elle's clit growing harder in my mouth. "Suck my cunt, Elle. I want to feel you cum in my mouth as I squirt all over your face."

Elle nodded enthusiastically, trying to mimic the stimulation I was giving her on the other end. She was a quick study, and before long I felt my orgasm approaching as West's balls suddenly tightened and Elle began bucking wildly on top of my face. Within seconds, all three of us were wailing at the top of our lungs, signaling we'd reached the height of pleasure.

As Elle's clit began twitching in my mouth, I grabbed West's balls and squeezed them tightly while he tensed his buttocks and came inside Elle for the second time that day. I could feel his pelvic floor muscle contracting as he emptied his seed inside Elle's pussy, and the combination of sensations was too much for me to hold back. As Elle and West groaned in mutual climax, I tilted my hips and sprayed my juices all over Elle's face planted between my legs. We shook and grunted in unison for what seemed like a full minute before collapsing together on the floor in exhaustion.

But just as I was looking forward to a relaxing respite in the arms of my new friends, the elevator suddenly lurched and the lights came on as it began to descend.

"Holy shit!" Elle said, realizing we only had seconds before the doors opened and we'd be exposed to anyone waiting on the ground floor. "We better get ourselves put together before we're found out!"

We scrambled to put on our wet and wrinkly clothes, and as the elevator jerked to a stop, we looked at each other and smiled.

"That was one hell of a ride," Elle grinned.

As the elevator doors opened, we grabbed each other's hands and nonchalantly strode past the alarmed maintenance crew and rescue workers. The large wet spots and undeniable scent of sex on our clothes left little doubt what we'd been up to in the elevator. When we swung open the main exit doors and walked out onto the building courtyard, a large crowd was waiting to greet us. Without skipping a beat, they spontaneously erupted into a loud ovation.

I guess we weren't the only ones being entertained while we were locked up this whole time, I grinned.

Elle and West peered at one another, then leaned over and kissed each other passionately. I was happy to see that I'd been able to create more than one new connection among my friends at the Ogilvy & Mather Advertising Agency.

BOOK 20

LADYBOY

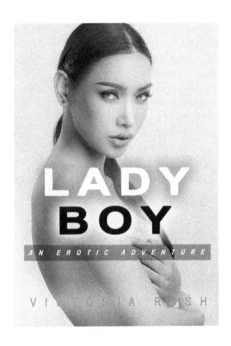

1

I'd been looking forward to this night out for a long time. It had been ages since I'd been out to a show, and the live cabaret act that my best friend Hannah had invited me to promised to be a lot of fun. Starring female impersonators, there'd be plenty of singing, dancing, comedy, and campy good fun.

In the spirit of the theme for the night, Hannah and I had agreed to dress up in cross-gender outfits, and I was eager to see what she'd chosen to wear. I'd found an old padded-shoulder pantsuit in my closet and paired it with a see-through chiffon blouse, skinny red tie and matching high heels. Deciding at the last moment to go topless underneath, the lapels of my blazer and the narrow strip of silk down the front disguised just enough of my bosom to look half-convincingly like a man. To accentuate the appearance, I'd trimmed my hair and slicked it back over my head with some heavy gel. Of course, the six-inch-high Louboutin pumps and my curvy figure in the tight suit left little doubt as to my real identity. But something told me not many people would be looking at my *shoes* this evening.

When my doorbell rang, I finished applying mascara and blush then ran downstairs excitedly to greet Hannah. But as I swung open the door, I gasped and had to hold onto the handle to steady myself. She was wearing a Scottish kilt, replete with high white knee socks, leather sporran, and a glengarry hat. But instead of the usual argyle jacket or waistcoat up top, she wore a thin plaid sash running diagonally over the front of her bare chest. Covering only half of her torso, her right breast poked brazenly out next to the flimsy tartan strip.

"Holy fuck, Hannah!" I said. "I didn't know you were going to go full *Mel Gibson* on me tonight!"

"You *told* me to dress up like a man," she deadpanned.

"Um, well yeah–dressed up in a man's outfit, but not with your *tits* hanging out!"

"Well, technically I've only got *one* tit hanging out," she said, stretching the ribbon to pull it over her other breast. "But at least the sash is pleated, so I can look a little more demure if the mood pleases me.

"Besides," she said, glancing at my see-through blouse. "You're not exactly leaving much to the imagination with that outfit. If it weren't for that skinny tie barely covering your cleavage, you'd be putting most of it out there on display too."

"Not quite as blatantly as you," I huffed, pulling my lapels tighter over my shoulders.

"Come on," she winked. "Tonight's all about having fun, remember? What good is it going to a queer revue if we can't let our hair down?"

"Speaking of," I smiled, tracing her strawberry-colored ringlets down over her bare shoulders. "I like your hairstyle. It goes nicely with the tartan theme."

"Yours too," she said. "Kind of minimalist, but it matches the power suit, and it highlights your cheekbones."

"Thanks," I said, looking at my phone to check the time. "Are you ready to do this? We better leave soon if we're going to get there in time for the start of the show."

"I've been ready all day," she said. "Let's go get our Vogue on."

W hen we got to the theater, there was already a long line stretched along the side of the building, but we found a spot to park on the side of the street not far away. As we approached the venue, the crowd was pumped up, chatting and joking boisterously in flashy drag costumes. With their heavy makeup, colorful wigs and over-the-top costumes, it was hard to tell the men from the women. Everybody seemed to have gotten into character, mimicking the campy personas of the female impersonators inside.

"Looks like a raucous crowd," I said, pulling up at the end of the line.

"These shows typically involve a lot of audience participation," Hannah nodded. "Kind of like the Rocky Horror Picture Show. That's part of the fun."

I looked up at a neon sign flashing on the brick wall above us.

"'*Lips?*'" I said. "Isn't that a bit of a strange name for a cabaret show?"

"Not for a *queer* cabaret show," Hannah said, smiling at a pretty girl wearing a feather boa next to us in line. "If you think about it, it's actually the perfect name for a female impersonator act. It's mostly about the singing, but it's also a metaphor for a woman's anatomy. These girls take their act pretty seriously."

"Except they're not really *girls*," I chuckled.

"You'll be amazed at how authentic these performers look and sound. You'd never know they were actually men under all their makeup and bodily enhancements."

"Enhancements?"

"Some of these performers take hours to get into drag. Between the makeup, wigs, and all the extra padding, it's quite a production. But the final results are quite astounding. Some of them are actually quite gorgeous."

"You make them sound almost fuckable."

"Well most of them are *men*, after all, under all their entrapments. It's kind of fun imagining taking a pretty girl to bed only to find she's equipped with a real functioning cock."

"Like in the song by Lou Reed, *Take a Walk on the Wild Side*?"

"Yeah, kind of like that."

"You said most of them are men. What about the others?"

"It's hard to say, because everybody's so well camouflaged. They're all *gay* of course, but I suspect there's a fair number of transgender girls who are transitioning one way or the other. That's just another aspect that makes it all the more interesting. You never really know what's going on behind their stage personas. But it's all very inclusive and accepting."

I glanced down the line, surveying the mix of primping and preening theatergoers. Everybody seemed to have taken the theme to heart, dressing in provocative outfits. Whether adorned as a man or a woman, they all looked sexy and hot. As I squinted my eyes trying to decipher each person's gender, my eyes stopped at a platinum blonde dressed in a tight corset with cone-shaped cups and black garter stockings. With her hair pulled back into a tall pony tail and pointy eyebrows, she looked like a dead-ringer for Madonna during her *Blind Ambition* days. She caught me staring at her and shook her chest from side to side, playfully twirling the tassels hanging from the tips of her bra as she smiled at me. I pulled my shoulders back, stretching my suit lapels to reveal the erect nipples showing under my sheer blouse.

"I see what you mean," I said. "I'm already getting excited about meeting some of these girls."

When we got inside the theater, the hostess escorted us to a table near the front of the stage and we ordered some cocktails as a loud buzz began to fill the room.

"How'd you score us such primo seats?" I said to Hannah. "I was afraid showing up so late, we'd be stuck in the bleachers."

"Nothing a little extra *lubrication* can't fix," Hannah smiled, rubbing her fingers together, indicating she'd tipped the hostess handsomely. "The closer we can get to the action, the more immersive the experience will be."

"Mmm," I nodded, as the room lights dimmed and a spotlight lit up the stage.

Suddenly a tall redhead wearing a feathery costume with black fishnet stockings and high hells pulled the drapes aside and strutted out onto the stage.

"Good evening, ladies and *wannabees!*" she shouted into the mic. "Are you ready to have some fun?!"

"*Woo hoo!*" the audience wailed, stomping their feet excitedly on the floor.

"My name's Ginger Snaps, and I'll be your MC for the evening," she said. She placed the side of her hand over her eyebrows and peered out into the crowd. "Do we have any *queens* in attendance tonight?"

Another loud cheer arose from the crowd as many patrons waived their hands proudly over their heads. I peered up and down the MC's figure, inspecting her long slender legs, curvy hips, and full bosom. With her arched eyebrows, pouty lips and bright red wig, she looked just like a sexy, full-blooded woman.

"That's a *man*?" I said, whispering into Hannah's ear.

"Uh-huh," she nodded, smiling up at the MC.

Ginger caught Hannah's gaze and moved closer towards our table.

"I see we have a few other Scarlet O-*Hair*-ahs in the room," she said, flipping her poufy mane dramatically behind her shoulder.

"What's your name, sweetheart?" she said, kneeling down and extending the mic in our direction.

"Hannah," my friend blushed.

"I like your costume," Ginger said. "Goes nicely with your fiery hair. Why don't you stand up and show the audience what you're wearing tonight? Don't be shy, sweetie. We're all queens tonight."

Hannah stood up and turned around, pulling her sash to the side to flash her bare breast then jerked her hips, flipping up the leather pouch between her legs. The crowd hollered its approval and Hannah sat down, as a crimson flush spread over her chest.

"That's pretty hot, honey," Ginger said. "But do the curtains match the carpet under that kilt of yours? Have you got a tinge of the *ginge* in your minge?"

Hannah glanced at me for a moment, contemplating lifting her skirt for everybody to see what lay underneath, but I shook my head in horror, already embarrassed enough by all the attention we were getting from the bright spotlight focused on our table.

"Do you guys want to hear some good redhead jokes?" Ginger said, turning to the crowd.

Everybody hollered in encouragement and Ginger stood back up, raising the mic to her mouth.

"What do you call it when a redhead squirts when she comes?"

"*A Fanta blast.*"

The audience roared in laughter.

"How many redheads does it take to screw in a lightbulb?" Ginger continued.

"*None. They prefer to hide in the dark.*"

Hannah grinned good-naturedly, but I could tell she was beginning to feel the sting from the pointed jokes.

"What's the difference between a ginger and a brick?" Ginger said.

"*At least the brick gets laid.*"

Hannah placed her hands on her hips and pouted, pretending to be hurt.

"But that's not true, is it Hannah?" Ginger said. "We gingers know better. We get plenty of action. You've heard of *yellow fever* for people who like to have sex with Asians? Except in our case, the obsession with carrot tops is called *gingivitis.*"

As the crowd chuckled and howled, Ginger finally turned away from our table and motioned toward the red velvet curtain at the back of the stage.

"Enough redhead jokes," she said. "Who's ready for some *diva delights*!?"

"Woo hoo!" the audience hollered.

"Well then, let's hear a big round of applause for the hottest girls this side of the Mississippi!"

She waved her hand toward the curtain, and it suddenly parted as five flamboyant girls strutted forward in unison singing *It's Raining Men*.

Hi, hi, we're your weather girls and we've got news for you, they warbled.

As they swiveled their bodies in harmony to the women's empowerment anthem, I ran my eyes over their sexy figures. Every one of them had long slim legs, curvy hips with narrow waists, and full, realistic bosoms. As they belted out the song in full soprano voices, I watched their lips trying to detect if they were lip-syncing to the music. But I didn't notice any gaps or disconnects between what their mouths were saying and what the music was projecting.

I turned to look at Hannah, dumbfounded. Besides having pitch-perfect, exquisite feminine voices, every one of them was drop-dead gorgeous.

"You've *got* to be kidding me," I shouted over the music. "You can't be serious that these are *men* dressed up as women?!"

"I told you they took their act serious," Hannah nodded. "They go to extraordinary lengths to play their part convincingly."

"But," I protested. "Their legs, their asses, their *breasts*. They look like real women!"

"It's part diet, part genetics, and the rest is just good makeup."

"But those hips! And their tits! How can they make them look so real?"

"It's amazing what a little bit of strategically placed padding and waist-cinching will do. Do you like it?"

"I guess so," I said. "I mean, there's no denying that they're all hot. It's just weird knowing they're actually men underneath all that makeup."

We've got news for you, you better listen up, the girls continued singing.

"Don't think about any of that," Hannah said. "Just sit back and lose yourself in the fantasy. Enjoy the ride!"

I nodded at Hannah, then turned back to watch the performers.

Get ready all you lonely girls, they sang.

And leave your umbrellas at home...

As they twisted their bodies and shook their hips to the beat, I watched the muscles in their arms and legs, looking for the telltale signs of any masculine features. But their limbs were smooth and slim, and their calves as long and skinny as any woman's. Even their tits and asses giggled like a real woman's. As each girl took a turn singing a solo part, I studied her facial expression and skin tone, looking for any evidence of a five o'clock shadow.

'Cause tonight, for the first time in history, a sexy brunette wailed, *it's gonna start raining men.*

As they all joined together in formation to sing the song's chorus, moving to within a few feet of our table, I felt goosebumps from the excitement of witnessing such an electrifying performance.

It's raining men, hallelujah, it's raining men, they trilled.

I'm gonna go out to run and let myself get wet, absolutely soaking wet.

As I began to get caught up in the act, a strange feeling came over me. Even though I identified as a lesbian, I was beginning to get wet myself watching these female impersonators shaking their sexy bodies and singing such an empowering song. By the time the song was over and the MC came back out to work the crowd with some more light-hearted jokes, I was already shifting uncomfortably in my seat, feeling the wetness in my tight-fitting pants spreading down my thighs.

"Pretty sexy, huh?" Hannah said, noticing my disequilibrium. "Bet you never thought you'd get this excited watching a bunch of guys performing on stage."

"I still can barely believe it," I said. "They just don't have any of the normal manly features. No sinewy muscles, broad shoulders, or square jawlines..."

"I suspect a lot of them are drawn to this line of work because they're already blessed with naturally effeminate features. If you look closely, you can see their Adam's Apples when they turn a certain way. But who cares, anyway? All the power to them if they can entertain a whole room full of admirers to this degree."

"They're *entertaining*, alright," I said, adjusting my tight pants bunching up around my moist crotch.

"Don't tell me you're actually getting *turned on* watching these guys?" Hannah said, raising an eyebrow. "I thought you just liked women?"

"I do, for the most part. I guess my mind is just playing tricks with my body. When they're doing their schtick, I can't help imagining them as sexy women."

"I suppose they've accomplished their goal then," Hannah nodded. "For all intents and purposes, when they're on stage, they *are* women."

The MC suddenly raised the volume of her voice, interrupting us.

"What do you guys think?" she said. "*Are you ready for some more T-girl action!?*"

As the crowd roared, she stepped toward the side of the stage, swinging her arm back toward the red curtain.

"*Let's spice it up then!*"

The curtain parted again, and the five performers sashayed slowly onto the stage, while the music from the Spice Girls' hit song 2 *Become 1* filled the room. As the opening verse started, one of the girls separated from the rest, slinking toward the front of the podium. Everyone had changed their costumes to look like one of the original Spice Girls, and this time it was 'Sporty Spice's' turn to introduce the song.

Candlelight and soul forever, she purred.

A dream of you and me together,

Say you believe it, say you believe it...

I marveled at how beautiful and authentic her voice was, and before long I found myself swooning at the intoxicating lyric.

Next, it was the Scary Spice character's turn, looking for all the world like a young Mel B in her caramel-colored afro wig.

Free your mind of doubt and danger, she crooned.

Be for real, don't be a stranger,

We can achieve it, we can achieve it...

I'd always thought Scary Spice was the sexiest Spice Girl, and as she warbled the suggestive lyrics, I crossed my legs together, squeezing my throbbing clit, remembering how I'd fawned over her as an adoring adolescent. By the time her set had finished, I was feeling so hot I had to take my blazer off and hang it over the back of my chair to let my body breathe. With the spotlight focused on the girls on the stage, I felt confident in the shadows that no one would notice my rapidly hardening nipples under my flimsy see-through blouse.

But it was the *next* performer that really got my juices going. As the spotlight swung to the other side of the stage, the performer resembling Baby Spice began singing the next verse. With her parted pony tails and tight lamé dress, I practically melted when she began walking toward our table and locked eyes on me.

Come a little bit closer baby, get it on, get it on, she teased.

'Cause tonight is the night when two become one...

As I stared at her with wide fawning eyes, she gazed at my chest, noticing my nipples protruding like doorbell buttons under the glow of the spotlight cascading toward our table. By the time she'd finished singing her part, I'd already begun to fantasize about joining together with her every way I could. But as much as I tried, I couldn't see any sign of an Adam's Apple in her throat while she flexed her muscles belting out the song. Even her *hands* looked feminine and petite as she caressed the microphone erotically, tormenting me with her dark brown eyes. When the five girls came back together and began to sing the chorus, I'd already transported myself back twenty years when I used to fantasize as a teenager about making love to each of the Spice Girls one at a time.

I need some love like I never needed love before, they sang.

Wanna make love to ya baby,

Wanna make love to ya baby,

Set your spirit free, it's the only way to be.

Even though each of the T-girls had her own individual vibe going on, there was only one I was fixated on now. As I watched Baby

Spice mouth the words sexily to me, I felt the puddle between my legs expand further and further down my pant leg, and it took everything in my power not to mouth the words back to her.

I want to make love to you too, baby, I dreamed.

For many days after the cabaret show, I dreamed about the sexy T-girls prancing around the stage, crooning their songs as they took turns shimmying up to my table and peering into my eyes. I imagined going to bed with each one, but in every case I ended up disappointed when they disrobed and revealed their fake padding and flapping dicks. It wasn't so much that I was turned off by them being men under their suggestive costumes–after all, I'd enjoyed my fair share of hard cocks in my life. It was that the fantasy bubble I'd created in my mind's eye had been so rudely popped.

But my thoughts kept returning to the pretty blonde one who seemed so much more feminine than the rest. Even though Hannah had warned me that she was probably just another gay guy dressed up in a convincing outfit, I wanted to *believe* that she was something more. Maybe it was the sweet Spice Girls character she played in one of her sets that had got me going, but there was something about her that I found different, and highly alluring.

I was already planning to go back to the venue to take in their next show and wait by the exit door after the performance to see if I could catch sight of her out of costume. I wasn't sure how or whether I could approach her, I just needed to know one way or the other what her deal was. I knew that I was probably deluding myself into thinking we'd made any kind of meaningful connection during her performance, knowing that she, like most of the rest of the performers, was just play-acting for the benefit of their fans' prurient fantasies. But my steadily throbbing pussy whenever I thought of her told me I couldn't let it go.

Trying to take my mind off my never-ending obsession, I decided to go grocery shopping at my local supermarket to find a temporary distraction. When I walked into the store and saw all the bright produce displayed on the stands and smelled the aroma of freshly baked bread, I smiled knowing this was just the remedy I needed. Collecting the ingredients for a home-cooked meal would soon refocus my attention on my rumbling stomach instead of my other aching body part.

As I began assembling the ingredients for a cucumber salad, I couldn't help imagining each item as a symbol for the female impersonators I'd seen a few days before. I picked up a large red onion and squeezed it to make sure it was properly firm, wondering if their silicone implants felt equally hard. Then I ambled over to the refrigerated display case and lifted a tuft of fresh dill to my nose. It smelled grassy with a hint of licorice, and I closed my eyes wondering if that's the way my Baby Spice T-girl might smell if I got her naked.

Naked, nothing but a smile upon her face, I hummed the melody to their hit song Naked.

I grabbed some garlic powder, sour cream and white vinegar to make the dressing, then angled back to the produce section to pick up some radishes and cucumbers. As I approached the cucumber stand, I smiled inspecting the long green tubers which always reminded me of a certain well-hung porn star. I occasionally liked to use English cucumbers as a substitute for rubbery vibrators, reveling in the natural texture and flexibility of the phallic-shaped objects. I picked up one of the larger ones and bent it sensuously in my hands, sensing another customer hovering behind me, waiting for me to finish fondling the merchandise.

"Are you more interested in *length* or *girth*?" she said with a sultry voice.

I swung around to see a pretty blonde woman about my height, smiling at me as I held the long vegetable upright in my hand.

"Oh, ah, *yeah*," I stammered. "It *does* have a certain suggestive shape, doesn't it?"

"I prefer zucchini squash, myself," she said, running her fingers delicately over my cucumber's shaft. "It's a little shorter and stubbier, but it has that lovely bulbous tip that makes it feel a little more authentic."

I blushed, suddenly feeling embarrassed by her cheeky manner.

"Oh, I'm just planning to use this to make a *cucumber salad*," I lied.

"Whatever you say, sweetie," she smiled. "It works well for *that* too."

I darted my eyes back and forth across her face, recognizing something familiar.

"Do I know you from somewhere?" I said. "It feels like I've seen you before."

"I don't think we've met," she said, holding out her hand. "My name's Shae. But I get around quite a bit, so there's a good chance we've crossed paths one place or another."

"Jade," I said, I squinting my eyes trying to place the recollection.

Then my eyes suddenly flew open. Her pointy nails gave it away. *It was Baby Spice from the cabaret show*! And she looked even prettier and sexier in street clothes. Wearing a tight wool sweater and skinny jeans, I ran my eyes shamelessly over her curvy figure.

"Oh my God!" I gushed. "You're one of those girls from the *Lips Cabaret Show*, aren't you? I barely recognized you out of costume. I absolutely *loved* your act! If you don't mind my saying, I thought you were one of the sexiest performers."

"Thank you," she said, lowering her voice. "I try to keep a low profile when I leave the stage. There's a lot of fanatics out there who are obsessed with T-girls. You never know when you might run into someone who's got a more insidious intention in mind..."

"Sorry," I apologized. "I didn't mean to invade your privacy. You must get accosted everywhere you go..."

"It's okay, honey. You're one of the few people who've recognized me offstage. And besides," she said, scanning my pointy nipples pressing against my cotton T-shirt. "You don't strike me as one of the dangerous types." She glanced around her, noticing other super-market customers eyeing us suspiciously. "Why don't we continue this conversation in a quieter place? There's a Starbucks just a few blocks down the street."

S hae and I drove our separate cars to the coffee shop, then we went inside and ordered a pair of lattes, finding a quiet table in the corner to chat.

"I hope you don't mind my asking," I said, pulling up a chair. "You don't seem like the other performers. I mean, you look like a–"

"*Woman*?" she chuckled. "Most of us girls put on a pretty convincing act. It's all part of the game. It takes quite a few hours behind the scenes to get into character."

"It doesn't look like you need much *help*," I said, still intrigued by her evasive answer. "You're already gorgeous and plenty curvy..."

"I guess I've been blessed with some natural genetics," she said. "Some of my gay friends have to work a little harder to create the look. May I ask what brought you to our show? Were you just looking for a little fun, or are you another one of those drag queen groupies?"

"I guess I was looking for a little change of pace. I've been flitting from one flighty relationship to another, and I needed a little distraction..."

"Are you attracted to *T-girls*?" Shae asked. "How do you identify, sexually?

"I've tried it both ways," I said. "But I seem to have settled into a comfortable groove with other women. Though I *have* had the occa-sional fling with a transitional girl."

"*Oh*?" Shae said, raising an eyebrow. "Which way? I mean, was she transitioning from a boy to a girl or a girl to a boy?"

"Boy to girl, I think. She looked for all intents like a woman, but still had all the functioning boy parts."

"Did you *like* having it both ways?" she smiled.

"It was definitely interesting," I nodded, happy to see her becoming more interested in my sex life. "Ever since then, I've been kind of intrigued with the whole *ladyboy* thing, if I can use that term. I even dressed up at a masquerade ball once wearing a strap-on dildo, and I've fantasized more than once about being one for real."

"It sounds like you're a little obsessed with ladyboys," Shae said, running her eyes over my chest. "I think I remember you now. You were the hot chick sitting near the front of the stage with the slicked-back hair and the chiffon blouse. I'd recognize those tips anywhere."

"Yeah, sorry," I said. "It was getting a little hot in there and you were kind of getting me worked up–"

"Maybe that's why you came to the show," she grinned. "To live out your fantasies of getting it on with a real T-girl?"

"I dunno," I said. "There's something strangely arousing about being with a transsexual person. I get to imagine them as a woman while still experiencing the act of penetration..."

"Mmm," Shae nodded, adjusting her position in her chair, obviously getting as excited as I was by our conversation. "You're not alone. There's a whole subculture of futa-loving fanatics out there. Both men and women."

"Does that make me a freak or something?" I said. "It doesn't quite seem normal..."

"No less than the people plying their wares on the other side of the coin. Everything's pretty gender-fluid these days. Nobody can seem to make up their minds what they want to be, or who they want to be with."

"You almost make it sound like a *bad* thing," I said, still searching for clues as to her real sex. "How did you get into this line of work anyhow?"

"I kind of fell into it. I have a lot of gay and bisexual friends and when I went to my first T-girl revue, they thought I'd be a natural at it. It's kind of fun to vamp it up and put on a different persona for a bunch of adoring fans. I find it very invigorating to receive that kind of affirmation from the crowd."

"How do you identify *yourself*, if you don't mind my asking?" I said, growing more confident with her increasing transparency. "I mean, do you consider yourself gay, bi, or trans?"

"I prefer not to pigeonhole myself into any particular corner," she said, placing her elbows on the table and leaning forward to gaze into my eyes. "I consider myself *pansexual*–I enjoy having sex with anyone who turns my crank."

"I feel exactly the same way," I smiled, sensing an opportunity to move our conversation to the next level. "Are you feeling hungry? Maybe we can get out of this place and find a bite to eat."

"I'm absolutely famished," she said. "I could really go for a cucumber salad about now."

"Oh?" I said, raising an eyebrow playfully. "Would you like to come back to my place? It would be a shame to waste all those tasty vegetables on just myself."

"I thought you'd never ask," Shae said. "But something tells me you won't need that cucumber after all. I think we might find some *other* ways to satisfy our appetite..."

———

The moment we got to my place and I set the grocery bags down in my kitchen, Shae and I fell into each other's arms as we groped each other and pressed our bodies together against the island. I could feel her tits mashing against mine and all I wanted to do was get her naked as quickly as possible to ravish her body. Besides, I was dying to see what she'd been hiding so carefully from me ever since we met. I still wasn't sure if she was a natural woman, a pretty boy pretending to be a woman, or someone transitioning from one gender to another.

"Let's go upstairs where we can get more comfortable," I said. "I'm dying to touch you *everywhere*."

"Same here," Shae panted. "I want to have you every way I can."

I held her face, plunging my tongue into her mouth, then grabbed her hand, pulling her down the hall and up the stairs into my master bedroom. We both dropped down onto the bed and I ended up lying next to her with her back leaning against my front side. Feeling all the more excited still not knowing what I'd find, I began taking off her clothes.

I reached around and pulled off her sweater then unclasped her bra, squeezing her breasts tightly in my hands. They felt full and natural, and I ran my fingers around the base of her mounds, trying to feel for the telltale ridge of a silicone implant. But they felt as soft and natural as any woman's. Then I lifted my fingers and rolled them gently over her areolas as she sighed and arched her back in pleasure.

No sign of scars either, I thought. *Whoever did her boobs must have been a very skilled surgeon.*

As I traced my fingers down her quivering abdomen, her skin felt as smooth and soft as a baby's. I didn't detect any sign of hard abdominal muscles or any stubble from recently trimmed hair. I could even feel the thin indentation of her linea alba running down the middle of her stomach, something I'd always found attractive in fit women. As I traced the line toward her crotch with my middle finger, she grabbed my hand and stopped me just above the top of her jean's waistline.

Instead, she slowly unclasped the button and pulled her jeans down over her hips, then shimmied out of her panties and threw them near the base of the bed. Shae was now completely naked facing away from me, and I could feel her hot body radiating next to me. I was dying to reach around and touch her loins to see what surprises lay in wait for me, but I decided to go slow and torment her just as much as she was me.

She pulled her right knee forward, separating her legs a few inches, and I caressed the inside of her thigh from the base of her knee all the way up to her curvy, tight buttocks. I felt a slippery film of fluid as I got close to her crease, and I rubbed my fingers and together, trying to divine its source. It didn't feel thick and mucousy like a man's precum, and I pressed my hips harder against her ass, rejoicing in the knowledge that I was holding a real woman in my arms.

She turned her head around and we kissed softly while I caressed the curvature of her ass, inching my hand toward her steaming cleft. When I felt her slippery slit, I pressed two fingers deep inside her hole, and she moaned into my mouth as our tongues swirled together in delight. As I began to fuck her with my fingers, she rocked her hips along with me, and I felt her juices begin to trickle down over my knuckles. Eager to please her even more, I removed my fingers and traced them forward along her valley, seeking to caress the sensitive nub at the top of the fold.

But when I reached the base of her mound, instead of finding a little clit, I felt a huge, throbbing phallus pointing upward toward her stomach. Hardly believing what I was feeling, I placed my fingers around the shaft and squeezed it tightly to see if it was real. Unlike any strap-on dildo or faux penis I'd ever felt before, this one felt warm and spongy in my hand. And unlike the plastic or silicone fake dicks, this one *pulsed* in my hand as I felt the rush of blood coursing through its shaft.

I suddenly felt a charge of electricity running through my body, realizing I was lying next to a true hermaphrodite for the first time in my life. My pussy gushed in excitement as I traced my fingers further up her shaft, feeling the flare of the coronal ridge encircling the crown at the tip of her cock. Her head was coated in a viscous layer of precum, and she groaned as I swirled my fingers over the sensitive tissue.

"Oh my God, Shae," I whispered. "I had no idea–"

"You said you had a *thing* for ladyboys," she smiled, turning around to face me directly. "Well now you've got your wish. The real question is, have you got the skills to take full advantage of my special equipment?"

"*Fuck* yes," I growled, ripping off my clothes, pressing my tingling body up against hers.

3

"What do you feel like first?" Shae smiled after I'd removed all my clothes. "There's a lot to choose from."

"Mmm," I purred. "Indeed there is. Do you mind if I play with your big thumper first? I've never experienced a real cock attached to a girl before. Just plastic dildos and other artificial toys–"

"Like long *cucumbers*?"

"Ha, yeah–sometimes. But it's not quite the same," I purred, stroking the underside of her shaft with my fingers. "This one you can actually *feel*..."

"Yes, I can," she sighed. "Have at it. That's all anybody seems to want, anyways."

I lifted my hand from Shae's crotch and looked into her eyes, realizing I was treating her like a piece of meat.

"I'm sorry," I said, pulling away. "I imagine this can be awkward for you sometimes. With your fans already expecting to find boy parts under your clothes, they must be even *more* obsessed with your body when they discover you're more than you seem."

"You mean a full-fledged *tranny*?" Shae said. "*Dick girl*? Anatomical *freak*?"

"No," I said, caressing her face softly with my fingers. "I'd never call you any of those things. To me, you're just a girl with a bit of a...*twist*. A very sexy, *surprising* twist."

"Mmm," Shae said, leaning in to kiss me back. "I like the sound of that. I didn't mean to sound so defensive. It's just that I kind of–*like* you. I was hoping we'd have something a little more meaningful than a quick fling."

"I feel the same way," I said. "We can slow down if you want and take some time to get to know one another before we escalate things any further. I've got some food downstairs if you're hungry–"

"No," she said, pressing her hips against me, coating my belly with her dripping cock. "I only want *you* right now. I want to feel your lips all over my body..."

"With pleasure," I purred, kissing my way down her neck. As my face nestled between her cleavage, she arched her back and moaned.

"Suck my tits, Jade," she mewed. "Take my girls into your mouth and tease them like you do your other lovers. Make me feel like a real woman."

"You *are* a real woman to me Shae," I said, peering up at her. "I love your body–*every* part of your body."

I traced my hands down over her shoulders and encircled her full breasts, squeezing them gently. Then I lifted my head and sucked on each of her nipples, making a playful popping sound.

"Yes," Shae moaned. "That feels so good. You're not like most of my other lovers. They just want to *fuck* me or have me fuck them. I like the way you make love to my whole body."

"Mmm," I hummed as I swirled my tongue over her fat teats. I could feel them lengthening in my mouth and I sucked on them like lollypops as she writhed in delight on the bed.

"I need you Jade," she groaned. "My *cock* needs you. Make love to the rest of my body the way you're worshipping my tits."

I didn't need any further encouragement, and as I slid my body down the front of her slippery abdomen, I pointed her member between my breasts and pressed them together, feeling her heat throbbing between my flesh. The precum dribbling down the underside of her shaft provided ample lubrication, and I proceeded to caress her cock with my melons as she rocked her hips in pleasure.

"Oh God, Jade," she moaned, lifting her head to watch her purple tip poking in and out of my cleft. "I love fucking your tits. You look incredibly hot."

"So do you," I smiled, watching her big pole sliding between my cleavage.

Part of me wanted to continue fucking her with my tits, intrigued to see if or how much she could cum when she reached orgasm. But by now I was burning up with desire also, and I had to feel her in my mouth. I wanted to make love to her most sensitive part and feel her jetting inside me when she came. I lowered my body a few more inches, kneeling between her legs, and looked up at her with a devilish grin. Her pole was bouncing in excitement between her legs, and I grasped it with two hands, beginning to jerk her off slowly.

As she threw her head back in ecstasy, I watched her body writhing on the bed. There was something incredibly erotic about watching a beautiful woman squirming in pleasure while I felt her burning sex in my hands. It was strange to see her breasts jiggling on her chest as I stroked her cock with both hands, her nipples peering up at me like two beacons in the dark shadows of my bedroom.

"Jade," she panted. "You're going to make me come soon. I've never had someone give me such a delicate hand job before. Look into my eyes when I come. I want to see your pretty face."

"Yes, Shae," I hissed, feeling my own juices beginning to run down the inside of my thighs. "Come for me, baby. I want to watch you cum in my hands."

Shae began rocking her hips more urgently then she slammed her hands down onto the bed, clenching the covers between her fingers as she curled her body up toward me, staring into my eyes. Suddenly her cock erupted, spewing ropes of cum all over my tits and face, as I gushed simultaneously all over the sheets. The intense eroticism of watching her beautiful body come alive as I held her tightly in my hands had turned me on so much that I'd come along with her even without any direct stimulation.

As I watched Shae's chest heaving in excitement as she recovered from her powerful climax, we clasped hands, and she pulled me down gently on top of her.

"That was incredible," she panted. "I've never had someone touch me like that before."

I lay down beside her, pushing some loose strands of hair back over her face.

"You've never had someone give you a hand job before?" I asked.

"Not like *that*," she said. "Usually they just want to see me cream, like I'm some kind of robot. But this time it felt like you were making love to me with your eyes. Knowing you were watching me that way made me cum a thousand times harder."

"I could tell," I said, wiping some of her cum off the side of my face with the back of my hand. "I enjoyed watching you respond to my touch just as much as you did."

Shae slid her knee forward, feeling the big wet spot I'd made on the sheets.

"So it would appear," she said, wiping my face to remove the last traces of cum from my skin. "I've never seen a woman squirt so much before."

"You're not the *only* one with special powers," I smiled.

Shae grabbed my head and thrust her tongue deep into my mouth, pressing her dripping cock up against my stomach.

"I want to return the favor now," she said. "It's *my* turn to watch you while I give you some pleasure."

"I won't say no to that," I purred, rubbing my slippery tits against hers. "What did you have in mind exactly? Like you said, the combinations and permutations are practically limitless."

"As much as I'd like to focus entirely on you, I desperately need to make love to you. I want to be *inside you* this time when we come together."

"Mmm," I smiled, grabbing her ass and pulling her tighter toward me. I felt her burning cock resting against my abdomen, and I swiveled my hips to see if she was still hard. "Are you ready to go at it again this quickly?"

"I've been ready from the moment I met you," she said. "As long as you're lying naked next to me, I don't think there's any risk of my cock flagging."

I reached between our two bodies and squeezed her throbbing member in my hand.

"Should we be taking any precautions?" I said, pinching my eyebrows.

"You mean regarding pregnancy?" she said. "We don't have to worry about any of that. As you can see, I don't have any balls, so I can't produce sperm."

"But you produced plenty of fluid–"

"That comes from something else. Just like a man, I've got a prostate and seminal vesicles. Ninety percent of a man's ejaculate is produced by those glands–it's just that in my case it's *all* of the cream."

I pulled back momentarily, intrigued to learn more about her unique features.

"What about the rest of the package, if you don't mind my asking?" I said. "You seem to have all the other lady parts. Do you have a uterus and ovaries, like a regular woman?"

"The chromosomes got a little mixed up in my case," Shae said, shaking her head. "I got a little bit of this and a little bit of that when they were handing out the DNA. Every intersex person is born differently. Some have mostly boy parts, some have mostly female parts, and some have a few parts of each."

"Well, I think God endowed you with the *best* combination of parts," I said, tracing a line down the side of her jaw with my finger. "I can't imagine a more perfect specimen than you. You look more beautiful than any woman I've met, and you *still* get to have it both ways."

Shae chuckled softly, then her expression turned more solemn.

"For the longest time, I felt like a freak. When you're a kid, you want to be like all the other kids. But I've learned to make peace with my situation and I hardly think twice about it anymore. I'm just Shae–unique and special in my own way."

"I couldn't have said it better myself," I said, beginning to feel closer to her as she grew increasingly candid. "But I know there's a lot of gender-confused people out there, even without your ambiguous anatomy. Did you ever consider–"

"Surgery?" Shae said. "Not for a moment. I kind of *enjoy* having two sets of organs to play with. You have no idea how much experimenting I did growing up."

"I can imagine," I smiled, thinking about all the different ways I'd found to self-pleasure myself. "But what about your parents? Didn't they want you to fit within society's expected stereotypes? Wasn't there a lot of pressure to choose one clear sex or another?"

"Thankfully, I had pretty progressive parents," Shae nodded. "They loved me for who I am and never pressured me one way or the other. I can't imagine being any different than the way I turned out."

"Neither can I," I said. "I love you just the way you are."

"*Love*?" Shae said teasingly. "Isn't it a bit early to be using those kinds of words? I mean, I just *met* you..."

"I know," I said. "But it feels like I've known you my whole life. There's something deeply spiritual about you. You're unlike any other woman I've met before–"

"That's because you've never met another woman with a real cock before."

"That's not what I mean," I said. "I just feel a special connection with you. I knew you were different the moment I laid eyes on you. I've fantasized about being with you ever since the cabaret show–"

"Being with me, or *being* with me?" Shae said, furrowing her brows. "I don't want you to love me the way all those other ladyboy fanatics do."

I shook my head as I wrapped my arms around her back and pulled her closer.

"I know it's weird to say so soon after we've met, but I want to be with you forever. As friends, partners, lovers. I'm stuck on you like no one I've met in a long time."

"I feel it too," Shae said, gazing into my eyes. "Let me make love to you properly now. I'm thinking of *another* way for you to be stuck on me."

"Mmm, I like the sound of that," I said, rolling on top of her. "Stick me with that big cock of yours. I want to feel you creaming inside me this time."

Shae tried to turn me over so she could be in the superior position, but I pinned her arms on the bed and smiled mischievously at her.

"Let me be on top. I want to watch you when we join our bodies. *All* of you."

"Same here," Shae smiled. "This time I want to watch you to gush all over my cock when you come."

"Damn straight, girl," I said, rubbing her throbbing pole against my wet labia. "This time I'm going to surround your cock with a *different* part of my anatomy."

"*Yesss*," Shae purred. "Fuck me, Jade. Fuck me with your wet pussy."

I lifted my hips over her quivering dick, then I pointed it toward my hole and slowly lowered myself over her shaft. As she penetrated deep inside me, we both groaned in pleasure. It felt strange having a woman's cock inside me, not just because of the absence of testicles slapping against my ass. The combination of her pretty face, sexy tits, and throbbing hard-on was something I'd never experienced before. As I began to pump my body up and down over her throbbing organ, I gasped when I felt her reach the end of my tunnel.

"*Fuck*, Shae," I groaned. "I've never felt so filled up like this before. Fuck me with that big tool of yours."

Shae grabbed my hips on either side and pulled me harder toward her as she began thrusting deeper inside me. I tilted forward and grabbed her tits, squeezing them tightly. It was nice to have something substantial to hold on to while I bounced on her joystick, and we both smiled at how perfectly we'd melded together.

"I love looking at your pretty face while I fuck you," I purred, gazing into her eyes as my juices dribbled down over her slit and between her ass.

"I want to look into your eyes when you come this time," Shae said. "I haven't felt this close to anyone in a long time. Make love to me, baby."

I lifted my arms and held my hands out to her, and she grasped my hands again, interlocking her fingers tightly with mine. As we rocked our hips together, gazing lovingly into one another's eyes, our grip grew progressively tighter the closer we edged toward orgasm.

"Fuck, Jade," Shae hissed. "You feel so good. Squeeze my cock with your tight pussy. I want to watch your tits shaking over top of me when you come with me."

"Yes, baby," I panted. "I'm almost there. Pound me with your big dick. Let me feel you spurting inside me."

"Oh God, Jade," Shae grunted. "It's coming. Look at me while I come inside you. Oh *fuckkk*..."

Shae squeezed my fingers so tightly they began to turn blue and her whole body began shaking as she fell over the precipice. With her tits shaking in orgasmic tremors, I arched my back, pointing the tip of her cock against the G-spot on the front side of my pussy. As I watched her mouth gape open in the throes of a powerful climax, I clenched down hard on her pulsating prick and sprayed all over her quivering pussy. Feeling me come on her slit, she angled her hips toward me, jetting her cum hard against my cervix. Feeling her touching my furthest reaches heightened my pleasure all the more, and I shuddered in joy as we gripped each other's hands and peered at one another with watery eyes.

As I collapsed on top of her feeling her warm body pressed against mine, I closed my eyes and rested my head on her chest. For the first time in ages, I felt like I'd found my soulmate.

4

For many long moments, Shae and I lay next to one another, softly caressing each other's skin. I could feel her heart pounding next to my head on her chest, and I wasn't sure if it was because she was still coming down from her high, or if it signaled her joy at being next to me. Either way, I smiled, knowing we'd made a powerful connection and that this was just the start of something wonderful. After a few minutes, I felt her heartbeat returning to normal, and I peered up at her.

"How are you feeling?" I said.

She peered into my eyes and smiled.

"Happy. Content. Euphoric."

"It's probably just the endorphins still floating around your system," I said.

"No," she said, shaking her head. "It's much more than that. With all my other partners, it was mostly about the sex. Like they were using me as a novel plaything. But with you, I can feel something special. I haven't felt this close to anyone in a long time."

"Did you know there's a special hormone that's released when we have an orgasm with someone? It's called oxytocin, sometimes referred to as the love hormone. It creates feelings of belongingness between partners and promotes a sense of togetherness. Psychologists believe it's an evolutionary adaptation in humans to encourage couples to stay together long enough to raise their children. I've often thought it plays an important role in same-sex relationships too."

"Oxycontin?"

"No," I chuckled. "That's a whole other type of drug. That one produces an intense artificial high, much like heroin. This one's all natural and lasts a much longer time."

"Are you saying these feelings we're developing for one another aren't *real*? That it's just due to the hormones produced when we have sex?"

I could feel Shae's heart racing again under my ear, and I reached up to squeeze her hand reassuringly.

"No, I just think it's interesting how it's all interconnected. How sex and love are mutually interdependent. But true lasting love is something that develops over time. You have to work at it. It's a give-and-take process, where each partner supports one another as they learn each other's wants and desires and learn how to make each other happy in more substantial ways."

"Well if love depends on sex, and sex depends on love," Shae mused, "and the strength of our bond depends on getting to know each other's desires better, then we better get *busy*. Tell me what you like—in *bed*, I mean. What turns you on?"

"Until I met you, I thought I knew. But you're kind of a game-changer. Suddenly, I have so many more...*options*."

"Because I have a cock?"

"Kind of. With other girls, it was all about tribbing and licking and that sort of thing. You know, mostly focusing on the external organs. But with you, I can feel you *inside* me. I've got a whole new exciting toy to play with. Now I can throw away all my vibrators and dildos—"

"Not so fast," Shae smiled. "I enjoy playing with those things as much as you do. Sometimes it's just as much fun to watch your partner pleasure herself. Besides, I can think of a number of ways we can incorporate those into our sex life to keep it fresh and exciting. Starting with that big vegetable of yours..."

Shae's mention of the cucumber got me thinking about all the new ways I could use it with her. After all, she also had a fully functioning *vagina*, and there was nothing I loved more than using a double-sided dildo with my partner while we ground our pussies together. Only this time, I could watch and play with her pecker too while we fucked each other.

"Mmm," I said. "I like the sound of that. Shall I run downstairs and bring it up for us to play with? I want to fuck you so bad right now."

"In a little while, maybe," Shae said. "First, I want to taste you and make love to you with my mouth. I'm dying to suck your pussy."

My cunny suddenly twitched at the thought of her going down on me.

"I've been dying to take you into my mouth too," I said. "Maybe we can do it at the *same time*. Do you feel like a little sixty-nine action?"

Suddenly Shae's heart began thumping rapidly against the side of my face again.

"Yes," she nodded. "We'll be able to rub our bodies together and hold each other close that way. *Fuck*, yes. I want to bury my face between your legs."

I lifted myself off her body and turned around, lying beside her on the bed with our faces positioned in front of each other's crotch. Her flagpole was already ramrod straight and bobbing inches away from my mouth. I grabbed it gently with my fingers and rolled my tongue around her crown in slow circles.

"Oh God," Shae groaned. "Lick my cock, Jade. Make love to me with your mouth. I'm gonna suck your pussy and taste your honey. I want to feel you gush all over my face when you come this time."

I spread my legs and felt Shae's face press against my dripping hole as she began lapping her way up toward my clit.

"Yes, baby," I panted. "Lick my pussy. Taste my love for you while I suck you off. I love your beautiful rod."

I grasped her prick with two hands and engulfed her head in my mouth, sucking her pole feverishly while I slathered her shaft with my tongue. At the same time, Shae wrapped her arms around my ass and pulled me tightly toward her, encircling my bud in her mouth. We both moaned, thrashing our hips against each other's faces.

As we pressed our bodies together with our tits sliding against each other's abdomens, I rejoiced in the knowledge that I was making love to someone I'd never imagined being with in my wildest fantasies. It felt strange to be sucking a cock that didn't belong to a man for a change and to feel someone kissing me in my most intimate areas that wasn't a regular woman. It was like she had some kind of superpower, like she was my very own *Wonder Woman*.

As our moaning began to rise in urgency and volume, and our pleasure arced inexorably toward orgasm, I slipped my hand inside Shae's pussy and curled my fingers toward her G-spot. She hummed excitedly, thrusting her cock deeper into my mouth, and I tried to relax my throat to take as much of her as possible. Normally, I'd gag on a man's dick this size, but somehow with Shae I didn't have the same sense of fear being taken advantage of by someone far stronger than me. I knew that Shae would be gentle with me, not fucking my face just to get her rocks off. We were truly making love to one another, and I savored every moment feeling her warm, throbbing organ in my mouth.

I could feel myself nearing the point of no return as she teased my burning clit with her tongue, sucking and teasing my nub as she squeezed my buttocks with her hands.

"Mmm-mmm," I grunted, signaling that I was about to come.

"Mmm-*hmm*," Shae nodded, clenching her buttocks as I relaxed my throat while she sank her cock all the way into my mouth.

Suddenly, the walls of her pussy began contracting against my fingers as I felt her pole pulsing while she poured her jism down my throat. Feeling her coming both ways soon put me over the edge, and I groaned as I clamped down hard and sprayed my juices onto her face, coming in a series of powerful contractions that never seemed to stop. All the while, we gnashed our tits against each other's tummies, feeling every square inch of our bodies tingling in euphoria.

I held Shae in my arms until her contractions subsided then I drew my head back, closing my lips around her crown. I wanted to taste her for the first time–even her *milk* tasted sweet and creamy.

"Mmm," I purred, feeling her pussy twitching as I milked the last drops out of her trembling hard-on.

Shae kept her face planted between my legs while she caressed my ass and nibbled on my jewel. As we held each other lovingly in our arms, there was no longer any doubt in either of our minds that we'd created something special and neither one of us wanted to pull away anytime soon. Within a few minutes, we both drifted off to sleep, dreaming of nymphs and mermaids gliding through an ethereal realm.

5

When we woke up a few hours later, we snuggled next to each other, kissing softly and talking about our plans for the future. We were both giddy as schoolgirls talking about all the places we wanted to go and all the different adventures we wanted to have. But before long, we realized how much of an appetite we'd worked up, and we went downstairs where I cooked up some fresh seafood and prepared the cucumber salad. When we finished, Shae looked at me and smiled.

"That was a lovely dinner, Jade," she said, raising a playful eyebrow. "But now we don't have one of your favorite sex toys to play with any longer. Whatever are we going to do with ourselves?"

"Oh, I've got plenty of *other* toys to play with," I said, looking at her with a mischievous grin. "Why don't we go back upstairs and see what we can find to work with? I'm intrigued to see how we can incorporate some of them with your special features."

"I'm guessing you don't have too many cock rings or Fleshlights in your bedroom," she grinned. "They're probably all designed for clitoral or vaginal stimulation."

"I think we might be able to find a way to make a few of them work for both of us," I said, grabbing her hand. "Come on, I've got a few ideas I want to try out."

When we got back upstairs, I pulled open my nightstand and showed Shae my collection of sex toys and dildos. Most of them looked like the normal female stimulators you'd find at any sex shop, but there was one that she seemed particularly interested in.

"What's this thing?" she said, picking up a long silicone wand with a bulb on the end and a mysterious hole in its base.

"That's one of my favorite sex toys," I smiled. "It's called an Osé vibrator, and it works in a very unique way."

"How so?" Shae said, placing the tip of her finger into the little hole.

"Let me *show* you instead," I said, pulling it away from her. "I've got a special idea for how we can adapt it for you to use." I shimmied up against the bed's headboard and spread my legs, tapping the mattress between my thighs. "Sit in front of me and rest your back against my chest. I think you might kind of like this."

Shae peered into my eyes and smiled.

"I'd like *anything* we do together," she said. "As long as I'm lying next to you."

"This time, it will be a little different. It'll give me a chance to stim-ulate and explore *every* part of you at the same time."

"Mmm, I like the sound of that," Shae said, shifting her ass up next to my crotch.

I could see her cock angled at half-mast, unsure of what to expect. I grasped the Osé vibrator and slowly bent the flexible wand in the reverse direction. Unlike its normal use in the missionary position with the wand curled upward to stimulate a woman's G-spot while the other part caressed her clit a few inches higher, in *Shae's* case we'd have to make some adjustments. For one thing, she didn't have a clit to stimulate, but she was also faced in the opposite direction, so the wand would have to be turned the other way around.

I reached down and caressed the sides of her lips to prepare her for the insertion. She'd have to be good and wet to enjoy the tool's unique movement, but I also wanted to get her fully hard so I could play her *other* part while she was being stimulated internally.

"Mmm," she purred. "I like it when you stroke me like that. It makes me feel very...womanly."

"Oh you're a *woman*, alright," I said, slipping my fingers inside her box to see how wet she was becoming. "A *super* woman–my own very special action hero."

"Mmm," she panted, rocking her hips against my fingers deep inside her. "You know I'd protect you against anyone who'd try to take you away from me."

"You don't have to worry about any of that, sweetheart. I'm stuck on you like glue now, remember?"

"Right, hormones, and all that," she smiled, turning her head toward me. "But right now, I'm stuck on you in a very different way."

"You *like* that?" I said. "Do you like the feeling of my fingers fucking your pretty pussy?"

"Yes, Jade," she sighed, resting her head against my chest. "Fuck me with your fingers while I play with my cock."

As she moved her hand up toward her throbbing pole now flapping straight up against her tummy, I batted it away gently.

"Let *me* have the pleasure," I said. "I'm going to have my hands freed up soon enough."

"Oh?" Shae teased, looking at the strange sex toy lying on the bed a few inches from her watering pussy.

"I think you're about ready to try this thing," I said, picking it up and pointing the bulbous tip toward her opening.

I turned it around with the hole facing her anus, then inserted the tip slowly into her slit. Shae tilted her hips forward to accept the instrument and hunched down a few inches to allow it to penetrate all the way inside her.

"Mmm," she purred. "That's a pretty big cock you're wielding there, my love. But I'm not sure it can do all the things your fingers can do for me."

"I wouldn't be too sure about that," I grinned, reaching down to tap the button on the base of the unit with my finger. The device began humming, and Shae's body jerked in surprise as she twisted her head to look at me with wide eyes.

"What the *hell*?" she said. "What is that thing? It doesn't feel like any vibrator I've used before."

"It's not really a vibrator," I said. "As you're about to see. It's more of a human *simulator*. Can you feel it caressing the inside of your pussy?"

"Yes," Shae said. "It feels like a finger stroking me. A very long and *soft* finger."

"I knew I'd be able to make you forget about my own fingers soon enough," I smiled. "I've got other plans for them."

Part of the attraction of using the special vibrator with Shae was that it would free up my hands to play with her cock while her pussy was being stimulated in other ways. I wanted to feel her burning flesh in my hands again while I watched her hips trembling from the feeling she was receiving inside. In her position faced away from me, it gave me an opportunity to caress every part of her body while the sex toy did its work on her lower parts.

I poured some baby oil into my palms and encircled her python with both hands as I began pumping her shaft up and down while the Osé finger caressed the inside wall of her pussy. Shae threw her head back against my chest in pleasure and I plunged my tongue into her mouth, kissing her passionately while she was being serviced below. I could feel her hips cavitating wildly against my crotch as she received stimulation simultaneously in both of her erogenous zones. As she rocked her body against my hands and the finger probing deep inside her pussy, I watched her pretty tits bouncing on her chest.

"*Fuck*, Jade," she hissed. "That feels incredible. I've never–"

"Been fucked and caressed at the same time?"

"Not like this," she panted.

"Mmm," I said, taking one hand off her cock and squeezing her breast while I twisted my other hand around the tip of her pole. "I like being able to feel and touch all of your parts this way."

"Fuck yes," she squealed, pumping her big dick into my hand. I could see precum pouring out the top of her slit, and the mix of her creamy emission with the watery baby oil made for an even silkier lube. "I can't imagine anything more heavenly than having you caressing every sensitive part of my body."

I grinned at her devilishly as I reached between her legs to tap the button on the base of the Osé vibrator one more time.

"I'm not quite sure we've finished caressing *every* sensitive part of your body," I said.

Suddenly, a snake-like appendage hidden under the hole of the vibrator emerged and began licking her twitching anus with its realistic tongue-like action.

"*Uhhn!*" Shae groaned, flexing her abs as she pressed her hips harder against the device. "What the hell is *that*?"

"I told you this was a special vibrator that was capable of stimulating you in many places. Just sit back and enjoy while you let *both* of us pleasure every part of your sexy body."

Shae leaned back against my chest and rested her head against my shoulder as I watched her face grow redder and redder from the rising tide of pleasure within her. I glanced down at her throbbing member and saw some pulses of precum dribbling over the top of her crown and down the underside of her shaft. I placed my other hand back on her throbbing meat and began pumping it tightly between my two fists. As I watched her purple head poking in and out of my hands, a bright flush began to spread over the top of her chest.

Suddenly, her face tightened up and her stomach muscles flexed as her body jerked against mine. While I pumped her raging dick and the Osé wand caressed her G-spot, with its tongue teasing her quivering rosebud, she wailed at the top of her lungs and wrapped her hands around mine as her prick jetted thick streams of white cum high into the air. I watched with amazement as she ejected one long string after another, arcing high into the air before landing with a loud plop onto her shaking chest.

When she finally stopped cumming, I took my hands off her cock and rubbed the creamy dew all over her plump tits and hard nipples.

I'd never seen anything so erotic in all my life, and to have held her in my arms while I beheld the spectacular fireworks show was just icing on the cake. I turned my head to kiss her gently, and she squeezed her hands three times against mine still wrapped around her throbbing member as if to say 'I love you.'

I squeezed her pole three times back to return the sentiment as I watched the last bit of cum dribble over the tip of her magnificent flute.

That's one instrument I'm never going to get tired of playing, I said to myself as I held her softly in my arms.

R eady for more erotic chills and thrills? Enjoy the next volume in *Jade's Erotic Adventures (Books 21 - 25):*

Sneak Peek (Book 21 - Peep Show):

Chapter 1

After going over a week without any type of intimate contact, I was feeling especially horny today. In such circumstances, I'd normally go online to find an outlet to relieve my built-up sexual tension. But lately, I'd been finding that internet porn wasn't doing it for me. Sure, the girls were always hot and sexy and I could generally find something new and interesting to get me in the mood. But it all seemed so impersonal, so *manufactured*. Even my favorite lesbian webcam site had become a disappointment, with viewers swiping from one partner to the next, often right in the middle of a hot-and-heavy session.

I needed some real flesh and blood contact, or at least be able to *see* someone live. But I didn't just want to see and hear her, I wanted to smell her, feel her, *taste* her. Somebody who wouldn't exit the scene at the first sign of boredom, or as soon as she got her rocks off. I wanted to be with someone I could take my time with and enjoy the experience on my own terms. And *Tinder* was out of the question, since I didn't have the time or the energy to vet the candidates, nor string along the ones whose profile never seemed to align with their real personas.

After trolling through the usual online sources, I decided to try something new. I clicked on the latest issue of the Windy City Times, Chicago's long-time LGBTQ newspaper. At least here, I knew I knew I'd be able to find authentic lesbian, bi, and trans girls. Among the litany of gay bar postings, I found an unusual listing in the classified section. Under the headline *Nude Casting Call* was an ad for open auditions at the local theater company. Intrigued, I clicked on the Details tab and began to read the full description:

The Bijou Theater is looking for uninhibited people who are interested in staging solo performances in the nude. With a king-size bed as your primary prop, your goal is to arouse and titillate a live audience using only your body and your wild imagination. There will be boys-only, girls-only, and mixed couples events, so you can cater your performance to your own sexual preference or mix it up as you see fit.

A winner will be chosen after each audition based on audience response, with the winners moving on to regional semi-finals and finals. The Grand Prize winner will win an all-expense-paid vacation for two to

the Desire Riviera Maya Resort in Puerto Morales, Mexico. Exhibitionists
and voyeurs alike are encouraged to attend. Come one, come all!

Holy shit, I thought, suddenly aware of the growing dampness in
my panties. The idea of watching someone perform an erotic routine
for a live audience definitely got my motor running. This wasn't some
sleazy dive bar or strip club where the girls performed nude dances
in front of a bunch of leering men. This was a legitimate theater
where amateur performers volunteered to display their naked bodies
to a group of of anonymous strangers in a darkened auditorium. And
I could *choose* the target audience—no sweaty old men, no creepy lap
dances, no private rooms where the girls were paid for private favors.
I could just sit back and enjoy the show in the privacy of my own
darkened alcove.

But what exactly did they mean by *solo performances*? Just how far
did these performances go? Did they touch their bodies only superfi-
cially, simulating sex acts like a typical stripper? Or did they caress
themselves in their most private regions, with the purpose of
genuinely getting themselves and their onlookers off? The presence
of a bed on the stage suggested it would be more than just a typical
erotic dance. And how much audience participation would there be
in the production? Were spectators allowed to actively stimulate
themselves in the dark while they watched the performers on stage?

The more I thought about it, the more turned on I got imagining
how exciting it would be to take in a live performance. Hell, if the
conditions were right and the security was good enough, I might be
tempted to give it a go myself. But first, I needed to check it out from
the protection of the viewing gallery. At least there I'd be able to get
my rocks off watching somebody else in the relative safety of a darkened auditorium. We could *both* take our time to ramp up our desire,
knowing the only consideration was maximizing everyone's viewing
pleasure and satisfaction.

I clicked on the Calendar tab and noticed a selection of dates
highlighted in different colors and markings. Pink shading signified
ladies-only nights, blue was men-only, and green was open to both

sexes. A downward-sloping diagonal line through the box meant the show was sold out for new audience members, and an upward-sloping line meant auditions had been fully booked for that day's event. Scrolling through the pink-shaded boxes, I saw that the next three week's events were X'd out, indicating there was no room for either performers or attendees. The next available ladies night only had one line crossed through it, so I click on the date and booked a ticket immediately.

As I leaned back in my chair, imagining myself watching a pretty girl caressing herself on stage, I pulled down my panties and began rubbing my inflamed clit.

This is going to be interesting, I thought.

Jade's Erotic Adventures - the complete series:

Volume 1 (Books 1 - 5)

Book 1 - The Dinner Party
Book 2 - The Dark Room
Book 3 - Naked Yoga

Book 11 - The Personal Trainer
Book 12 - The Dominatrix
Book 13 - Webcam Chat
Book 14 - Paint Me
Book 15 - The Toy Party

Volume 4 (Books 16 - 20)

Book 16 - The Costume Party
Book 17 - Swedish Sauna
Book 18 - The Therapist

Book 26 - *The Spa*
Book 27 - *Parlor Games*
Book 28 - *The Exchange Student*
Book 29 - *The Hostel*
Book 30 - *The Harem*

Don't go away - more to come!

CPSIA information can be obtained
at www.ICGtesting.com
Printed in the USA
LVHW111459110722
723209LV00005B/109